ZDRAVKA EVTIMOVA (Pernik, 1959) is a Bulgarian writer and translator, and winner of numerous literary accolades, including Bulgaria's Favourite Writer in 2021. Her novels and short story collections have been published in Bosnia, Canada, China, Egypt, Greece, Israel, Iran, Italy, Spain, North Macedonia, Serbia, UK and the USA. Her short story 'Vassil' was one of the award winners in the BBC international short story competition. The short story 'Blood of a Mole' is included in a literary anthology for middle school education in the USA as well as in Danish high school textbooks. The short story collection 'Pernik Stories' won the Balkanika award for Best Book of the Year. Evtimova's novel *Thursday* was published in Serbia (Arhipelag, 2023) and North Macedonia (Antolog, 2021). The novel *The Same River* was published in Bosnia (BuyBook, 2024).

YANA ELLIS found her ideal career in her middle years and graduated in 2021 with a merit in an MA in Translation from the University of Bristol. She was shortlisted for the 2022 John Dryden Translation Competition and in the same year was awarded an ALTA Travel Fellowship. She translates fiction and creative non-fiction from Bulgarian and German. *The Wolves of Staro Selo*, recipient of the PEN Translates award, is her first full-length literary translation.

ZDRAVKA EVTIMOVA

The Wolves of Staro Selo

*Translated from the Bulgarian
by Yana Ellis*

HÉLOÏSE

PRESS

First published in English in Great Britain in 2025 by
Héloïse Press Ltd
Canterbury
www.heloisepress.com

This book was first published in Bulgaria under the title
Резерват За Хора И Вълци
Copyright ©2022, Здравка Евтимова (Zdravka Evtimova)
Published by arrangement with Sofia Literary Agency
All rights reserved

This translation ©Yana Ellis 2025

Poem 'September' by Geo Milev (1924) originally published in Bulgarian in *Пламък*
Our edition includes the English translation by ©Tom Philips:
Geo Milev: Poems and Prose Poems, trans. Tom Phillips, 2025, Worple Press, p.56

Cover design by Laura Kloos
Edited by Dženana Vucic

Text design and typesetting by Tetragon, London
Printed and bound by TJ Books, Padstow, Cornwall

The moral right of Zdravka Evtimova to be identified as the author of this work has been asserted in accordance with the Copyright, Designs and Patents Act 1988.

Yana Ellis asserts her moral right to be identified as the translator of the work.

All rights reserved. Except as otherwise permitted under current legislation, no part of this publication may be reproduced or transmitted in any form or by any means, electronic or mechanical, including photocopy, recording, or any information storage and retrieval system, without permission in writing from the publisher.

This book has been selected to receive financial assistance from English PEN's PEN Translates programme, supported by Arts Council England. English PEN exists to promote literature and our understanding of it, to uphold writers' freedoms around the world, to campaign against the persecution and imprisonment of writers for stating their views, and to promote the friendly co-operation of writers and the free exchange of ideas. www.englishpen.org

ISBN 978-1-7384594-2-1

This book is a work of fiction. Any resemblance to names, characters, organisations, places and events is entirely coincidental.

For Vasko and Grandad Vasso

'Leave,' Grandma Elena told my mother.

'I'll leave, but your son will buy cockroach poison. And take it.'

'Entirely his business,' snapped Grandma.

Grandma Elena's son is my father.

Grandma Elena is like that, doesn't like idle talk. She picked up the poker, the one she sometimes used to threaten our dog Gasho, my best friend, but which more often strolled with her at night around the cherry orchard where it brought thieves to their senses.

Would it bring my mum to her senses now?

Who's that venomous woman dragging frost under her skirts and poisoning the melon fields? the people of Staro Selo asked about Grandma Elena. As if they didn't know. They had decided long ago to break her. But one day around noon, shrieks and wails came from the direction of the cherry orchard – as though the whole of Staro Selo was in its death throes. It wasn't the whole of Staro Selo turning its head towards death, just four men – enormous, big as barns, their hands and legs tied with rope (I recognised the rope; my father kept it in his tool cupboard before he left to earn money in Spain). Commotion ensued.

'Who did this, you thieves?' the mayor asked.

Two of them were Roma. Though bandits, they were honourable and didn't snitch on anyone, but the Bulgarians – Pavko and Ginger Dimitar – burst out together: 'Elena.'

She hadn't just tied them up. She had painted them with the poker too. Purple blotches glistened on their backs. And on their foreheads – I have no idea how she had heated it so white-hot that it branded the skin.

At sunset that day Ginger Dimitar burst into our kitchen, swathed in bandages and gauze from the neck up. Only his nose persisted, glowing like a naked light bulb. Grandma Elena and I were alone. She was clinking pots in the sink.

'Oi, loony!' the redhead shouted, and shoved Grandma. 'I'm gonna gut you. Tomorrow.'

'You can try,' Grandma Elena invited him, carrying on with the washing.

The redhead looked hither and thither, nose in the air, then left. Cleared out.

'I'm going to buy a rope for your neck, you old hag,' he yelled from the gate.

Every evening Grandma Elena makes me read a page from *Pippi Longstocking*. I don't go to school yet and I have no reason to read, but if I don't open the book, she won't give me dinner.

'Read!' she orders, but the letters wobble their naughty heads.

They escape; I can't get them to stick together, and because I'm so hungry that my stomach's about to run to the larder all by itself, I start making it up: 'Pippi was very hungry. She went to pick tomatoes from the garden together with the dog Gasho, so that Ginger Dimitar wouldn't frighten her.'

'There's nothing about Ginger Dimitar in *Pippi*.' Grandma Elena pulls *Pippi* out of my hands and bundles me into the bedroom.

'Give me some bread, Grandma,' I plead, but she doesn't open the door. 'I can't fall asleep.'

The door stays shut.

I know I can bleat until the cows come home but no bean soup will come my way. So I say, quietly and composedly, as if I'm not about to die from hunger: 'Grandma, please, let me read *Pippi Longstocking* to you.'

She opens the book on page eleven; I sit down on the chair next to her and start slowly – like a headless caterpillar – to spell out the words. They are long, weighing a hundred tons, but until I read to the very end of the chapter there'll be no bread or cheese.

One time, much to my surprise, Grandma gave me a piece of chocolate. 'You read very well, and you didn't stutter,' she said. 'There!'

Since then, I learnt that if you want to avoid starving in a dark room and get a pudding after your bean soup, you have to speak clearly. That's why I asked Mum the other day – very clearly, without a single stutter – 'Are you going away forever?'

I know that *forever* begins behind the bakery of the twins Dida and Dona and doesn't end, ever. Your mother packs her socks in a suitcase; you're dropped into *forever* and get nothing for lunch. Your tummy hurts. Grandma Elena might even chase you away to sleep in Gasho's kennel because you missed the opening of Dida and Dona's shop and failed to buy bread. That means you'll eat sand.

'I'm leaving for good,' said Mum. 'Stay with your grandma. Anyway, you'll never amount to anything but a bean picker.'

In that moment I spotted Grandma Elena grip the poker – the one with which she had tattooed the backs of Ginger Dimitar and the other bandits – and touch it to Mum's shoulder.

'If you say that nothing will come of this child one more time, I'll cut out your tongue,' Grandma said serenely, and even more serenely pulled out a knife from the sideboard drawer.

The haughty air that surrounded Mum when she walked through the town square evaporated. 'I'm not saying anything out of order to the child,' she declared flatly. 'There's nothing wrong with picking beans.' Then she fell silent. I would've fallen silent in her shoes too.

Grandma lay the knife on the table.

Mum left. Suddenly I felt sorry for her. She would let me use her make-up and say: 'What a pretty little girl you are! What a shame you're growing up in this godforsaken place.'

'Mum, I love you. I don't want you to leave!' I'd be picking beans for the rest of my life anyway. But at least if she were nearby... She was very pretty.

'Your mother's beautiful,' Grandma Elena said. And whatever Grandma Elena says is true. It's more than true – her word weighs a ton in Radomir. It was a shame that she added: 'But she's not a good person.'

I looked up to see what was happening to Mum, just in case she had turned into a sparrow or a banichka. I ran out onto the pavement and there it was: Mum was still a woman. Tall, blushing, she walked with her head held high as the European Union flag over the town square. The neighbouring housewives came out to their gates to watch her, as silent and still as if they'd been tied up with rope.

* * *

When Ginger Dimitar stormed into the house, I thought: *Grandma Elena's poker is nowhere to be seen. The End. Mum's long since hoisted her skirts like a flag and left; Dad's working to earn money beyond the Black Sea, beyond the ocean even. If they kill Grandma Elena, what will happen to me? I have precisely two lev and thirty-two stotinki and a slice and a half of bread.* Raw and angry, the wound carved by Grandma's poker on Ginger Dimitar's forehead looked like a crater.

I noticed: Grandma Elena has no cane, no knife, no poker, she's drowning in her brown dress. She'll probably die like that – in that ugly garment. And what will I die in? Since she beat the hell out of the four thieves, no child will play with me. As if I was the one who thrashed the burglars. In our neck of the woods pummelling bandits is risky business; within a couple of days, it's you who'll be beaten black and blue, smeared across the pavement.

I cast a frightened glance and what did I see? Grandma Elena neither flinched nor coughed.

Ginger Dimitar pulled a knife out, clicked something on the handle, and the blade sprang out like a snake about to strike.

Grandma Elena didn't even notice but carried on peeling potatoes as if the sky would do a somersault if she didn't peel that damned spud.

'Where's Siyana?' Ginger Dimitar asked.

Siyana is my mother.

But how could I be sure he was really after my mother? The neighbour who worked as a cook in the kindergarten was also called Siyana – Grandma Siyana the Quarrel – and lived nearby. Which one of these two Siyanas was Ginger Dimitar looking for? His knife, thirsty for blood, touched Grandma Elena's cheek and I thought, *He'll chop her into pieces*, but she continued to peel that potato as if its skin was made of granite and she couldn't carve it.

'Where's your daughter-in-law?'

'Ask one more time and I'll cut off your ear,' Grandma declared. Her voice was like that potato – granite. No way to bite into it.

'Oi, you old hag! She chose me. Dumped your stupid son,' Ginger Dimitar yelled. 'Your son's a lump of suet, and beautiful women don't eat suet. Where's Siyana gone?'

'If she's not with you, then she must've eloped with some other toerag,' Grandma Elena pronounced, her voice slow and clear. 'Siyana will never sleep under my roof again. Make a note of it.'

Then I – because I'm little and not worth anything, with no gemstones or gold – quietly took a step towards the window and saw them: Pavko and Vova, the two bandits, lurking by our gate.

Whenever those two hang around a house, the building spontaneously catches fire even before the evening news starts on TV.

'If my house catches fire,' Grandma Elena began, calmer than the news presenter, 'I'll mix a flesh-eating potion. The wounds I inflict do not heal. Those on your little friends won't heal either. You'll be cursing till the end of your days if you set my house alight.' I'm always afraid when Grandma speaks in that tone. Each word is a tongue of flame. So I lie on the floor in case it sets me on fire too.

Ginger Dimitar loosened his grip on the knife, which was no longer a knife but a worm.

'Where's Siyana?' he repeated, just to say something.

Grandma Elena carried on with her work without looking at him and probably only I saw how Ginger Dimitar waved his hand in the air.

The two standing on the pavement outside our gate burst into the garden.

'Cut!' Ginger Dimitar ordered.

Wielding axes, they sprinted to my cherry tree, which bore fruit the size of eggs.

'No!' I screamed.

I loved that cherry tree. I have no siblings and the other children don't play with me since Grandma picked trouble with the bandits; when I sit under the cherry, I feel that the stars are perching on its branches just for me. All summer long I bring it water from the river with a little bucket.

'Don't!'

'Stop squealing,' Grandma Elena snapped.

The words hadn't yet dried in her mouth when she pulled out the pistol. It was my dad's gun – poor man, he had bought it on the black market for a truckload of money. He must've wanted to scare Mum out of running away with some clown like Ginger Dimitar.

Mum wasn't the scared type though.

The gun was as empty as my wallet. But I still walked down the street with my wallet dangling around my neck on a golden chain. Everyone was jealous; they had no clue that the chain wasn't gold, nor the wallet rich. It was lonely, like me. My father had 'slung his hook' to earn some money, Mum explained, which apparently meant he had gone to chase the wind. Poor man didn't know that death by money is crueller than death by gun.

But Grandma Elena lifted the gun calmly to Ginger Dimitar's head and said, 'If an axe touches my cherry tree, I'll shoot you here, Ginger Dimitar.'

'The pistol's empty, you old hag.'

I also knew there was no gunpowder or bullets in it.

But there came a surprise.

Grandma fired towards the sky; the gun thundered. Ginger Dimitar fell against the sink.

'I didn't shoot at you, you idiot,' Grandma Elena said. 'I'll shoot at you if you touch my cherry tree. Do you understand?'

Ginger Dimitar opened his mouth, but nothing came out. Grandma emptied a pot of water over his head, and then the poker appeared – I have no idea from where. Maybe she'd hidden it among the watering cans we kept in reserve in case the water stopped. She struck Ginger Dimitar's buttocks with the poker.

'Out,' Grandma said. Ginger Dimitar scrambled up. 'I haven't invited you. So you'll leave on your knees. Or you'll die.'

And I watched a grown man with a bunch of carrots for hair crawl on all fours along our path towards the gate, his body twisting into eights and thirds, like a snake. Grandma Elena unleashed the poker on his heels. If I were her, I wouldn't have tortured a grown ginger man, making him crawl like a toddler before my eyes, but then I'm not Grandma Elena. I felt sorry for him.

'Don't torture him, Grandma,' I pleaded.

I have no idea how it happened; I just felt the back of her hand flash across my cheek. Suddenly I was rolling on the ground, not far from the creature crawling out of our house.

* * *

I'm Christo. Most people refer to me as 'that one, you know who I mean', or 'Elena the Healer's son'. I know what they say about me.

'Siyana moved in with Ginger Dimitar,' my mother said as she prepared some kind of potion for neck pain. Then, as if she had not opened her mouth, she added, 'Fetch me a bunch of dried mint.'

I didn't understand what I was supposed to fetch, I had forgotten what mint was; I didn't know where I was. Mother couldn't help me. She can fix broken bones, pull a pinched nerve from the grip of a creaky lower back and make you forget it ever hurt, the pain gone forever. She can appease an enlarged liver; her potions quieten angry intestines. But she couldn't work her magic on me. Mother hates the word *magic*. There is no *magic*. There are charlatans.

Siyana was my wife.

If she could've helped, would Mum have let me, her son, wander around like a lost soul without watching where he puts his feet; rambling incoherently, without grasping a word of what he's saying; seeing Siyana in the apple branches, in the water bottle; imagining biting into Ginger Dimitar's neck?

If it had been at all possible, Mum would've cured me.

My father was a very handsome man, drawn to parties and rakia, the first to turn up if there was music and laughter.

A gentle soul – a kite – no shouting, no grinding teeth. He would say, 'Christo, come sit next to me, son, so I won't taste the bitterness of the beer.'

Or: 'Christo, do you have money, son? If you don't have enough, take this twenty-lev note because a man without money is like a shrivelled donkey's hide. The donkey met his maker after pulling a heavy load all his life, toiling and moiling without a penny to show for it, only his hide hanging on the hook, dry as gunpowder. The only thing you can do with a miserable donkey is make him into salami. I don't want you to turn into salami, son. Look at me – do I look like salami? No, I don't. Forget that Ginger Dimitar. You're my flesh and blood. I hate watching you flicker like a candle.'

Dad was a very attractive man. Women knew it; they grasped his beauty and were forever wooing him: 'Kind, sweet-hearted, gorgeous. You're true as steel, Damyan. Top man!' And so as not to offend them, Dad would respond, but only up to a point, then stop.

Mum only needed to look at him for him to immediately walk away from rakia, women and merrymaking.

'Speak to me, *Dushichke Lenche*,' he would say to her.

That's also what they mockingly called Mum in Radomir behind her back – 'Sweetheart Lenche'.

I don't understand... When I close my eyes, beneath my eyelids I see Siyana – stardust spread on the street. Soft and gentle. Invigorating my blood, filling my lungs. They take the piss out of me to my face: 'While you're breaking your back building motorways in Spain for a little cash, she and Ginger Dimitar... Don't kid yourself; just because you have a daughter doesn't mean your wife's in the bag. No one can weave a rope strong enough to hold Siyana, boy, no one! Ginger

Dimitar's rich. Write that down somewhere and read it aloud four times a day.'

I can't forgive her. I can't live without her. I think the One who takes us all beyond will soon come for me. No matter where I end up, I'll see neither light nor darkness. In the blackest of blacks, in the whitest of whites, I'll only ever see her – Siyana.

My father stopped gazing at women; he no longer follows their silhouettes. Poor man, the older he gets, the brighter his face shines.

I've never heard them quarrel – he and Mum. Never.

I don't get it. A man – chased by every skirt in town, women ringing him up till his phone melts, all of them young and beautiful – chooses to stay with my mother. Why her? Because of the creams and potions? No, my father is as strong as the hill on the other side of the village. Quagmire or drought, frost or scorching sun, nothing bothers him. Maybe God was looking the other way when he should have shown Dad the turn he needed to take to steer clear of Mum.

It was Mum who figured out how to make ends meet and keep the wolf from the door. Her food was so delicious that you gobbled even the potato peelings before licking the pot.

'Siyana...' she started one evening.

'Don't bad-mouth her,' I protested.

Mum said Siyana had walked out on Ginger Dimitar and stopped by our house but left straight away. No questions. No answers. Not a word. I was in Sofia at the time, looking for car tyres. That's when I got sick.

Mum pulled me back from the grave.

On she carried mixing potions and brews, growing aloe and Chinese dates, concocting all sorts of potions from ash and flax seeds. Lame and crooked folk would come to our house; she would rub an ointment into their sore wounds and give them a herbal potion. People who'd been doubled over like a horseshoe would slowly lift their foreheads and stand up straight. They paid their bills. We always had money, but it wasn't the money that had lured my dad.

When he did have money in his pocket, he would buy himself and everyone around him drinks until his pockets were empty. When he was broke, he would pin back his ears and go cadge a drink from a friend.

'Your father's very handsome,' women young and old would say to me, giving me a letter to pass on to him. He never read them but threw them away as if they were smeared with engine oil. Every so often though, one of those damned letters would drop into his pocket and Mum would get a whiff of it.

I have never once heard Mum raise her voice or scream. I have no idea how she did it. My father, poor sod, would bow his head like a sack of ashes and call to me, 'Christo, let's eat, son,' then read me a story.

He was a good man, I'm telling you, clean, pure, mineral-spring water through and through. Under Mum's sharp eyes he would be sad until the second page of the story; by the time the prince rushed in to slay the dragon, he would start laughing out loud and I would join in his laughter. When someone asked me, 'What is childhood?' I would answer, 'My father, Damyan, reading a fairy tale about a dragon.'

It wasn't the money that glued him to Mum, because when he got his pay cheque, he would say, 'Come on boy,' and we would go to Sofia together. We would catch the train – brilliant train! My father – twice as brilliant! In one of his pockets there would be a chocolate, and he would bend over so I could find it. In the other pocket would be a honey cake. He would take me to the most expensive shop, get me to try on the most expensive pair of trousers, buy them for me, then say, 'Come on son, let's go to the cinema.'

I never understood the films we watched. It was enough to hear him laugh. I laughed with him.

He once told me, 'Your mother doesn't worry when you're with me, since she knows no other woman is glued to me.'

But the women, all of them audacious individuals, would sneak up on Dad even if I was with him; they would step on his toes or pinch him, but I would defend him with my fists so he could relax around me. They wouldn't leave him alone. That's why I would slap him on the neck too, so we could get going. God was probably checking on his humans, and in an absent-minded moment made some people impossibly beautiful. My father was one of those people. No one called him 'Damyan', only 'Beautiful'. Later they nicknamed him 'Big Beautiful' and me 'Little Beautiful'.

I understood what it meant to be beautiful – it meant women circled around you, like ants on an anthill, while you only had eyes for Siyana. It all started in the Graovtse kindergarten in Radomir. Girls in pink dresses, even boys, would write letters to you, but Mum, the moment she saw a letter in your pocket, would lock you in the larder. No yelling, no arguing, just one look at the larder and in you walked on your own. A whole day without food, just for one letter. At the back of the larder, Dad would throw bread and sausage through the window facing the chicken coop. Mum caught him once, my partner in crime, and kicked him out for a week.

I said to myself, *Well done, Dad! For a week you can enjoy women, go fishing, play poker or the lottery.* But he, poor man, returned in the evening, a bunch of wildflowers in hand – not even flowers, more like weeds – and handed them shamefacedly to Mum.

'Dushichke Lenche, please! I'll die without the boy.'

Then I noticed Mum crack a smile, but a very thin one; her face was a fast mountain stream, you never knew which way it would flow. When a torrent smiles at you, you're done for. But then Mum forgot to be her usual iron-poker self. It frightened me. Was she ill? Who would feed us if she fell ill? Who would cure all the lame and crooked folk, make ointments, look after Dad and me? Dad was a train driver; he didn't earn much, and whenever he laid his hands on some money, he would buy everyone a drink.

Mother never looks at me. Especially when I start babbling about Siyana.

'Your son is as soft as dough,' she would say to Dad, and not let him near the house.

It's possible he had been up to something; I couldn't be sure. But as far as I was concerned, there was only room for Mum in his heart. Dad could endure anything – soft dough, crusty bread, feast or famine. He would fall asleep on the bench outside with a smile the size of the full moon. He would forgive and move on. He was like the wind and bore a grudge no more than the wind did.

Whenever I was banished to the larder, Dad would come to the back window and pull out the torch we had bought at the fête in Staro Selo and nicknamed 'the electric blue butterfly'.

We were so happy with this butterfly that we went out three times to celebrate its purchase: once with kebabs, two days later with tripe soup, and then with tulumba and boza. Dad would pick up the butterfly, sit under the window and start reading the fairy tale about the dragon. By the second page he's in stitches, and even though he's been kicked out and I've been sentenced to the larder, we both laugh out loud, and I'm no longer scared that Mum might find another love letter in his pocket or mine. Dad and I would always laugh and if I could stop seeing Siyana everywhere, I would take him for a beer straight away. I don't know where the book about the dragon has gone, though. Never mind. He bought another one with 'The Wolf and the Seven Little Goats' and 'Puss in Boots', 'For your gorgeous little daughter.'

So, back to the matter at hand. When I brought Siyana home for the first time, Mother didn't utter a word for a whole hour. I knew she had prepared a rabbit with potatoes and baked bread, but she didn't move. Dad on the other hand – I'm so happy I named my daughter Damyana after him – got up, divided up the meat, arranged it on to plates, served Siyana first, then me. Broke the bread into pieces. Gave the first one to Siyana. Only then did Mum say, 'Christo, there's a lot of suffering in store for you.'

'Why is he going to suffer?' my girl asked, my Siyana. 'Why do you say things like that?'

'Because I can see through you,' Mum said. 'In the morning with one, in the evening with another. Tomorrow... who knows.'

Mother is a tall woman, almost as tall as Dad, and thin as a rope. She turned a formidable back on us, on the plates with roast rabbit, on the home-made bread.

'Well…' I could see Dad trying to crack a smile and finally succeeding, because his heart is a July wind; tears itself away from evil and rushes towards joy. 'Well, let's eat then.'

I suffered and I'm still suffering, Dad. But even if I had known back then that Siyana would leave, that Ginger Dimitar would whistle behind me, and his cronies would mock me… I'm still your flesh and blood. I would still do it – take a bite from that roast rabbit, from that home-made bread. I would still hold my girl's hand, because without her, I don't have enough air.

'Christo, what a golden child you have.' My father would always steer the conversation towards something light.

Dad and I never disagreed. I'm just wondering how come he didn't like Siyana.

'This one will play games with you,' he sighed.

Why did he say that? He's not a coward. He wasn't doing it to please Mum so she wouldn't kick him out of the house again. I'm sure.

'Brace yourself,' Mother said when I heard about Siyana and Ginger Dimitar. Fever swept over me. I had just come back from the building site in Spain. My girl had left. 'Look at your beautiful daughter.'

Of course she's beautiful.

Siyana is her mother.

* * *

I'm Siyana. Still married. To the same man, Christo. And this is what my mother thinks of my life:

'Now listen to me, you fool, and remember my words.'

Mum's really beautiful and people say that she has the most remarkable profile south of Vitosha. And south of Vitosha, apart from mud and thugs, there are snakes in summer and leeches in autumn.

'If you want to stay here, if you insist on your eyes drying up from reading textbooks, then you might as well go buy a rope and hang yourself now. Wear glasses, turn into a slug, owe money to every Tom, Dick and Harry and graduate from university with honours – you go right ahead! You'll become a teacher at the state secondary school for hospitality. In other words, you'll be educating illiterates at the Mangiata. For the rest of your life, you'll earn just enough to buy clothes from the second-hand shop. Your house will stink of cockroach repellent.' Mum pinches her nose and carries on calmly: 'Once a year you'll go on a trip to Ruse, and then for weeks you'll boast about it to the other teachers. Your students will whisper, "What a stupid tart that maths teacher is," and they'll be right, even though they'll be coming to your lessons drunk or high. While you rhapsodise about Pythagoras and his theorem, they'll plonk their heads down on their desks, yawn and snooze – and that's if they bother coming to school at all. Every other day some bigwig will call you to test "the child". And if you test "the child" and carve out the number two, i.e. the failing grade he deserves – no, for which he's screaming at the top of his lungs – the tyres of your eighteen-year-old car will be deflated. Words like "rag", "garbage" and "cow" will be inscribed into it with a screwdriver. And these are the mildest terms they'll use. I'm not even going to mention the obscenities that will blossom on your car bonnet. One night on your way home, they'll corner you and break your neck; your nose will bleed till you're anaemic.

Even if you only give "the child" less than top marks, it will go like this: the father will be outraged at you for grossly underestimating his progeny, since according to the parental body he's a genius. The town will boil over with gossip, and you'll end up in a psychiatric hospital. They'll note how you bought a coat from the seedy Second Chance shop where all the clothes once belonged to dead grannies. But, if you award "the child" full marks, you'll receive bottles of whisky, fine chocolates, the finest Hermès scarf; you'll be invited to shop at a discount in the grateful mother's boutique; you'll be given a free holiday to the seaside; and you'll be expected at the birthday party of the distinguished successor to the family business. He's innovative, he hates boredom and spells the word "address" as "adres", while under his exquisite hand the noun "mother" is transformed to "moter". And what's more, the young gentleman will graduate from school with higher grades than you had, my darling girl, who has been poisoning her eyes and brain with algebra, geometry and literature. Tomorrow, my darling, this individual will become the headmaster of the school where you teach.'

Mum chews a few hazelnuts and smiles.

'Pity you, Siyana! Pity the poor, stupid kids like you. Creatures who work their socks off while their mothers are in Munich scrubbing toilets for wealthy Germans and their fathers are in Madrid laying tiles in the apartments of the señores and señoritas. Meanwhile, the children live with their grandmothers. Deteriorating. Mouldering among books like you did. Are you sure you still want to live south of Vitosha?'

My mother doesn't usually talk this freely, which made me think she'd downed a whisky. She doesn't do that often, but when she does, it makes me happy, because then she talks to me for a long time. It's always been just the two of us. She divorced my father, which doesn't stop her sending me to him to drill for financial support. She taught maths before becoming an accountant and financier. After my father, some engineer lived with us. He got sick very quickly, no idea with what – he smoked and coughed. Mum despatched him speedily to his maternal home. Not long after, another engineer appeared. He was loud and arrogant, and had an unpleasant voice but plenty of financial resources. The problem was that his daughter often visited, chasing injections of euros.

The aforementioned daughter was a brazen girl who claimed my mum had broken up their family. Good thing this gentleman became sick too. I couldn't tell from what. Mum asked me to collect his clothes in a bin bag and the two of us took the engineer back to his ex-wife. Actually, they weren't divorced yet, but the wife still refused to take him back. Mum left the man at the entrance to their block of flats and I took the bin bag with his clothes – the ones I had personally gathered from the bedroom – upstairs. I kept only one of his scarves – silk, from Japan – and his almost-new trainers, which I gave to a boy. I met up with the boy a few times, decided he wasn't worth it, and took the trainers back. They were size forty-five – that's why I needed to inform myself which of his classmates wore a size forty-five.

To my delight, one of the boys was tall, handsome, didn't take drugs and didn't even smoke. The trainers were almost new, so I gave them to him. We split up after a few months – he was oppressively jealous. I took back my present. Wonderful that size forty-five was so common among the pupils in the Secondary School of Mathematics. I didn't have to search long. Mr Jealous' best friend received the trainers. We stayed close for a very long time.

But let me go back to Mum's second engineer. His wife refused to take him in, so Mum explained, 'I have no commitment to this gentleman,' and dumped him outside the block of flats. But since I had kept the trainers and the Japanese silk scarf, I called his daughter, that gadfly who kept pestering us with the aim of enhancing her financial prosperity. She cut me off: 'You take care of my dad. I have a test tomorrow. Call an ambulance.'

I called the ambulance, but Mum couldn't wait – she had a meeting at the school or a private lesson, I can't remember which. I would've forgotten that gentleman if he hadn't turned up on our door a few months later to ask Mum for a loan. Mum has an unshakable core principle – she does not lend money to anyone. I get that. The man asked for a bowl of soup. 'I haven't cooked tonight,' came the answer.

Sometimes she would say that no one can take away from you the knowledge you have amassed in your head through education. That's why I studied hard and wanted to be the best. Mathematics attracted me, I felt happy alone among the numbers. While the others were still reading the assignment, I had already come up with the answer. I could see the white threads – no, the white ropes! – that held it all together. I took part in maths Olympiads, where I shone. My ambitions had no limit, but God obviously had a thing about me conquering the peaks of science. My skills were decent, but decent doesn't get you to the top. I thought: *Well, I'm going to carry on until graduation exams, and then what? Maths teacher at the local school?* I had relationships with brilliant men, but only one – lacking any brilliance – proposed to me.

Christo.

He was as beautiful, as innocent, as an icon. And unbelievably stupid. I'd tell my baby daughter, to whom I had imprudently given birth, 'I married your father not because he was beautiful, although I hoped you would be beautiful like him. I married him because he was naïve.' He would give me all his wages. To the last penny. If he hid something, two days later he'd bring me a gift – perfume, reprehensibly cheap, but somehow this made me happy. Or he would buy some jewellery with no value whatsoever, as if he wasted his money on cow shit – but I liked that too. Many boys wore that pair of trainers, size forty-five, but no one looked after me like Christo did.

'Siyana, my love, do you want me to pick you up and carry you to the top of Golo Bardo?' he would say to me.

'Why carry me, silly?' I would ask.

'Just because.'

We would buy something to eat, pork chops for example, and Christo would eat all the fatty bits and save the best meat for me, 'Eat, eat, Siyana my love.'

No one had ever done anything like this for me before – that's how I got fooled. I thought I could checkmate my miserable life, just for once. One evening Christo bent down and kissed the earth.

'What're you doing?' I asked.

'I'm kissing your footsteps.'

'Why?'

'Because they brought you to me. I hope I can teach them to bring you back to me too…'

I feared Christo's mother – Elena. She and my mother were like chalk and cheese.

Rumours went around that Elena earned a tidy sum

mixing potions for creaky knees and sciatica. Feeble folk, something's always the matter with them. Apparently, if a child had a fright, the old crone would sprinkle flour on him. And she would adjust displaced bones and crooked spines. People said she had a gun.

She was tall and thin, like the muzzle of a shotgun, with dark eyes – the iris as black as the pupil – and a narrow face with no room left for a smile.

'Here,' she said one time. 'This is a ring. My mother-in-law gave it to me.' Then she repeated it in case I hadn't understood. 'Get on with your husband. May God give you healthy children.'

'Very well,' I said. I didn't approve of how those eyes watched me, as if they were cut from the sole of a boot. 'I'm not going to call you "Mother". I have only one mother, remember that, Elena.'

The shotgun muzzle didn't utter a word, only sat down, pulled the plate of boiled potatoes towards her and started eating.

'Ah, well... fine,' my future father-in-law began.

Christo, whom I was about to marry, was very handsome. But Christo's father... silver temples, a deep chasm in his green eyes, such a proud, high forehead – I had never seen such a specimen.

'Come... well... come on, eat, girl, eat,' said this handsome man and served me some food. His voice was beautiful, a bottomless lake. Immediately pouring me some water, he asked me with a smile, 'Care for anything else, love?'

'What shall I call you?' I asked. I knew his name was Damyan. Good in character, meek – led sheeplike by that rake with bullets for eyes.

'I'm Damyan, girl,' the man answered. 'You can call me Damyan or Dame, as you wish. I don't really mind.'

'I can call you "Dad",' I said, then sank into deep thought, but it wasn't necessary. As I mentioned – while other people were reading the assignment, I would already have calculated the answer. I took the ring that the rake had given me out of my pocket.

'Take it back. You'll be angry you gave it to me if I don't have children.' It was autumn then; the leaves persisted, fighting the wind and pressing against the branches; silence suffused the plates of roast rabbit.

'The town is small,' said the eyes, black like the last night of a patient with high fever. 'Rumours are going around.'

'What rumours?' I asked her. Then something snapped in her gaze and spilt out of those sharp eyes. I was terrified. Not a little, a lot.

'Mum!' Christo exclaimed, getting up from his chair, the glass of red wine still in his hand. To me that glass looked like a disembodied head.

'Well, there was a boy who couldn't stop vomiting.' Her black voice dug slowly as if it were a mole. 'He came to me for a cure. He said you had given him some trainers, then took them back. The boy was ready for the loony bin. Didn't know if he was coming or going, drinking or sleeping.'

'I expect his parents paid you well after you cured him,' I suggested. 'I hear your services are pricey.'

'The boy was all puffy from the drugs they had stuffed in him. Called my dog "Siyana", day and night. In the end he got better. It took six months.'

'Well, you've become even more famous then,' I remarked. 'You've earned plenty of honest lev.'

'You gave the trainers to another boy,' continued the eyes. 'But he was a bit stronger, got better in two weeks. He also called my dog "Siyana". The animal started to go downhill. Lost his fur.'

It was as if the rabbit on my plate was on fire.

'My dog died,' said the old crone. 'I got a new one. Gave him the same name – Gasho.'

'That's wonderful,' I congratulated her. I could've left – perhaps I could've remembered I had a maths lesson, or simply walked out. But I didn't want to run away. I imagine my hands were shaking, but I knew what to do if someone made me tremble. I started to eat the rabbit, then I sipped some wine that the old crone's impossibly beautiful husband had poured for me. In the end I addressed myself to her. I'm not sure if my voice trembled, but it didn't matter anyway.

'Elena, could you pour me some water, please?'

I rejoiced at her open-mouthed look of astonishment. I enjoyed watching her like that. She didn't pour me any water. The beautiful man with silvery temples leapt like a squirrel and scurried back with a glass in his hand. 'That's the most beautiful glass we have,' he explained. 'The only one that's real crystal. I bought it for my son's wedding.'

'Merci, Dad,' I thanked him. Very slowly and very quietly I ate all the food on my plate. Then I walked to the stove. Elena's oven was glowing. 'If I have a child, I'll name it after you – Damyan or Damyana.'

I imagined my mum's fury if she could hear me.

The hobs were gleaming. If it were possible, everything would have exploded from cleanliness. Out of spite, I served myself more food and chose the best portion of meat. I sat back down on my chair and started to eat slowly. I ruminated and ruminated, poured more wine for myself and drank it amid a deadly silence, feeling eyes of tar on me. When I was done chewing, I wiped my mouth with a napkin – not a serviette, but a hand-embroidered cloth napkin. It had probably been a present from Elena's poor mother-in-law too. I stood up suddenly, without warning.

'Christo, let's go. Take my bag.'

Christo got up, took my hand, and we stepped outside. The autumn danced as if it had never seen trees before, tossing gold and crimson onto their leaves. The wind blew, eagerly, as if trying to lift the slabs off the pavement.

'Christo! Carry me.'

And he embraced me. Lifted me up in the air, high above the wind, above the pavement, above this town where everybody knows everything, where the neighbours know the size of your socks.

Christo kissed me – quietly, gently – and I cried. No sobbing, no screaming like the tragic heroines in movies. I find them obnoxious. I curse us for having paid so much money for a satellite TV just to watch that rubbish. He was kissing me timidly, as no one had ever done before. No one. Ever. Drank my tears, drank my eyes, drank my pain and hatred, and the thought of the trainers, size forty-five. Perhaps he whispered 'I love you'. Anyone could say that, but no one could carry me over autumn, over sadness, over the knowledge 'you're good, but not good enough to get away from the Mangiata,' from that miserable land south of Vitosha. Yet it was beautiful, the land, because that fool Christo lived here.

The neighbours wanted to know everything. They watched and watched but I didn't give a damn. That was the first time in my life I was happy. Perhaps this is happiness – November, warm like a pool with sun-kissed water, like a newborn's cry, like a dish with roast rabbit and a very handsome, very naïve man. A November street. Happiness is born in November.

Christo, why did you go building motorways in Spain? Are you paid that much in Zaragoza? In Madrid?

'Wonderful! The idiot will leave and you'll get rid of him,' was Mum's response.

My daughter is called Damyana. She eats little. A sparrow. Such a beautiful child. As beautiful as her father, even more so. As if I'm looking at the old light-minded Damyan, gentle as a butterfly, with the temper of candyfloss – the little one looked like him. A child you would be crazy to leave behind. You'd have to be an idiot. But where you're going is no place for children.

'Give the child to Elena,' my mother suggested. 'Let her look after it. Serves Crazy Elena right.'

If it weren't for this stifling heat and those crickets, crying all night long. If it weren't for... If it weren't for Ginger Dimitar. He had kept those trainers, size forty-five.

* * *

I would go out with the purse Grandma Elena gave me. She even gave me a few coins so they could clink like church bells and the other children would hear them. I wanted to buy tulumba for the kids from the neighbourhood just so they might play with me. But they wouldn't. It all started after Grandma told the police that the bandits Ginger Dimitar and Pavko stole our peaches. They robbed us three times and we endured three times, but when they snapped the smallest peach trees in the garden, I came down with a fever. I vomited for a week or two, I'm not sure how long because I'm a stupid child. At one point Grandma said, 'We're not going to stand for this,' and reported the robberies to the police.

Around here, you never know what might happen next. If a kid is fooled into playing with me, Pavko could break their neck.

That's why, the moment they see me on the street, the kids hide. If they don't run away immediately, they turn their gaze to the clouds, to the brambles, to their socks or to the frogs in the ditch.

'Marche,' I called out to one of my friends, 'look!' and rattled the coins. 'Come, I'll buy you boza. Come!'

But Marche spat on the pavement.

I walk all the way down the street, as long as the road to the end of the world, the asphalt burning hot. I walk and listen with my most expensive purse hanging on the gold chain, the one Grandma Elena took an hour to choose for me at the celebration on the feast day of Ivan Rilski. I rattle the coins. The moment I see a child I wave, but the child pretends they haven't seen me, turns their back to me or steals a glance in my direction and quickly averts their eyes. My hand stops mid-wave, suspended there.

In the evenings, all the kids usually go to the hill at the end of town. At one point they had begun to build an open-air cinema there, with grey bricks. Before Grandma Elena reported the bandits to the police, I used to climb on the building site with the other kids. We would catch lizards; field mushrooms had sprung up in the grass, and we crawled, trying to find at least one. The one who found a tiny mushroom, even if it was the size of a button, was the happiest ever – the rest of us pretended to be happy, but we were *so* jealous. Vasko, the Roma boy who was as skinny as a roof tile, found the most.

Once, a long time ago, when summer was still young and couldn't clamber past June and couldn't find the heat and was basically still a spring with rains, Vasko found a field mushroom the size of a jam jar lid. He said to me, 'Damyanka, here, eat some.'

At first I thought, *he wants to poison me*, but he added:

'I'm not trying to poison you. Look!' And bit off half of the mushroom. 'That's for you.'

I couldn't believe it. Such treasure for me – for me, the girl who didn't even have gemstones or a single lev, only thirty-two stotinki and a purse in which they could clink. Even the chain, which I believed to be gold, was made of ordinary wire. I squeezed and twisted that chain in my fingers so much that the poor thing lost its gold in the torment, turning as grey as the stones. That's why I couldn't believe Vasko was letting me have a bite from his mushroom. I asked him:

'You sure you're not after my purse with the thirty-two stotinki for half a field mushroom?' And at the same time I was thinking, *If he wants it, I'll give it to him*. I *so* wanted to have a bite of the mushroom that I was sure angels had roasted in butter. Angels only ever roast something for you if you've won a million on the lottery, after you scratch the winning ticket with two stotinki.

'I don't want your purse,' Vasko said. 'Eat this giant mushroom. It's delicious. You've never eaten anything so tasty. Believe me.'

'What do you want then?' I pressed. He might get the idea of jumping over the fence into Grandma Elena's strawberry patch. I knew he went around stealing stuff, but Grandma might smack him with that poker or set the dog on him. 'Don't you dare come picking our strawberries, because Grandma will break your spine with the poker, you know the one.'

'I don't want anything. Go on, eat.'

Then I thought, *This one has probably caught some mental illness, like that girl, the handicapped one – the only one who waves at me when I say 'Hello', the one who can't talk and just smiles.* I was just about to say, 'Are you sick in the brain, Vasko?' but had no time, he gave me half of that massive mushroom. I shoved it into my mouth and I'm still wondering how I didn't melt from the sweetness. I had eaten bananas oranges tangerines cherries as large as footballs, I had eaten lamb goat pork and beef, but I had never eaten anything as amazing as that giant mushroom Vasko gave me.

'Thank you, Vasko,' I said, once I'd come to my senses after such beauty and deliciousness.

'Damyanka, what's the matter with you?' he asked, worried. 'We only ever say thank you when someone's about to kick the bucket.'

Because of the huge mushroom I ate, they called Vasko 'sissy' and beat him. *He's soft on that one, you know, the one whose grandmother reported Ginger and Pavko to the coppers, imagine what a fool the old crow is. She'd better not ask questions if her barn catches fire tomorrow.*

They gave Vasko a thrashing.

I went to the town square, outside the disco and the bankrupt pharmacy which someone had set fire to (we all know who sets fires around here, they are not 'persons unknown' as Slavcho the policeman insists). There was a tile, half of it stained brown, blood from Vasko's nose, the drops all dried up. I decided to go to his house to find out what was going on, and since no one wanted to play with me, I stared at the ground. Four children live in Vasko's household – the twins, already enrolled in the Mangiata, another girl in Year 3. Vasko is the only boy. Suddenly, from nowhere, a gang of kids appeared before me and lined up in two rows. A few of the older girls blocked my way. I couldn't go anywhere, so willing or not, I started picking my way between the two rows. One of them pushed me, but I managed to stay on my feet; another one kicked me, even though we had searched for mushrooms together on the hill. The blonde, Evelyn, who was supposedly my friend, tripped me.

I went to Vasko's house but didn't dare enter in case I caught the mental illness too.

'Auntie Valya, how's Vasko?'

'You're not scared of getting fleas or the flu, are you? Why're you standing out there?' she called from inside.

'I'm scared. How's Vasko?'

'Well, they beat him up because of you,' she said. 'Have you brought him something?'

'No,' I answered and got annoyed with myself because I gave half of my cheese sandwich to our dog Gasho. I could've saved it and brought it to Vasko. Why didn't I think of it? Stupid me!

'Go away then.'

I was just turning to run away when a dishevelled head appeared – swollen blue green purple.

'I'm OK, Damyanka. Absolutely fine.'

'You! Straight back to bed. And you, young lady, clear off,' his mother barked.

That evening all the kids gathered in one big happy pile on the hill, a mountain with a hundred eyes, a hundred legs and a hundred arms, and there I was, on my own, like the empty purse that had lost even the gold on its chain. I sat a donkey's length away from them. The grass was tall, but I could still hear their laughter. Grandma Elena had commanded:

'Get out a bit, Damyana, go and have a walk.'

'Where should I go? The other kids don't want me.'

'They will. Sit near them.'

I sat a donkey's length away from them, and how far is that… Almost as long as the motorway. They chatted among themselves, and I sat on my own, like that dog that died of old age and remained in the fields until the sun and rain took his fur, hair by hair. I sat and thought, *The sun and rain will take my hair too*, even though at the time it wasn't raining at all. *Grandma, please don't make me go with the kids any more. I'm even prepared to eat spinach or rice pudding, but please don't make me go to them any more.*

Grandma Elena would force me to graft trees. 'You must know,' she said, 'if you carry the name Damyan or Damyana, you are to graft trees. That's it. Start.'

'I don't want to graft trees, Grandma Elena. I want to explore.'

'No food for you then,' she would say and wouldn't give me as much as a breadcrumb unless I went grafting with her.

Once I managed three days without food and thought I might just drop dead and hoped that when she saw me, she would give me bread and milk. Grandma saw me fainting, but she still didn't give me anything. So, willing or not, I got on with grafting a wild damson onto a Victoria plum. I cut myself doing the first three trees, but I managed the fourth one without an injury. The damn things even took.

I was thinking about the grafted damsons so I could ignore the kids, hoping it would get dark soon and I could go home. With night falling, Grandma Elena was unlikely to make me go back to them on the hill.

While I was wondering what else to think about, someone tapped me on the shoulder.

Vasko.

His face was still blue green purple, like a sunflower with all its seeds prised out. 'Damyanka, I'll play with you,' he said.

I looked at him – tall and lanky, his neck skinny like a dead dog's – and said, 'Vasko, they'll beat you up again.'

'No, they won't,' he said. 'I told them last time: "Give me a double beating. I'm going to go play with Damyanka again." I've had my beating in advance, just so you know.'

His face had become even rounder.

'Come on then,' said Vasko. 'Let's go looking for field mushrooms.' Then he bent to my ear and whispered very, very quietly, like the tail of a fox following its owner: 'I found a special place yesterday. I haven't said a word to anyone. I'm saving it for you.'

We started walking to the special place and I was imagining, since I'm as greedy as our dog Gasho, that we were going to find an enormous mushroom – the size of a Volkswagen Golf's tyre. Suddenly it started raining. Argh, bastard rain!

'What're you getting angry for, Damyanka? Rain for mushrooms is like sausages for you and me,' Vasko said, trying to calm me down.

He was right.

* * *

Three shadows crept towards the garden, which was surrounded by an old drystone wall. Saplings grew in the orchard – in this rocky region you could do nothing else but graft wild damsons onto Victoria plums. That's what they make the rakia from, Victoria plums. There was a cherry tree in the garden too. If the late frosts didn't creep up on it, it bore fruit like stars. The shadows, quieter than torchlight, crawled towards the saplings. Each shadow held an axe. Someone had grafted the wild damsons two or three years ago and now the young trees, protruding into the hollow of the night, were showing off, even after midnight. The axes aimed precisely at these presumptuous deities. Everyone in Radomir knew whose garden this was. They knew only one person who could graft trees and prune them so that even in this hideous soil – though it's called soil, in truth it's stone – Victoria plums would take. And not just take; they bore plums the size of your dad's fist.

All the kids from Staro Selo – its name might mean 'old village', but this backwater is really a neighbourhood of Radomir – and from Vladovo and Stefanovo villages would eat them before they were even ripe. Later, if some fruit managed to reach maturity, flocks of opportunists swooped into the garden, but lately even they thought twice before stealing from that garden. Crazy Elena had planted bushes with poisonous thorns around the wall, and if an abominable spike scratches you, you swell to the size of a mountain, get nauseous, and before you know it you're throwing up your throat, lungs and liver until someone takes you to A & E in Radomir. If the doctor at the hospital is sick, which happens often because he's old and can barely walk, by the time you get to the hospital in Pernik only your dead arse completes the journey.

They have to take you to that same Crazy Elena so she can smear her ointments and infusions on you. The following day you can walk unaided – even though you'd rather never walk again – and you pray for an ordinary death.

It's true, some boys in hoodies pushed over the drystone wall belonging to Crazy Elena or Dushichke Lenche (what they called her depended on the anger or gratitude of her fellow citizens) and burned whatever poisonous bushes they found around it. But it turned out that Dushichke Lenche had played a prank on them: she had stuck some purple-looking sloes about – if one of their spikes gets into your hand or elsewhere, you immediately turn purple yourself. The doctor in Radomir is old and sick and might even die while the ambulance is taking you to the hospital in Pernik, yet you are struggling to breathe as your tongue stiffens. One night, five hoods burned the filthy sloes to the root, and now nothing can stand in the way of their black tracksuits.

One of the axes, the fastest one, flew towards the first tree; a second axe, strong and shiny, sped towards a second. Its blade slit open the moon. Then something clanged – clang, clang – twice. It turned out that the two shadows had voices. They roared and screamed. The third, the clumsiest shadow, heard the noises and was quick on its heels – it turned and ran, jumped over the wall that was now free of bushes, and vanished.

'Idiot! Come back!'

'Come back, you cretin!' the two apparitions shouted over each other. Quicker than machine guns a minute ago, they were now crawling. One of the apparitions barely managed to move. Pulling itself forward, one of its legs dragged something round with metal teeth clamped onto its foot. The second shadow wasn't so lucky – the round thing had bitten both the arm and the leg of the poor creature, and it was turning over and over like a roll of carpet.

But that wasn't the only thing. At one point the first shadow, the lucky one, fell to the road like a brick and its friend, the fabric roll, couldn't even get to the wall. An old grandad, awakened by the commotion, appeared, then a man, then another man and a woman.

Had the old doctor in Radomir already taken his sleeping tablets? Would he be able to lift his head from the pillow? He was a wise and good man, but very old, bless him. What were they to do with these two – it was clear who they were: Ginger Dimitar, with a trap around his leg, and Pavko, famous for burning down all the rakia distilleries in the district so that his could flourish, now with his arm, leg and axe bitten by traps.

'Elena! Get up!' shouted the old grandad, who was the first to reach the yellow house that was quietly dozing as if it couldn't hear what was going on two metres away from its front door.

A tall, grey-haired woman emerged, her nightgown dragging across the floor. She didn't ask, 'What's going on?' If someone was banging on her door before the first roosters crowed, that meant either someone was dying or someone had been killed.

'We're bringing you bandits, Elena. They were screaming in your garden. The trap even caught one of their axes, Pavko's. You know him.'

The woman remained silent.

'Did you set the traps, Elena?'

'These are traps for wolves, not humans,' the woman retorted.

'Then why're these two growing cold, as if they're dying?'

'Because of the burning bush,' the woman said. 'I couldn't kill a trapped wolf on my own. With burning bush, it dies by itself. Once the poison gets in it, the wolf's gone.'

'What wolves in your bloody garden, Elena?!' interrupted a woman wearing a man's jacket over her nightgown.

'There are wolves everywhere.' Elena enunciated every syllable. 'I'll have to burn around the wound, otherwise… take them to Pernik if you want.'

Another woman – tall, spindle-thin, elderly, hair dyed bright orange – ran forward and shouted:

'I curse you, Elena. I curse your granddaughter to fall into the traps you've set!'

'To fall into the traps, you say?' Grey-hair asked. 'Well then,' she said and stopped heating the knife on the candle.

'Heat the knife, Elena! I'll curse you, but you heat the knife. If Ginger Dimitar dies, I'll find your granddaughter. I'll strangle her with these two hands here.'

Silence ensued. The moon was embroidering the clouds with a silver needle – zigzag zigzag. None of the spectators in pyjamas and galoshes over bare feet budged.

'So you're going to strangle her?' Grey-hair muttered and put the knife in the sink.

'Elena. Make that cut! Quick… I won't be strangling anyone.'

The knife suddenly shone over the light of the candle. Then it touched the black trickle of dried blood where the trap had bitten.

'Ooooo,' groaned the man, but the knife wasn't interested in the groans. It was slicing. After the knife, Grey-hair's brown hand poured some mush from a round bottle which was emitting an odour that the people of Radomir had never smelt before.

'Please, Elena! Cut my boy too,' cried another, smaller woman. She wasn't dyeing her hair yet, but she had curled it like old bedsprings. No one used sprung mattresses any more, everyone in this modern district had switched to modern ones.

'I have told you that I'll never heal Pavko again,' Grey-hair said. 'Since he slaughtered a kid, I promised myself, Diana, that I wouldn't heal your son. He cut the head off my baby goat and threw it into the kitchen. Just as the child was having breakfast.'

'Please, Elena! Please!' The woman was about to fall to her knees. 'Look! He's gone all pale! Cut, please! Cut! I'll buy you another kid. I'll buy you two. I'll buy you a car!'

'One kid. He slaughtered one, I only want one.'

'Oooo,' cried the one the trap had bitten on the leg and the arm. He had thick hair – a hedge overgrown with nettles.

The brown hand was pouring stench from the round bottle over the blood, the blood was sizzling over the wound, the wound opened and shone menacingly. The throat under the thick hedge gurgled, as if the kid the youth had slaughtered was coming back to life.

'Would the boys have really... hmmm... died while we drove them to Pernik?' the grandad who had first appeared on the street in the middle of the night muttered. 'Poor things, suffering so much. Have you done that on purpose, Elena?'

'Now you can take them to Sofia, if you want,' Grey-hair announced. 'That thing I poured will protect them for four hours.'

'Bitch! You're a bitch, Elena!' the woman who was still bent like a torn bag whispered. 'You won't see a kid from me. You won't even see piss from a kid. Is that clear? Know that. Even write it down.'

Grey-hair rinsed the knife and wiped it with the towel that hung on a hook on the wall.

'A kid. And make sure you wash the blood off the tiles. Next time you knock on my door, I may not put my galoshes on.'

'Let's hope worms feast on your flesh in the grave next time,' the woman with the perm hissed, straightening up. She started to leave, took a few steps, reached the gate, then scratched her head, her neck, and turned back.

'Gimme a rag,' she snarled.

'Get one from your house,' Grey-hair answered calmly.

At that moment a young child in pink pyjamas approached the group of adults. Smiling from their chest was a printed image of Anna from *Frozen*, and on the back Elsa was looking thoughtfully and intently.

'Is he going to get better?' the child asked, but no one answered. A cranky old Volkswagen pulled up outside the yellow single-storey house. The two injured youths were loaded into it. That weird round bottle was going to help for four hours. God knows what Crazy Elena had poured into it.

'Bitch!' the woman with the curly nettle-like hair repeated, holding a rag in her hands as if she wanted to strangle it. She started scrubbing the tiles but didn't really clean them.

'Here's some water,' the child in the *Frozen* pyjamas said. 'It's easier with water.'

* * *

Every day the young woman would dress the girl in an ever more expensive dress and ever more expensive sandals and walk further and further away from the single-storey yellow house.

'Siyana, when are you going to leave the child with me?' asked a tall, rope-thin old woman one Saturday.

'When I'm in a good mood,' the mother answered and, clutching the girl's hand, began walking. The child wanted to say something, even ask a question, but never got the chance.

Mother and daughter wore the same dresses, sandals and hats. The girl was chattering and pointing at trees, the road, the houses. The woman didn't talk, it wasn't necessary. They had reached the ice cream van when a gentleman with spiky orange hair approached them. His trainers were orange, his vest was orange, his shorts – an even brighter orange. Not human, but fire.

'Two ice creams for these beauties,' the man ordered and didn't even wince at paying for the largest and most expensive wafers available. 'This is for the most beautiful lady,' the man carried on, and after a minute the orange trainers ran towards one of the posh houses.

In this town all houses were grand; someone in the family always worked in Italy or Spain, and even the ones in Greece often sent financial support. Every Tom, Dick and Harry bought a used car first, then painted the outside of their house. In this way, according to the price of the paint, it became clear who worked where and how much they earned. From one of those houses, which boasted in a loud voice to the others, 'We're rich and you aren't!', appeared the orange vest holding a bouquet. He didn't work abroad. His house sparkled suspiciously. Where did the money come from? The bouquet didn't even look like a bouquet. It was a huge sheaf of orange roses.

'They're for you, Siyana. Every single one of them.'

'You do know that my darling mother-in-law will note what happened,' said the woman who wore a dress identical to the girl's.

'You don't seem to be the worrying kind,' remarked the orange vest.

'Those roses are expensive,' the woman assessed.

'Are you going to give me something?' the kid asked.

'I brought chocolate for you.' Apparently the orange vest had come prepared and added: 'You know, Siyana, I'd love to show you my collection of…'

'I bet you don't have any collection,' the woman laughed. 'I bet you don't even know what the word "collection" means.'

'I'll show you a collection I haven't got. I have something else for you.'

'And the kid?' the woman asked.

'The kid? Of course, the kid… we'll take the kid to the Willow Play Centre. What do you say, little princess? Do you want to go to the Willow Play Centre? I'll buy you face paint and lipstick. Would you like that?'

'Yes, yes!' the child cheered so enthusiastically that the Bulgarian flag embraced the European Union flag, then both flags bowed to each other and began dancing with the wind, perched on their long poles.

'We don't have much time,' the woman commented.

'I know. Why didn't you leave the kid with the old crow? She could've made her some soup or something.'

'Just to make your life difficult,' said the woman. 'You see, I've made you reach into your pocket for a ticket to the Willow Play Centre. You've already bought her an ice cream and chocolate, and when we leave, you'll buy her roller skates too. My daughter takes size thirty-two. Remember – size thirty-two.'

* * *

The girl was quite happy at the Children's Play Centre, part of Café Willow. The man with the orange forelock gave fifty lev to a pimpled teenager and encouraged her to pay special attention to the girl in a dress that cost her father at least a month and a half's salary. He was a naïve man who aspired to get rich from construction in Spain. The pimpled teenager was grateful for the cash. She was probably doing her teacher training and clearly money was a bit short, otherwise she would've bought anti-acne lotion.

The girl sank into the soft pink balls, glided down the slide, played with purple ribbons for queens and fairies. The teenager with the unattractive skin drew cat's whiskers on the child's face, then wiped them off and drew blue butterfly wings. The kid was having fun. The young employee with the ugly complexion read her the fairy tales 'Puss in Boots' and 'Snow White'. There were no other children's books in the play centre, but the girl in need of a beautician told the little one fairy tales she remembered from her grandmother: 'The Three Little Pigs' and 'Dyado vadi ryapa', the one about the impossibly big turnip that grandad couldn't pull out.

At some point the child cried: 'I want my mummy.'

'Shall I buy you a chocolate?' the caring employee asked.

'No. Ginger Dimitar already got me some.'

'Shall we play piggyback then?' she offered. 'I can be a stallion, you can saddle me and shout, "Go, go, chase the wind!"'

'OK then,' the child agreed. 'I'm a skinny kid. Grandma always wants me to eat more, but I don't. Grandma also shows me how to lift the skin, so it doesn't hurt you if you have a trapped nerve. Am I too heavy, kind horsey?'

'You're as light as a feather,' the pimpled teenager assured her. They played piggyback, then pretended to be hippopotamuses, then frogs, 'croak, croak.'

Suddenly the girl screamed: 'I want my mummy!'

It was a normal child's scream to start with, then her head started bobbing back and forth as if it was on a spring. That was barely tolerable, but when the little one began to choke, and after a while to suffocate, the frightened employee gave in: 'Calm down, my little gold nugget. Would you like me to take you to Mummy?'

The acne-ridden teenager turned out not to be so strong after all and couldn't carry the little one. She carefully removed the damp strands of hair from the child's face, took her hand, and after swaying here and there on the road, which was hot like sunflowers, they eventually arrived in front of an ostentatiously painted house, several storeys high with windows from floor to ceiling. That was the latest fashion to sneak into this small provincial town where the earth was devoid of soil and filled with stones.

Suddenly the employee from the Children's Play Centre started coughing. So hard and intensely that one of her sandals flew off and she tripped on the path to the house. Despite this, she carried on coughing harder and more intensely.

'Are you choking, Petya?' the little girl asked. 'Would you like some water from my bottle? Look how pretty my water bottle is, Dad sent it for me from Madrid.'

The teenager didn't even glance at the water bottle from Madrid, in which according to the label in English, *Your child's water remains radiantly clean.* The face conquered by acne turned scarlet from the racking cough.

'What's the matter? Please don't die,' the child said, frightened. 'Do you have bronchitis? Grandma makes potions to cure it.'

For no apparent reason, the teenager grabbed the child's head and turned it back towards the street, though there was nothing to see.

Behind the glass of the enclosed marble terrace, a woman and a red-haired man were asleep on the floor.

* * *

Hello, Siyana!

I'm writing you a letter in my head.

It's hot here. Temperatures reach forty degrees, but don't worry about me. I bought a hat for seven euros. It's synthetic but it does the job. Good hats cost thirty-four euros and with them, you don't even know that the sun exists. I really wish you were here with our little girl. Have I dreamt of you or not, I'm not sure, but I see you next to me. It's lovely, but the moment I realise you're not near, it all turns ugly. Please write. Sometimes after midnight I read my mail, and if there are two lines written by you, it's as if I haven't been digging holes all day. I feel better. Do you remember, you once showed me that special equation of yours — apparently super easy to solve? The equation of happiness.

$-3y + 4x = 11$

y + 2x = 13

I tried to solve it. I don't know why I think of it so often. You are my difficult equation, Siyana.

It's better that you and Damyana are not here. It's really expensive. If we lived around Madrid, it would cost us four times more than in Bulgaria. Sometimes I get fed up. I don't know how I manage to hold myself back from jumping on the bus back to you. I want to see you. Even if it's for half an hour. I've sent you two hundred and seventy euros. Maybe you could pop over for a bit? I can arrange for half a day off work. There are budget airlines. Please come. For two days. I've lost seven or eight kilos.

I'll put them back on when I return.

If Mum gets on your nerves, don't pay any attention to her. If you can't cope with that, move out. I'll send you a hundred euros every month. I'll help with the rent.

I watch videos of you and the child. You are beautiful. My x and y joy. If you can't find an apartment in Radomir, or rather if you don't want to, take an apartment in Pernik. It's far enough that you won't get annoyed by Mum.

Does Damyana ask about me?

Kisses. Christo.

Don't fear poverty.

More kisses.

Christo.

* * *

All the grafted Victoria plums, each and every one of them, were cut right down. *That's not axes*, Elena thought, *they used a saw.* Some of the ruined saplings were stuck in the ground next to their barren roots, others were strewn about, their buds still not formed, the place where they were grafted slightly thicker, the trunks carefully whitewashed. The stronger trees had been chopped into equal length branches. Big feet must've jumped on the branches to squash them. By the front door of the house a pair of men's trainers were left behind – old, battered, size forty-five.

Elena observed the devastated garden, her gaze caressing the cut saplings. She had gone to Kyustendil for the grafts, then grafted early in the morning, ten minutes before sunrise. She cherished every tree that took, she pruned them, treated their injuries with a special fruit tree potion. Tall, thin as a snake, the woman stood in her barren garden – a withered snakeskin thrown under the miserly sun. She was motionless, not a person but an iron rod covered in rust. Beneath the rust though, the iron was intact.

She bent over one of the cut trees, picked it up, and with severed steps, black as the plague, carried it to the house. She returned, piled one, two, three, four broken saplings, grabbed the sheaf in her hand and squeezed it in a strong grip, dragged it to the barn, then removed the small twigs and arranged the stems into a neat pile. She went back to the garden, bent down, bit her lower lip and began to gather the rest of the ruins. Around that time a child with shoulder-length light brown hair, a girl wearing pyjamas with the image of Anna from *Frozen* on the front and Elsa on the back, came out, her bare feet shoved into large galoshes.

The child saw her grandma, looked towards the garden where the severed plum branches lay like kittens run over on the road. She didn't say anything. Just started whining like a dog hit on the head with a shovel. The old woman didn't come to comfort her.

'Granny,' the girl whispered.

Her face was a small muddy puddle, a trampled page from a fairy tale. Snotty nose. A river of tears down the *Frozen* pyjamas.

'Granny, they've cut our Victorias.'

'Yes, they have.'

'We won't have any plums.' The child began whimpering again. The beaten dog in her voice groaned, and if anyone glimpsed the child, they would probably think that the poor dog's days were numbered.

'Go wash your face and shut up,' snapped the tall woman. 'Then come back to help me, Damyana. We'll dig holes. We'll plant new trees. Cherries.'

The child tried to stop crying, didn't quite manage but at least hushed a little, and wiped her face and nose with a sleeve from *Frozen*.

Exactly at that moment, right by the gate, a tall, toned man with hair so red it looked like the burning centre of a hearth, a man dressed in an orange jacket, orange jeans, orange trainers, more of a tulip than a person, called in a loud voice:

'Oi!'

The tall woman turned to face him, then locked her gaze back on to the pile of severed saplings.

'My compliments, Elena!' the man said and waved.

'Thanks!' the woman answered. 'I'll remember it.'

She picked up the flat shovel, then slowly examined something with her eyes. Without hesitation she stabbed the shovel into the soil.

'It looks like you're having fun, huh,' remarked the orange tulip.

Elena didn't respond. With measured, concentrated movements she carried on digging, first shaping the hole – fifty by fifty centimetres – then making it deeper. The child, now dressed in a worn pink coat, faded jeans and wellies (exactly the right clothing for accomplishing important jobs), joined her.

'Bring the pickaxe,' the woman ordered.

After couple of minutes the little girl appeared from the cellar. She couldn't lift the heavy pickaxe, so she dragged it. Grey-hair didn't go to help her. The man with the orange jacket leant on the drystone wall surrounding the garden. The child didn't look at him, just carried on – a small digger pushing hard to excavate rocky terrain.

'Your daughter-in-law is advancing fast, huh, Elena?' remarked the orange voice.

* * *

Sometimes I dream of her eyes: black, freshly dug graves. I wrote to Christo that I'm going to move out. I don't want to live in this town. I hate her trees, her flowers. Now all twenty-one trees are on the ground.

I thought of Christo. Of the heat enveloping Madrid. Of how he showed me that in a second a person could become greater than death. Ready to give their blood for someone, for the one who made them shine. Things like this rarely happen, so rarely that you doubt they ever do. Just for a moment, for less than a moment, I wanted to give my life to Christo. I thought a century wouldn't be enough to thank him. I thought he made me, without even intending to, touch something other people couldn't know, something more powerful than the sky, than sex, than callous gossip and envious glances. He was my equation of happiness. He was the x and the y.

I could have endured hunger with Christo. I could have washed his shirts by hand and been happy to have done it. But he left me to a scorched life inside Elena's black eyes.

Ginger Dimitar is robust, a bull with iron horns, and I've discovered that I enjoy being a matador. I like it when someone crawls in my shadow, kissing it. The further my thoughts descended, the thirstier my shadow became.

Every so often I would go over to Ginger Dimitar's house. His dad spat in my direction. His mother, red-haired like her offspring, even brighter ginger since she had started dyeing her silver hair, would hiss: 'What do you want, here, huh?'

'Not you,' I would reply.

I would slip into the hallway. Ginger Dimitar waited for me behind the door. It took me a month to notice the rug on the floor. I would push him on top of his own orange trainers. Malice oozed from my skin. There was no malice with Christo. For Christo I would jump into an abyss. For Ginger Dimitar? Please, don't make me laugh. There is a Ginger Dimitar on every corner, on every floor, under each stone. Each one with biceps I could drain with a single touch. Ginger Dimitar would fall asleep, meek, beneath me. The hunk of muscle, which had broken more people than there were slabs on the footpath, would wait for me behind his front door and whisper, 'I love you.'

… All my clothes, topped by a pair of old socks chewed up by the obnoxious dog Gasho, were stuffed into a black sack from Kaufland and thrown outside her gate. Ginger drove me there. I had mentioned to him that I wouldn't set foot in the piece of junk that was his six-year-old Audi. Two days later he bought a Jeep the size of a train carriage. The monster shone; I liked stepping out of it onto the street. I have a penchant for power and powerful cars. When I drove the Jeep, teenagers with pimples, gentlemen with glasses, men in elegant suits and beggars would all turn their heads after me. I asked Ginger to stop outside Elena's house. He rammed the snowplough to a stop in front of her gate. I waited. Finally, she came out – a plank in a blue apron. She spotted me. Her shoulders tightened like a rope on the gallows; the asphalt melted and flowed under the wheels of the Jeep.

A sack from Kaufland in which some old granny had stuffed my clothes is unlikely to have a negative effect on my mood. I pushed the gate. It was locked. Elena occupied herself in the garden. I watched her. She was chopping the butchered saplings, cutting them into twigs, each around thirty centimetres long. With the big axe she split the trunks, as thick as my daughter's arm, then with the small axe removed the side branches.

I had made coffee in two plastic cups and called her: 'Elena, would you drink coffee with me? You look out of breath.'

She came over.

I was hoping she would slosh the coffee at my feet, but she just stood there – an old giraffe awaiting death in Staro Selo. Her black eyes bored into mine. She stretched her arm over the drystone wall, took the cup from my hand and sipped. In that moment I regretted I hadn't sprinkled something poisonous in that coffee.

'Elena,' I said flatly, 'why have you locked the gate?'

I stood next to the Kaufland sack; the Jeep was towering behind my right shoulder. Elena suddenly stopped seeing or hearing me.

Immediately next to the fence, on the inside of the wall, glimmered a narrow white cement patio. I had asked Christo to paint it that colour. I used to splash water on it, bringing up the heady scent of rain, rain that was still months away from summer and from me. Along with the imaginary rain, Christo would return to my thoughts. Christo loved the clouds; he would pick me up in his arms and let the sky bathe me. I would smile and he would say, 'I dressed you in laughter.'

I jumped over the fence and landed on my white rain patio. I waved at Ginger; he waved in response and then looked out of the Jeep's open window.

I attempted to get into the house, but even before opening the door to the vestibule – that awful word 'vestibule', which Grey-hair used, brings thoughts of a plastered limb; I call the tiny space 'passage' or 'entry' – even before I could slip into the passage, the blue apron, without hurrying, without fussing – I had the feeling an excavator was digging a hole nearby – stepped forward, hands slack. Before I could ask myself what she was going to do, she pushed me and slowly, with the hideous indifference of a landslide, drove me beyond the patio where I used to wait for the scent of rain and think of Christo.

Elena was strong: she massaged backs, swollen ankles, arms; she split wood. An ox of a woman. She pushed me as if I were an empty basket in her arms.

I didn't shout. I didn't speak.

I saw the snowplough Jeep approaching me in reverse.

'Mum!'

That's when I saw her. She had climbed onto the wall. Slim, delicate like a snowdrop. Two brown hands grabbed her by the waist – a tiny waist, the size of a champagne flute.

'Mum,' the child called from the patio where I once summoned the rains.

* * *

They had found Ginger Dimitar in his orange jacket and orange jeans outside the post office. I saw him when they brought him to Grandma – his hair was wet in places and looked like a dying fire; in places it was dry, the orange stove still burning.

'Not good,' Grandma said and prised open one of his eyes with her thumb and index finger. It was bloodshot, but that wasn't dangerous, even I knew that. The danger was that the eyelids had swollen like pillowcases. And they were yellow.

'He's been given hellebore root,' Grandma Elena said.

'Are you trying to say that someone has been putting a root in his eyes?' Ginger Dimitar's mother asked.

'I'm saying that he has been given hellebore root tea to drink. Dilated pupils. He could go blind,' Grandma explained so calmly that the woman, her red head sharp as a ball of barbed wire, jumped.

'Here!' she said, waving a wad of money. 'Here!' I had never seen so many hundred-lev notes in one place, more than the treasure in Elov forest from the fairy tale they were showing on TV. 'Here, cure him!'

'People say it was you who poured that nastiness down the boy's throat. Because he chopped down your plums,' Ginger Dimitar's father muttered so quietly his throat turned inside out, and the words fell murky and bloody onto the ground.

'If someone felled your Victoria plums, would you stroke them with a feather?' Grandma asked. She pronounced this in a level, deep voice, as if she was telling me, 'Tomorrow we'll be digging holes to plant new trees.'

'So it was you who poured hellebore down his throat then?' said the upside-down throat of the man, Old Ginger, who was taller than his son with the yellow eyelids.

'If it were I who poured hellebore root down his throat, he would have gone blind long ago. Believe me!' Grandma Elena said. 'Do you want him to go blind?'

Old Ginger was silent.

'I asked you something,' Grandma Elena repeated.

'I want him to see.'

'Twenty-one young cherry saplings, tomorrow. You'll deliver them to my garden. Twenty-one exactly. That's how many of my saplings your son ruined. Seven early Cristalina, seven Sonatas, and seven white Dame Nancy.'

'But...' Old Ginger's throat had returned to its place but was still struggling to find the voice.

'Then he won't go blind,' Grandma said.

'All right! All right!' the barbed-wire woman screamed.

'All right!' Old Ginger shouted.

'Damyana.' Grandma turned to me. 'Go get the bottle for eyes. Quick. Wash your hands and come here to keep his eyes open.'

I was frightened. I was very frightened; his eyelids were thick, as thick as the cover of *Pippi Longstocking*.

'Pull yourself together so I don't leave you without lunch, Damyana,' Grandma scolded me, and I forgot all about Pippi. I held the eyelids open as if they were the door to the chicken coop. Grandma was pouring from the eye bottle when suddenly she snapped:

'Damyana! Now close this eye and stop shaking if you don't want me to slap you across the face.'

'He's in pain,' I let slip without realising. 'He's moaning.'

'I'll slap you across the face,' Grandma repeated. 'Hold that bottle!'

I held the bottle firmly and she still slapped me.

'Can Grandad come and hold his other eye?' I stuttered.

This time Grandma didn't say a word, just pulled my ear very hard and ordered: 'Open the man's eye at once!' The eyelid of his left eye had gone from yellow to a terrifying light brown colour. I opened his other eye and nearly wet myself. It was red like the red traffic light – when it was still working two months ago – outside the bakery of the twins Dida and Dona.

'Pour from the eye bottle, Damyana.'

'I can't.'

'Pour!'

I clenched my teeth, actually I didn't clench them, I bit my right hand so it would stop shaking, and poured from the bottle into the red traffic light. The bloodshot red began slowly to turn into a human colour, very slowly; first yellowish, then it crawled towards pink, and finally turned white like a normal human eye.

'Can you see me?' Grandma asked. 'I'm asking you, you conceited dimwit. Can you see me?'

'Yes,' Ginger Dimitar moaned. 'I can.'

'If you set foot in my garden one more time... you will never ever see again.'

Then the barbed-wire woman threw herself forward and kissed Grandma's hand.

'I... I... was going to kill you,' said Old Ginger.

'And then you would've let your son slip away,' retorted Grandma and turned to me: 'Damyana, go read two pages from *Pippi Longstocking*. I'll test you. If you stutter, you'll be sleeping on the bench outside the town hall.'

Lord, I know You're somewhere far away, but do You think You could tell Pippi to take off that long stocking, so the book's not so thick?

'Twenty-one holes – fifty by fifty centimetres. Make sure they're dug by three o'clock tomorrow afternoon,' Grandma demanded. 'In the space where my Victoria plums stood, I expect to see twenty-one cherry trees.'

'All right then,' muttered Old Ginger. 'It'll be done.'

* * *

There were two men: one of them with silver-grey hair and such an intelligent, beautiful face that all the girls from the grammar school turned their heads. The other man, clearly younger, unshaven, stuffed into a crumpled jacket, was bent like a wasp with a spinal injury. His face was hidden behind a thick brown beard. The two dragged each other, like toddlers making their first steps. The beautiful man supported the one with the beard.

'I'm fine, Dad,' said the crumpled jacket, but either the words drowned in the beard or they weren't words at all, just a grunt. Beautiful squeezed his son's ragged sleeve tightly. That wasn't enough. He caught him under the armpit, but something gave way. The bearded man swayed and his dad helped him to sit on the ground.

Everything was wet – what else do you expect from mud?

'I'm going to be sick,' the bearded man said, this time clearly. 'I don't feel well.'

'Do you want to lie down? There's nothing wrong with you, son. Nothing… Christo…'

Beautiful helped his boy lay down, then pulled a phone out of his pocket. Everything about him was clean, new, beautiful, even this phone, though it wasn't the latest model like everyone else's in this town (all either bought second-hand or stolen and resold at a bargain price). But this handsome man could hardly have a stolen item in his hands. He uttered a few frightened words into the phone, listened tensely to what the electrons had to say, then responded, 'I hear you! I'm waiting!' The man choked on these words, couldn't get them out, his neck bent from waiting. He kept repeating to his son:

'I've got you, boy. I've got you; I'm telling you I've got you.' He was holding the lapels of the crumpled jacket as if he was trying to squeeze juice from it.

After a while, who knows if it was a little while or a long while, a tall, thin woman in rubber galoshes came up the street; she had no coat, just a cardigan. About ten or fifteen paces behind her scurried a little kid – a girl, thin like a clock's hand. She didn't have a coat, just a tracksuit, no hat either even though the clouds were of a mind to expel rain. They had a soul too; they had had enough of carrying hailstorms and deluges in their suitcases.

The kid shouted, 'Granny, Granny Elena!' but realised that only the wind caught her words in its cold net. No one paid attention to her, and she pushed on, trying to catch up with the tall woman. Elena reached the handsome gentleman with the clean phone, didn't look at him, bent down to the bearded man and said:

'Open your mouth, son.'

The man didn't open his mouth. His head lay very close to where he had vomited. His eyelids were shut. The woman opened his left eye with her thumb and index finger and ordered: 'Stop playing games. Open your mouth.'

The man couldn't hear her.

The child finally caught up with them. Whispered: 'Daddy.'

The beard moved slightly. It wasn't clear if it was a smile or something else. The beard moved again, really trying to smile. Failed. Then vomited again.

'Come on. We're lifting him up,' the woman said. She and Beautiful picked up the shabby young man, got him to his feet and dragged him down the street.

The kid shuffled behind them wearing huge rubber galoshes. One of them slipped off her foot, she put it on again, caught her father's jacket and began chirping: 'Don't worry, Daddy. I've got you. I'm holding you really tight. Really, really tight.'

When it started raining, the four of them hadn't yet reached the simple one-storey house, simple but pretty. No one paid attention to the rain. The kid opened her mouth and swallowed a raindrop. *I drank the spring*, she thought, frightened, then looked around and saw that spring was falling from the sky and said to herself, *Now I'm the spring*.

The group entered the house. Even while they were opening the door, the child didn't let go of her father's jacket. She was convinced that like this she was giving him the spring.

At one point the rain stopped for just long enough to gather more strength before coming rushing back to caress the street with its damp fingers. The sky trembled with thunder. Damyana had been told that when this happens, it was because the dear Lord had bronchitis and was coughing, so she poured a greenish liquid – a bit like a porridge and a syrup at the same time – into a spoon, walked onto the cement patio and said: 'Here, Lord, this is for You. It's not very pleasant, but it will cure Your bronchitis, honest.' The dear Lord coughed again, and the child insisted, 'Even I know how to mix this nasty concoction. You need seven herbs. Five of them have thorns, look I still have a splinter in this finger. Please, Lord, don't delay. The rain will drink Your medicine and I don't want You to suffer.'

Exactly at that moment the handsome old man said quietly (he was always softly spoken and had a beautiful voice, like chocolate): 'Damyanka, come on, come inside, my little moonbeam, *mesechinke moya*. The dear Lord is cured now.' He helped the girl out of her soggy tracksuit and gave her a dry one to put on; it was old and worn, but it knew its obligations. It worked together with the girl while she picked nasty thorny herbs and mixed potions under her grandmother's instructions.

'This tracksuit is for making quince seed syrup,' the child said. 'I should put on the blue one, Grandad. Grandma and I do the healing with it.'

'As you wish, mesechinke moya,' Grandad agreed, dabbed the moisture – or maybe it was spring – from the girl's hair and helped her put on the blue tracksuit. Anna and Elsa, the princesses from *Frozen*, had left this piece of clothing. They had faded, or maybe they had never wanted to be there.

'Where're you going, Grandma?' the child asked. 'Are you going to get lavender? Can I come too?'

Elena didn't answer.

'Your grandma's in a hurry, mesechinke moya. Come, the two of us will sit with your daddy until Grandma comes back.'

The woman who looked like a walking lightning rod ran, not paying any attention to spring, to the road, to the rain. She had no hat or umbrella but had slipped into the huge red galoshes the girl had just been struggling with.

She reached a smart house, a show home, in front of which a well-maintained garden lay like an obedient pageboy ready to perform his duties, though Grey-hair didn't even notice it. The gates of such haughty properties are always locked. Wet to the bone, she pressed the bell. No one came. For a fleeting moment an enormous man with curly ginger hair, dressed in a shirt more elegant than he was, appeared.

'What's that old bag doing here?' the man asked. He added something but the words drowned in the mud, unheard. Behind the window, as large as an airport's, stood a woman. There was nothing special about her apart from the fact she was pretty: brown hair, brown eyes, like most women in this town.

The lightning rod leant on the bell. The air heated, the rain started bubbling, still no one came to open the gate. The ginger specimen and his companion seemed to have melted into the carpet on the floor. They stayed still. Their eyes, satisfied and confident, watched Grey-hair ring the bell as if trying to thrust it to the other side of the world, perhaps to Australia or India.

'Mad,' said Ginger, but he didn't yet know what 'madness' really meant.

The woman with the silver-grey hair, as tall as the down-pipe and no thicker than it, stepped onto one of the gate's horizontal iron bars and climbed onto the fence. The drystone wall was adorned with sharp iron spikes, a necessary addition in this flourishing town. The lightning rod was convinced that she wouldn't be able to get past the spikes but despite this, she continued upwards. She stood up, a piece of string in a wet cardigan and red galoshes.

She considered her next move. If she were a normal person, she would've jumped back down to the pavement, but clearly she wasn't a normal person. She stepped between two sharp spikes. Her trousers, black, made of cheap artificial fabric like the ones they sold in the popular Second Hand-Second Chance shop, swayed with the raindrops. One of the second-chance trouser legs got tangled in the spikes, but she unhooked it. Then, like a cannonball, like a bucket full of concrete, like a sack of potatoes, the woman jumped into the garden. It was over a metre and a half to the ground and she landed on a patch of lilac hyacinths. The flowers turned to mush under her weight, but the old crow didn't even look at them.

She picked her way down the neat garden path towards the house, from where, astonished and outraged, the unusual young woman and the ginger man were watching.

The lightning rod stalked forwards. She was probably badly bruised from her landing on the hyacinths. She reached the front door – made from expensive wood, engraved and polished, in tune with the fashion of this flourishing town – and started banging on it. The front door, as was habitual around here, was firmly bolted.

After a minute or two – but then who knows exactly how long – the door moved, without a squeak. It opened with dignity and definitiveness. First loomed Ginger, then, like the good fairy, smiling from top to bottom, the woman with the brown eyes appeared.

'What d'you want, huh?' the man said and, without waiting for an answer, pushed her backwards. 'Clear off!'

The lightning rod swayed, stretched out her arm, touched the sleeve of the good fairy and said: 'Siyana, I've come for you. My son is in a bad way.'

'First of all, I forbid you to talk to her.' Ginger pushed her again, but the tall, unpleasantly skinny woman ignored him.

'The father of your child is here, Siyana. He'll die. Come see him. Damyana is waiting too. Look. She's outside the gate.'

Ginger froze. 'Move on,' he growled.

'Siyana! Come with me. I cannot cure him. No one can. He's sick for you.'

'Why don't you ask politely then?' the young woman said.

'Please, Siyana.'

'You're not begging convincingly.'

The tall, unpleasantly skinny woman fell to her knees. She lifted her head towards the brown hair and brown eyes. 'I beg you.'

'Some people kiss the hand of those they beg,' said the brunette, and her brown eyes turned black.

The lightning rod folded into three. No, into four. Her lips, never touched by lipstick, cracked, thin, fell onto the soft palm of the brunette and kissed it. Then they crawled to the other soft pink palm, kissed that too and whispered: 'Please, I beg you, Siyana.'

'Some people, when they beg someone for something, they lift them and carry them to where they need them,' the brunette said.

'I'll carry you in my arms.'

'Ginge, love, run to open the gate,' the brunette ordered. The man, red like a November day, lowered his head and dutifully headed for the gate.

The woman with the brown eyes, which had turned so black they looked like cinders, whispered: 'Now then, pick me up in your arms, Elena.'

The lightning rod rose from the ground and stood up. No thunder raged. She grabbed the brunette around the waist, adjusted her position in the same way a groom carries a bride across the threshold, and turned. The rod swayed a little, staggered coming down the stairs. Then she began walking along the path – large steps, a little stiff, in fact very stiff; the one-lev trousers from the Second Hand–Second Chance shop hampered her steps. The brunette was silent.

'Mum,' a small child cried out in the rain.

The curly ginger gentleman, stuffed into his large shirt, stood and looked on silently. At one point the mass came to life and said through clenched teeth: 'The woman's mad.'

On a street of the quaint little town – it was spring, and it drizzled persistently, small raindrops the size of yellow coins – a tall woman, thin like smoke, advanced along the pavement outside the Golden Lion Bakery. She was wearing a cardigan and a nondescript purple top, bought for one lev, like the plastic trousers, like the red rubber galoshes. This woman was clutching in her thin brown arms another woman, you would say a girl, a much younger girl. She was almost running; her red galoshes splashed in the puddles like bullets hitting stone.

Who knows what business these two had – was the girl unwell, had she choked on something? Was that her mother taking her to Elena for a cure?

Wait… Is that Elena, long and thin like a wooden clog? It looks like her. Oh yes, it is her.

* * *

Listen to me, Dame-Damянka! You're the only reason I'm learning to read and write, and you're the only reason I go to school. It's nice and warm in school, but you have to sit still and the bones in my skull start hurting when I sit still. I could even get a nosebleed. The only reason I'm putting up with this is you.

I want to write you a letter so you can see that I'm serious. Letters don't fill your pocket with money, Mum says, and you know Mum – she's clever. She's also big. With one slap across the face she can cure you of flu, pneumonia, even your brain can be cured if there're lies in it, and if you deceive people with them. Out of all of Mum's kids, the twins and my timid younger sister, I'm the only one who's ever got a grade five, almost top grade! Like a complete plonker I go to school every day and every day I persevere. I've even been to see Mrs Petrova, so she can show me how to write the letter я - ya, because that letter я in your name is really hard, Dame-Damянka. But I'll learn it and I'll write you a letter with my own hand. The same hand that can take apart any lock can take apart and put back together an air rifle, can make a bench, mix a smoke bomb, and can beat up anyone too.

'You,' Mum says, 'you doin' a good thing clinging to Elena's granddaughter. The little one watches how her grandma makes potions against this and that disease. Stick with her and you'll learn too.'

But I'm not clinging to you 'cause of your grandma's potions, Dame-Damянka. I made you a mini moon shuttle from an old wire reel. It can creep, it can climb up places, and when it's on the flat, it runs like a motorbike. Lately, I haven't seen you go out to collect herbs for your grandma's potions. I want to write that letter to you, but I can't. I don't know how to write all the letters of the alphabet, that's why I just make it up in my head. I've written this letter so many times in my head that it's now full to the brim with letters.

I walked past your house yesterday. It was dark inside. They say your father's ill. How on earth is it possible for a man to get sick because his wife is stupid and ran away? How come he's ill, isn't he your Grandma Elena's son? And Elena can cure anything, she can even make medicine out of manure and fix whatever could possibly go wrong with a man. Your father hasn't died, has he, Dame-Damunka?

Look, even if he has, have no fear. Don't cry, I'm telling you.

Mum says there's heaven in the sky, just over the cross on top of the church. Your dad will wait for you there. You and I, when we get old and die, we'll go to heaven to be with him and it won't be bad at all, because the sun always shines over the church, it's never in the shade. It's sunny there and in the winter, we won't feel the cold even if there's no wood for a fire.

My dad tells me I'm stupid, Dame-Damunka.

'There're a hundred beautiful girls with Roma blood like ours, but you, Vasko, stupid boy, don't seem to notice them! What're you doing staring at that feeble-bodied granddaughter of Elena the Healer. Can't you see that girl wanders about like a lost calf and no one wants her? You're the only one who wants her, you idiot!'

'Only me, Dad,' I say to him. 'I don't know why I'm so stupid either.'

But let me tell you what I told Mum: a hundred years ago when the grandmother of my grandmother was herding goats, God came down to the river Struma and said: 'I am on my own and I am God, but I'm not happy. It hurts that I always sit in loneliness. That's why I'm going to give each human a special friend. In this way a human is never going to hurt because they don't have anyone to talk to or because they don't have anyone to make a mini moon shuttle from a wire reel for.' If the human's special friend wanders about like a lost calf, then the human should find them and say: 'Dame-Damunka, you are my special friend. God created you so I'm not on my own and so you're not on your own.' The important thing is that you prick up your ears and hear what God tells you — he came down to earth. He too wandered around like a lost calf, we met, and he said to me, 'Vasko, your special friend is Dame-Damanka.'

'You're an idiot!' Mum said and slapped the back of my neck, but not too hard. When she wants to prevent a lie from forming in my head, she hits hard. 'How come you saw the Lord, Vasko?'

'Maybe I haven't seen the Lord exactly,' I admitted. 'I saw his shadow. He lingered outside Dida and Dona's shop when it was closed, and he fancied drinking a Coke. I fancied a Coke too. That's how I understood what he was thinking. God looks a bit like Dame-Damanka's father.'

'And his wife tramples over him,' Mum snapped. 'Laughing stock.'

Dame-Damanka if your parents argue over who's the laughing stock and who isn't, come to my house. We have chips for dinner. No one is going to ask why you're eating our potatoes, don't worry.

Come out of your house, so I can see you, please.

* * *

'Siyana.' The man couldn't talk. His beard, long and brown like cordite, was suffocating him, the air was suffocating him. 'Siyana… you came. I didn't think you would.'

She was sat on the bed next to him, wet from the rain in this wild, weird March, though the sick man didn't see March. He managed to prop himself up.

'You came,' he said, or maybe he didn't say it. He was so weak he could hardly say anything. It was laughable to see a man in a crumpled shirt, even more crumpled trousers, a man reduced to a pile of bones and a beard, being brave, gritting his teeth.

'I didn't bring you anything from Spain. I earned nothing, Siyana. I failed.'

She was silent, a woman with brown hair, an extraordinary face and brown eyes, which had suddenly turned light brown, perhaps green.

She remained silent.

She didn't stretch her hand towards the crumpled shirt, didn't touch the matted brown hair.

'I wrote a song for you,' the man whose beard was the only thing left of him said. 'When we first met, you told me that you liked my voice. No one's ever said that to me before. Only you. There are no singers on either side of my family.'

It was afternoon or maybe it was morning. He didn't know what time it was out there. It was raining for the second week or the second year in a row. He wasn't even looking at her. A light glimmered in the room, an ordinary light, cheap, the bulb wrapped in something white or perhaps yellowish.

'I was thinking of you. That's why I survived.' The voice was small, soft like hot sand, like spring departing without bringing sunshine. The voice was quiet, didn't know where it was, nor when it would die away. 'If you're not here, why do I need spring? I don't. I give you my memories. There's a person inside them – you. If you're not here, why do I need tomorrow?' The voice fell asleep, turned into rain, into useless rain.

That wasn't a whisper. Just a voice, fading into a place of no return.

The eyes of the man – who would've been better off not saying anything, who would've been better off staying on that street in Spain, who would've been better off falling asleep on the pavement – those eyes became deep, thirsty. He was silent. A man is not born to cry.

'Perhaps I'll get better, but there's no point walking along the streets on my own.'

His face had become ugly, the gaze of a helpless, worthless creature. Someone who shouldn't be dirtying this bed with his filthy trousers.

But suddenly the woman (now she had an ordinary face and eyes that had become light green, like the leaves which were still afraid to show themselves in the March rain) bent over that creature and quietly, very carefully, as if he were a newborn, began kissing the yellow shadows under his eyes. She gently touched the huge brown beard, the matted hair.

In this grey town on the banks of the Struma there was a story about how lonely the Lord was up in the sky. He didn't want people on earth to suffer like He did, because the earth is big and much emptier than the sky. So, the Lord created a special friend for each human. In this neck of the woods people say, *Don't be afraid, loneliness will never cook you in its pot if you drink someone else's tears. That's when you know this is your special friend. You could meet a hundred acquaintances and be even lonelier that the Lord up there in His own sky. At least the sun lives there too and the Lord can talk to him. And for you,* people said in this mean, poor place, *your special friend will shine on you.*

'You shone on me, Christo,' the woman said. 'You.'

Behind the door, like the post of a gallows, stood a tall, thin woman. Elena the Healer. Next to her protruded another post, not really a post – a man, a very beautiful man, so beautiful that when he went out to buy bread from Dida and Dona's bakery, the mountains leant towards each other so they could have a good look at him.

'Our son will get better,' whispered the man.

The tall woman didn't say anything. Slowly, as slowly as if the air were iron and she had to rend it with a hacksaw, she sliced a piece of bread, put cheese on it and handed it to the beautiful man.

'Eat,' she said.

Then she cut another slice, and again put cheese on it. She went across the corridor, opened a door and walked into a narrow room where a little girl was sitting, her nose stuck in *Pippi Longstocking*, page eighty-three.

'Eat,' said the woman. 'When you've finished eating, I'll come to test what you've read, Damyana.'

★ ★ ★

'Grandad, tell me again how Daddy ate the chocolates you bought for your friends.' The girl held the hand of the tall man with silver-grey hair. She smiled, even though March – that peevish month – had just decided to sprinkle more snow over Radomir so that new, deep drifts could sprout. 'Grandad, are you my friend?' the child asked.

'Yes, I am your friend, Dame-Damyanka.'

The child smiled again but didn't say anything.

'Perhaps we can treat ourselves to some chocolate, what do you say?' the man offered. He was so beautiful that the sky looked down and almost stopped throwing snow over Radomir, and two women, whispering to each other and openly staring at the man, greeted them:

'Damyan, you're growing more beautiful by the day. The little one's taking after you and thank God she's not soaked up too much of her grandmother's genes!'

Damyan said, 'Hello!' and was just about to turn towards Café Zoya when the little one tugged at his hand.

'Grandma Elena said that we're not supposed to eat chocolate. It's bad for your teeth, your gallbladder, your heart and your blood vessels.'

'Blimey! Do you know everything about blood vessels?' the man marvelled. 'As long as your grandmother's not looking, chocolate isn't bad for you.'

'We shouldn't tell lies,' the child said seriously.

'We're not going to lie, we're just going to eat some chocolate,' countered the grandad.

The little girl's face shone. 'Do you want to play football?' she asked.

Grandad didn't fancy it because the whole town square was covered in mushy, sticky snow. 'Why don't you go play with the other children?' he asked.

'They don't want to play with me,' the child responded, and the street became as dark as night.

'Well, when your Grandma Elena was your age, she went about on her own too, so don't you worry yourself. Look at her now. The whole town runs to her, people from Pernik and Sofia and Stara Zagora even. When a person gets about on their own, they think all sorts of things and invent even more things, you see.'

'I'm the same, Grandad,' admitted the child. 'But if you're all alone, a witch could take you away.'

'No way! I'll give her such a punch I'll knock her unconscious for three days and three nights. Look at my muscles!'

The grandad clenched his fists to show his strength and the two of them laughed.

'Your Grandma Elena was an amazing child. Very tall! When we were younger, she was taller than me and I always dreamt of growing taller than her, of throwing stones further than her, of swimming faster than she did. The other kids didn't like your grandma, Damyanka. She was very clever too. In school, if she couldn't find the solution to an equation, she would glue herself to the desk and not move. The rest of us would leave, and she would sit there churning away at equations like a concrete mixer. We would take the micky out of her, saying she was "cast iron" and a nerd, but she wouldn't even look at us. She and I were in the same class. She used to sit at the desk furthest from the board because she was the tallest, and I sat at the first desk. I was the shortest. I only came up to her shoulder. Even I didn't know why I was constantly around her. I used to give her a bite from my buttered bread.

She hardly ever accepted it, but whenever I picked wild sorrel from the field – the one where they built the DIY store – your grandma would take the sorrel and smile, just like you're smiling at me now. She would eat that sorrel as if she were a lamb. I also picked her Cornelian cherries. The kids used to say, "You fawn over her just so she can solve your maths questions and let you copy her Bulgarian literature homework." It was like that at first, but beside the homework I began to notice how fast she ran and how she recognised all the different herbs, just like her grandmother. I used to bring her herbs, but she would throw most of them away, hardly ever accepting any of them.

I was up to her shoulder, and they made fun of me for being as small as a bottle of weak rakia.

"Tell me, Elena, what do I need to eat so I can grow taller than you?"

"Why do you want to be taller than me?" she asked.

"So I can ask you out on a date," I said, and that was the truth.

"You can ask me out, even if you're short," your Grandma Elena responded. "I don't think you'll grow taller than me, Damyan."

"Well, in that case I won't ask you out then," I declared. What an idiot, what an idiot! That tall girl, as she stood there holding the sorrel, suddenly burst into tears. I had never seen a girl do that before, sobbing without a sound. You would think she had choked on a sorrel leaf, yet the tears kept falling; her top got soaked. I still remember that top – purple, thick, as thick as three of my tops.'

'Couldn't you pick more sorrel for her?' the little girl asked, still clutching her grandad's hand. 'Why didn't you say that you'd ask her out? You've been a bit stupid there, Grandad.'

'Well, I didn't think of it,' admitted the man with silver-grey hair and smiled, but somehow inwardly. His face closed like people close their windows in February. 'But I thought of something else, you see. You know the saying we have here in Radomir, the one about God who is always on His own and even the sun, despite all the shining, can't bring Him joy?

God created a special friend for every person, man or a woman, so that all the people who can't talk to the sun, the stars, the clouds and the moon didn't suffer. Only that special friend can transform the loneliness into a river with warm pools, into joyous children playing at home and demanding to eat all the chocolates, into a sorrel soup and a clean, cosy house.'

'But we have a cosy house and chocolates,' the girl said.

'Yes, we do, because I found my special friend,' Grandad explained.

'You mean Grandma? How did you find her?' the child asked impatiently and just for a moment she forgot that she had wanted to play football in the damp snow of the town square.

'Well, I just told you the tale about loneliness we have here in Radomir.'

'That tale is a deception and a lie from end to end,' objected the child.

It was snowing, large lacy snowflakes. God was crocheting with clouds again. As if to trick Baba Marta into becoming His best friend and bringing the end of winter with her, He was grabbing the white yarn and throwing it over Radomir. Like this, the earth would be confused into thinking she had become the sky because she was wrapped with clouds, and the clouds would think they had finally managed to tread for a while – just like real people – on the earth. What else could a cloud dream about, except to walk barefoot on the streets, meadows and rooftops of Radomir? Maybe this tale is a deception and a lie, but why would that be? If a whole town recounts it, from grandfather to grandchild, then it must be sincere and true.

'Go on,' the child asked and stuck out her tongue to catch the snowflakes.

She knew there was only one thing tastier than snowflakes – icicles. But one was not to overdo it, because that's exactly what your throat is waiting for – for you to eat an icicle so it can put on its red coat. The stupid throat believes that if it turns scarlet, it would be prettier, and the icicle would like it better. Of course the throat is mistaken and in order to bring it to its senses, it's given an antibiotic. Grandma Elena had told the girl that antibiotics were harmful, it's a shame the throat doesn't know anything about medicine.

'As he sat in heaven alone and sad, God was deep in thought: what is to be done when a person is feeling blue and crying? Well, their special friend could turn sadness into chocolate!' said the grandfather. 'So, as I told you, your grandma began crying, silently. I didn't know what I was supposed to do. I couldn't exactly climb on a rock to hug her and calm her down. Her tears were falling, the size of hazelnuts. I wasn't clever at all, back then; I only ever got threes and fours out of six in school, a five only once, in Bulgarian literature, when I wrote the tale of God's loneliness. I had missed so many commas that the teacher scribbled all over my essay with a red pen. It's odd that she still gave me a five.'

'Well, you should be happy she didn't smack you with a grade two,' interrupted the girl. 'Leave the teacher. What did you do after?'

'I stretched out my hand and then remembered I hadn't cut my nails and if your grandmother were to see them, she was either going to run away or slap me across the face. Luckily, she didn't see.'

'Leave the nails. Tell me, what did you do?'

'I stretched my hand towards her tears. The tears ran off her cheek and onto my fingers, they even paused at my uncut nails. I… I drank them. All of them, all of them that had crawled onto my fingers. They were salty and didn't look like hazelnuts any more. I stretched out my hand again and drank them again and again until your grandma – a girl towering over me, but much slimmer, I was sure I was stronger than her – stopped crying. She smiled. Dame-Damyanka, have you ever seen a smile through tears? It's like that day the temperature plummeted to minus fifteen. The skin wants to quit your face and become a sheet of ice, but just before it peels away, the sun rises. The skin mutters to itself, "Why should I turn into a sheet of ice? Let's stay on this face. I have eyes here, and a nose, and a mouth, there's no better place to be!" See, this is a smile through tears – you realise you have eyes just so you can see how beautiful this tall girl is; her smile is a truck full of chocolate! You and I, Dame-Damyanka, we know what chocolate is, don't we?'

'It's the best!' the child shouted. 'And Grandma Elena? Did she become your special friend, the one who could turn sorrow into a pool like the one on the Struma where I dived head first?'

The grandad was tall and slim and with such a beautiful face that two women waved at him from the opposite pavement, saying, 'Oh, Damyan, are you ever going to get old?' This was an ordinary occurrence and he didn't pay any attention. Instead, he bent down and pulled his granddaughter's hat over her ears because one of them had escaped to March and the snowflakes. In fact, the snowflakes were small cloudcrumbs that had finally managed to get to the streets, roofs and gardens and with their long fingers comb and paint everything white.

Even the clouds – who are by no means human – don't want to be lonely and sad, so they turn the sky over Radomir into a nest full of stars. In this town even the youngest children, like Damyana, knew that the stars were in fact fish in the heavenly pool.

'Go on, go on,' urged the child.

After greeting the women from the opposite pavement, the grandad confessed: 'Yes, your grandmother became my special friend.'

'But... you were a whole head shorter than her?'

'Well, I grew taller just because of her. I stretched and flexed and ate ice cream and five years later I was a whole head taller than her. And now I'm even taller, you see?'

The child smiled, her smile stretching from here, Radomir, to the end of the world. Baba Marta understood smiles like this, and the snow stopped falling. The sun peeked from a corner of the sky, the size of a hazelnut wrapped in chocolate.

'Grandad, let's play football,' the child said and the handsome man with silver-grey hair couldn't deny her any longer. From his rucksack, he pulled out a ball, almost new because no one had had the time to kick it or throw it into the basketball rings in the school grounds. He patted the ball and threw it into the damp and heavy snow on the town square.

The football match commenced.

* * *

They found Pavko, his eyelids green, in front of Café Solaris. Two women from the council department Clean Streets saw him and couldn't believe their eyes: an enormous man, built entirely of muscle – even his forehead had muscles – lay spreadeagled, eyes open, gaze turned towards Radomir's town centre, his eyelids thicker than the twins Dida and Dona from the bakery.

'That man's about to kick the bucket,' said one of the women from Clean Streets.

'He's not about to kick it, he's collided with it,' corrected the other woman, already bent over and touching Pavko's forehead. It was still warm. That woman was Vasko's mother. Out of her four children Vasko was the child furthest away from his brain, and he was constantly blabbing about Damyana, Elena the Healer's granddaughter. That's why the woman said: 'Let's drag him to Elena, she might stop him dying.'

The women were not particularly tall, but very sinewy. In Radomir, if you're not sinewy they take you to the hospital in Pernik and in two weeks' time you've cosied up to the bouquet. So, the two experts from Clean Streets ran to the healer. 'Elena, come look at this one. We know he cut your Victoria plums but save him out of human kindness. He's an only child, even if he's a thug.'

Elena the Healer didn't bother saying, 'Get him in the dry,' even though the sky had gone mad. Not handfuls but wagonfuls of snow were pouring from the clouds, making sure the Clean Streets employees would have plenty to shovel and could not so much as take a peaceful drag of their cigarettes like decent women. Elena didn't appear by Pavko's side; probably grief was still gnawing at her insides since he had butchered all her plums. People say she had grafted twenty-one varieties. 'She's good with her hands and with her brain,' Vasko's mother said. 'Why does she have to have those eyes, though. As if someone's forging knives in them.'

Pavko was left lying on the street. Elena didn't come out, just that kid, as tiny as a flea, the same one that roams the streets of Radomir on her own or walks up the hill searching for herbs for her grandmother. A beautiful girl, with her grandfather's face, but in her eyes too, a blacksmith sharpens knives. *A raven must've pecked Vasko's brain, that's why he's constantly blabbering about her*, decided his mother. The woman saw the rest with her own eyes. That flea ran out with a round blue bottle. With her thumb and index finger she prised open Pavko's swollen eye and poured a bit of the stench into it.

Then she opened the other eye – really stretching it, as if she wanted to yank it out of his head – and lifted the bottle. She poured lots, no joke here, almost half the bottle went in. In the space of smoking one cigarette, Pavko began blinking, then his eyelids turned from green to yellow, yellow to grey, and then from grey to an ordinary eyelid colour, like yours and mine. A cigarette later, Pavko got up and screamed: 'I wasn't the only one who axed the old crow's plums. Vova and Ginger Dimitar were there too. And I cut the least, why did you just blind me?'

'Repeat the names of the other two,' the girl said.

'If I slap you one, there'll be nothing but a puddle of piss left of you,' Pavko shouted, and according to the two ladies from Clean Streets he was in the wrong, because that tiny flea fixed his eyes.

'She made them like new, she did. We witnessed it all, before God,' the women affirmed.

'If you don't tell me who the other two were, I'll pour a little more from this,' the child said calmly and pulled out of nowhere a tall, slim black bottle. 'One drop and you'll turn green.'

Pavko tensed all his available muscles, brandished his arm, but ended up not hitting anyone.

The girl spat. The Clean Streets employees saw her and made the sign of the cross. They went to Saint Ivan Rilski church and worshipped God. Now they prayed to God and the saint for everything around this affair with Pavko to go without a fight, but God was probably in some faraway place, and it all turned out the way it did.

'Oi, you little rat! Did you just spit at me?' Pavko roared.

'I certainly did,' the girl said calmly. 'If you don't rest while Vasko's mother smokes another two cigarettes, you won't feel too good. I'm warning you.'

Again, the two women prayed to God who – even though far away – had His wits about him and did the decent thing.

'Thank you, Ivan Rilski, but mostly thank you, God!' Vasko's mother uttered. She really didn't fancy seeing a child's blood spilt before her eyes, particularly the blood of a child who could turn an eyelid as thick as a rubber sole into an eyelid like yours or mine.

'Bye, Auntie Valya,' said the girl and looked at her with eyes in which a knife had already sliced through something. 'Say hello to Vasko from me.'

'OK, I will,' the woman from Clean Streets promised, even though she didn't really like this girl. It's not right for a little squirt to order around a grown man, who besides all the muscles had a Mercedes too. But Valya was glad that this little squirt had made Pavko straighten up like a plank on the street, right there in the snow.

That was it. That and nothing else. One of the employees swore she had heard everything with her big ears and now she knew why Vasko was all over that girl. She and her colleague only glanced at each other when, as they were coming back from the doctor a day later, in exactly the same place in front of Café Solaris, the two of them stumbled upon Vova. He was all muscle too, though his eyelids were fine and dandy as a magpie's wings... A young man, but a bandit. Good job there was God to take him if he were to get into a fight and drop dead someplace. Vova swayed and zigzagged. Two men dragged him to Elena's. Vova, muscular as a catfish, his eyelids strong as concrete, but his body – cold, ice-cold. Vova's mother ran to Elena, yet Elena, they say, didn't even put her slipper outside the door, just barked, 'I'm busy!' Instead, the tiny flea dashed out holding an ordinary beer bottle.

They also say that someone threw money over Elena's stone wall. Apparently the doctor from Radomir went twice to ask her the name of the weed for the eye potion and the other one, against the fever that makes the top jaw rattle against the bottom one. Elena told him she didn't know. As if anyone believes that.

'What do you mean you don't know, Grandma?' the tiny white flea asked. 'I know. How come you don't?'

The doctor's jaw dropped and seemed to nearly swallow his beard. Not just a coffin-dodger, but a bearded one at that.

A small truck pulled up outside Elena's gate and Pavko, using his own muscles – as seen by Vasko's mother and three other colleagues from Clean Streets – unloaded four large *kashpi* (what people around here call wooden buckets) full of saplings. By God the saplings were beautiful, all healthy and standing proud! Then the bandit handed Vasko and his friends fifteen lev to carry the kashpi to Elena's shed.

'The tiny white flea,' started Vasko's mother, 'her grandma's been teaching her all these doctors' tricks since she was born. The family's whole female line has gone off the rails and is crazy about scientific stuff.'

'True, true,' her colleagues agreed.

'When Vasko came home, his hands were no longer hands, but two large calluses from all the kashpi he'd hauled and he said to me, "Mum, my callus hurts. I'm going to Dame-Damyanka to treat me." All well and good, but Damyana wasn't there apparently. Look at my eye! As if! That boy of mine has lost it! The tiny titch must've put a spell on him. He can't breathe a day without seeing her.'

★ ★ ★

The girl tugged at his hand.

'Dad.'

The man, tall and lanky, was startled: 'What?'

'I'm hungry.'

The man just mumbled, 'And I, the idiot, drank them...' The man reached into his right coat pocket, delved into the left, then slowly rummaged in his trouser pockets, found nothing, stroked the child's hat, tried to smile, failed. 'Your mother will be back soon,' he said.

'Ginger Dimitar's rich,' the girl muttered. The man was hatless, the snow falling straight onto his hair – thick and brown as a ploughed field. 'Dad, I've got money.' Her father didn't hear her. 'Mum's not coming back,' she stated.

The man's face vanished. Just for a moment, it was as if he didn't have a face, just hair over a dreary autumn, even though icy March swirled around.

'Don't worry, Dad! I've got lots of lev.' She quickly pulled her glove off, reached into the pocket of her pink coat and pulled out two five-lev banknotes, each folded in four or perhaps in eight. God knows how she had managed to fold them so they fit into her tiny, tiny pocket. It looked almost like new, that coat. Well, it was new if you didn't count her grandad sewing on two buttons which were slightly lighter than the original ones, and also not counting that Grandma Elena had stopped boiling the quince seed potion for coughs, then cut off all the buttons and sewed on three new ones. So then the coat was much prettier than before.

'Come on!' The girl took the man's hand. 'I'll buy you a pizza – the biggest one they have in At Lunch. You'll give me just two bites, my tummy's the size of a worm's, even smaller.'

'I'm not hungry,' her father responded.

'Well, if a person doesn't have any stotinki, they're easily tricked into thinking they aren't hungry. Grandad says so and you know he doesn't lie. Come on, I'll take you for pizza.'

The kid tugged at the man's hand again and the two of them began walking along the pavement, where no one had walked yet. There was no path in the snow. The man and the girl in the most beautiful coat strode forward, towards a spring which was afraid to arrive.

'Do you know what Grandma says about medication?' the girl asked, but her father didn't know. That's why he remained silent. His daughter didn't get upset though. She never got upset with anyone. Her grandad, the cleverest person in the world, had told her that an argument gives you a headache. So, for example, if he got upset with her grandmother all the time, he would've hung himself by now. He had already chosen her, so what's the point? It's best to live peacefully. 'Grandma says that you shouldn't make evil medicine. Even if you hate the bandits. Even if the bandits are eviller than caterpillars.'

'What?' the man mumbled, his gaze fixed in the distance or maybe elsewhere. The houses were low, with thick walls. You couldn't tell if they were new or old under their snowy blankets.

'If you do evil with a potion you make, your hand will wither,' the girl said unexpectedly. She stopped abruptly; the snow reached up to her knees and squeezed inside her boots, but she didn't notice. She took her gloves off, tugged at the man's coat, then again, and again much harder. 'Dad, my hands have withered.'

The man didn't hear her. The girl clenched her fists and turned to her father. Her tiny fists punched the coat well below where his heart was.

'They've withered. Look.' She stretched her palms out, spread her fingers, as thin as colouring pencils from a seven-lev box, her nails cut short or rather gnawed almost to the skin.

'You're just fine,' the man said.

'I'm not though, Dad… I… I…' She fell silent, began sobbing.

'Shall we call your grandma, mesechinke?'

'They cut down my cherry tree. My cherry tree which bore fruit for the first time last summer!' the girl said. 'The cherries were as big as one of Gasho's paws. No one punished them. No one said anything to them. I… They were drinking in Solaris and I… I mixed an evil potion. It takes a long time to boil it… Hellebore root takes a long time on low heat. Then the pupils are scary to look at. The eyelids swell sometimes too. I brought water to my cherry tree with a bucket. From the river. Dad!' Snow and tears mingled on the girl's face. She went to wipe them with her hand but thought of something and said: 'Look!'

The man bent down, gently wiped the mess from her face. 'You're still young, mesechinke moya.'

'I'm not young. I knew their eyelids would swell.'

The man remained silent.

'I boiled it for three hours. That evil potion. Afterwards I poured drops from the good bottle. Because of Vasko. "Heal them, Dame-Damyanka," he said. "A person is bigger than a cherry tree." That's what Vasko said.'

The man embraced the girl, lifted her up and said: 'Your mother won't come back, mesechinke moya. Brew an evil potion for me.'

* * *

His father was coughing, his chest wheezing painfully with every breath. He was lying in bed. The doctor had told him over the phone to rub in some honey mixed with ammonium chloride, but the mixture didn't help and Valya, Vasko's mum, after running to three different pharmacies, was left penniless by the expense. The man just lay in bed, silent.

'How are you doing?' Valya would ask. Vasko wasn't worried; her face didn't say his father might die. The man was silent. If he complained, she'd only tell him off: 'Get on with it!'

And that's what he did – not groan, because he was a man who didn't huff and puff, he was a man who liked to be surrounded by peace. Vasko and his sisters tiptoed around, bringing their dad tea; even Vasko's mother produced a small bottle of rakia from somewhere and popped it on a stool by her husband's bed. Half an hour later, the rakia in the bottle still hadn't been touched and Vasko's mother gave her son a look that made the boy's heart burn as if someone had plunged him into boiling water.

'Dad,' the boy whispered. 'Why aren't you drinking? Look, rakia.'

His father shook his head. He had only one boy – Vasko, named for his Grandad Vasso, the most famous trumpet and accordion player in Radomir, Pernik, Kyustendil and pretty much everywhere trumpets and accordions are played in Bulgaria. At one point, Vasko's father beckoned him. That didn't bode well. The boy had heard that his grandad had done the same when he asked Vasko's father, 'How's your wife, son?' Valya had just given birth to the twins, each weighing as much as a loaf of bread. It had been a real struggle until those two loaves finally grew up and began to walk. All the honey they had to buy, all the scrap iron they had to sell.

Until recently, everybody thought that one of the twins had a tumour in her head. Back then, Vasko's father didn't have a taste for alcohol either; he just stood around staring out of the window as if the road had become a ravine full of poison. They all collected scrap and Vasko went to play the accordion, bless him, though his head was greener than an unripe tomato – he could neither make music nor sing. He was the most incompetent child in the whole family, and kept asking himself, 'Why am I so useless?' They didn't have a choice. His older sister, a tiny little thing, swept the town square for a few yellow coins.

'What gorgeous children I have,' Valya had whispered. 'Even the one with the tumour is beautiful. The other one, we'll send to train as a manager in Clean Streets or learn to be a singer.'

Fortunately, God is kind and compassionate, so He revealed to Vasko's mother: 'Listen, Valya! Don't be silly. Your child doesn't have a tumour, she has tapeworms, and not in the brain but in the stomach. Go to Elena the Healer.

She'll give you a cure and this daughter of yours will become the healthiest and most beautiful of all your four children.'

And so it was.

'Elena, give me herbs against worms. God told me my daughter doesn't have a tumour,' Vasko's mother said to Elena.

'Did you take Yanichka for a scan?' the healer asked.

'No, I didn't. But God Himself revealed it to me.'

'You need to take her for a scan.' Elena wasn't budging.

'Elena, listen, you and I get on. You're stubborn, you're bullheaded, but I'm even more so. When I tell you God Himself said this to me, then He did. Give me the herb for worms and we won't have to argue.'

Elena reached into a drawer, then another, rummaging through a total of six drawers, each one producing herbs. Finally, she reached into her blouse and pulled out some money. 'Here, Valya, take this. Get the child a scan, then I'll give you the herbs for worms.'

There's no point dwelling on this topic. The scan said: 'This girl doesn't have a tumour at all. She has a tapeworm, not in her head, but in her stomach.' The verdict was exactly what God had told Vasko's mother four days earlier.

Shame about all the money they had wasted on a scan. After that incident Vasko was converted once and for all. God knows more than any scan. But why was God not revealing to them now what they were supposed to do about his father's illness? Well, eventually it became clear why. Two days later, the last drop of the rakia in the bottle beside the bed was gone, meaning Vasko's father was slowly coming to his senses and would get better. He suffered quite a bit though.

Perhaps God was having a good drink somewhere and that's why the revelation was slow to come. Vasko understood God. Up there in heaven, there are no good drinkers like his dad, and drinking on your own is like someone slicing through your accordion. You can't play it, you can't earn money, and the honour of carrying your grandad's name is wasted on you. When Grandad Vasso started to play the Graovo horo, not just the people of Radomir, but even the boulders in Pernik, Radomir, Kyustendil and Blagoevgrad jumped up to join the local dance.

'God plays better than I do,' Grandad Vasso used to say. 'It's just sometimes He fancies a nap, so I play for Him, but He's a much better player than I am.'

'How do you know that, Grandad?' Vasko asked him.

'I can hear Him play,' answered Grandad. 'I hear Him every day. Every day, He plays new songs in my head. I just repeat them. But when you were born, Vasko, son, that's the only time I couldn't hear Him, so I made up all the songs myself. I said to Him: "God, a grandchild was born to me, and he's named Vasil after me. God, I thank You! Now I'll play so that the boy grows strong and learns to hear You just like I do, so that he'll make people happy at weddings, christenings and birthdays, so that he can comfort people at funerals, divorces, deaths and separations. You've given us a song for everything, God. You are almighty, You know that. I don't know where You get these tunes, I'm gobsmacked. The sky belongs to You, the earth and the people belong to You. Beauty has no end, no shore. You gave me such a beautiful grandson, strong and healthy. He's no good at singing but I'll teach him to hear You, God, so that he can comfort men and women in love and in hatred. Thank You, God, that my granddaughter didn't have a tumour but a tapeworm. You can leave me now. I can get on by myself. We have a crazy healer around here, Elena. She gathers herbs and stuff. Probably, just like I hear You play, she hears which herbs You gather to heal Yourself. That's why she runs around collecting and drying herbs. She's wicked though, I'm telling You. If she was my wife, God, I would be capable of killing her, bringing a great sin not only on myself but on the whole of Radomir. Then there wouldn't be anyone to hear what herbs You gather. I thank You, God, for my granddaughter. That crazy Elena cured her of the tapeworm.

Please God – I'll play music for You for another twenty years. Even if I'm drunk, I'll still play for You, if I'm dying, I'll still play for You. Protect that batty Elena. May life go with her. She gave us the money for the scan and the scan told us where to go: "Get out of here! That girl is perfectly fine." May life go with You too, God. I thank You.'

'Elena, the twin turned out to be exactly as God told me,' Vasko's mother had said. 'How will I ever repay you for the scan? If I give you two lev every week, it'll take a hundred years, and I'm not going to live that long. I hate digging gardens, Elena. If I come to dig in your garden but I hate it all the time, everything will die.'

'You'll pay me back when you can.'

'That means never then,' objected Vasko's mother.

'If it means "never" then it's never. But tell your father-in-law to stop calling me "batty Elena" in front of people. You know my brain's in the right place.'

'That won't happen. He'll carry on calling you "batty Elena". I heard him say, "Protect batty Elena, God. May life go with her. Please!"'

Elena rummaged in one drawer, then another, and another, to a total of six drawers.

'How about we steal you a mobile phone?' Vasko's mother offered, but even before her spit could dry in her mouth, batty Elena began putting the herbs back into the drawers.

'What are you doing?' shouted Valya, bewildered.

'I don't want a stolen phone,' said Elena. This was yet another proof, in black and white, that her mind had departed to faraway places where it shouldn't be.

'Fine, fine! We won't give you anything and we won't steal anything for you. Just give me those herbs for the tapeworm.'

Elena, as tall and thin as a knife blade, smiled – a rare occurrence. To see her smile was like winning the lottery.

'I'll make the potion for the child. I'll tell you exactly how many times she needs to take it,' Elena began to say. 'But you have to wait for it to cool down properly, that's the trick.'

'You do your tricks,' Valya said. 'Just tell me when to come to collect it.'

'It will be ready in an hour and a half.'

'Listen now, Elena! I'm going to go and make chicken and potato soup. You have no time for cooking. One more thing I'll do. I'll tell old Vasso to stop calling you "batty", but don't count on it. Probably won't happen. I'll make your son Christo one of those things to encourage good luck in love. Your daughter-in-law pierced holes in your boy like a colander, you know. When we want to make fun of a man, we always say, "The pussycats will walk over you just like Christo's wife walked all over him."'

Who knows what happened next. Most likely Elena began putting the herbs back in the drawers, because Vasko's mother said: 'Don't get all high and mighty now, Elena. I'm telling you the truth, honest. I'll try to make something for your boy, hopefully love will go from his head into his hands.'

Two hours later Vasko's mother brought the potion back home. Vasko sniffed it and nearly vomited. Good thing he didn't throw up, because he had just eaten a kebapche. He had fancied that kebapche so much that he had gone to the train station in Radomir and, because his head was as green as an unripe tomato, he got the idea to sing. He didn't just sing; he even began to play. An old man shouted at him:

'Hey, boy! Stop that. It's an insult to your grandad's music. He'd better teach you how to do it properly first. Then you can stand up and make a display of yourself.'

Vasko was upset, but never mind, that didn't help him play better, instead he embarrassed himself even more by carrying on. He knew only two songs: 'Night, night, children' and 'Djelem, Djelem', the one his mum sang. He couldn't play either of them well.

Vasko began hopping, raising his knee, stamping his foot on the ground, flying towards the skies, waving his right arm, throwing the left one up high – this is how you play the Graovo horo. According to Vasko, it was the best thing God ever invented.

Passers-by, old and young, threw coins in his bowl. Vasko had received only grade three in maths, and he'd struggled for a grade four, but the four was far away – as far as the train station in Pernik where people tossed twenty stotinki in your bowl, not just one or two. Often Vasko struggled to count how much money was in his bowl while he played the Graovo horo as God did. Afterwards, he had to work out how many grams of white brined sirene he could afford to buy. Some of the shop assistants were kind women. Vasko would drop all his stotinki in their hands, and they would solve the equation for him. But there were nasty ones too, who shouted in his face, 'You work it out yourself, you illiterate brat!' That's why Vasko started paying attention in maths lessons.

'Hey, Valya, are you sure that's our kid?' Vasko's father had asked after he'd recovered. 'Cause my blood pressure hits the roof when I work out eighteen plus twenty-nine, and Vasko comes home with top marks in maths. There's something iffy here. Not to mention, he can't sing; he bleats – people make fun of me. And he plays music as if someone's cut his hands off.'

'Cut his hands off, my arse!' Vasko's grandad had protested. He was nuts through and through and if anyone said a bad word about his grandson, he immediately took to fighting. 'You, Pesho,' declared Vasko's grandad, 'could neither sing nor play. And you never got more than a three in maths, but we didn't throw you to the dogs. That boy carries my name! Remember that and imprint it on your primitive brain cells: anyone who carries the name Vasil in this family can hear how God sings, and even if they sometimes fail to hear it, like when they've had one or two too many, their trumpet still listens to God! The song goes with the name, and if anyone dares say something against my grandson Vasko, I'll smash my trumpet and accordion on his head. Is that clear?'

Vasko was embarrassed. The dancing earned him enough to buy a sujuk, so tasty and appetising that he ate and ate. Eventually he saw reason and stopped eating. He decided to give the remaining half to a girl whose tears he had drunk – Dame-Damyanka. Isn't it true what God said, 'You, Vasko, have a friend who turns your head into a warm, soft bread roll. That girl is capable of knitting a jumper from the wind and making cures from all sorts of herbs.'

Vasko kept the better half of the sujuk, well, not exactly half, less than a half or even less than that, and headed to Dame-Damyanka. The weather was cold but it wasn't raining.

The sky had finally come to its senses and stopped fooling around, but a wind slunk in from the direction of Golo Bardo, covering the earth with ice.

* * *

The town despaired.

The surrounding villages despaired.

People began coming to tend to their allotments.

The fencing was missing; sometimes the metal stakes were taken away, sometimes they remained despondently in place; the gates were smashed; often a fire had been lit on the tables in the little caravans. Everything worth stealing was stolen – tools, clothes, cutlery, glasses, even old TV sets – and everything of no value was burned. The owners found cinders and ash on the floor. The walls greeted them blackened with soot, mute.

It was the same with the flats whose owners were known to have packed their bags and gone abroad to Spain, England, Switzerland. There were people from the district of Radomir everywhere, scattered around the world in search of more money. Serves them right! Let them earn, let them stuff themselves until full. People say their flats were turned upside down, gutted like a slaughtered calf from which everything worth eating – intestines, liver, kidneys, meat, skin – was taken. Police crawled everywhere. You would say, if you hadn't already swallowed your tongue from fear, that some terrible epidemic had broken out. Indeed it had. Yet the police cars left.

Instead of snowing, it began to rain, such fine rain that you wanted to grab the sky by the throat and squeeze until all the planets, comets and stars dripped from it, with the sun coming first. Then you would lock those shoddy constellations in a flat whose owner had gone to dig sewage drains in Spain. Let those planets see with their own eyes what kind of children Mother Bulgaria has birthed and continues to birth – children who tear the doors off of your wardrobe, set your blankets alight, pilfer the crockery from your kitchen cupboards, dismantle the bathroom taps, steal the springs from old beds, set mattresses on fire, defecate in the middle of your living room, shred the photograph of your daughter posing proudly with her primary school certificate to pieces.

Jesus, Mary and Joseph!

So what're you going to do, huh? You're just happy they haven't demolished the whole building, and that you can at least start renovations. Good job they haven't rummaged through the boxes in the bookcase where you had stored some old textbooks on electrical engineering, they would've burned them too. Your old underwear, the pairs you didn't take to Madrid or Manchester, have been crumpled into a ball and stuffed down the toilet. The doors of the built-in wardrobe in the hallway are smashed; if you had been born under a lucky star, they would have only been removed at the hinges. The carpet is torn and pulled up, the polished parquet floor has been chopped into pieces, most likely with a steak cleaver, which of course they brought with them.

'That's the way it is,' the twins Dida and Dona Ananiev would say to you. 'Since you are so... better not say. If you scarper to work abroad, and if you stretch your mouths to swallow the world without even knowing how to deal with thieves, then it serves you right!'

'How did you two clever clogs deal with things then, huh?'

'Well, just like this: like the erudite women we are, we left three one-litre bottles of rakia, full to the brim, outside the apartment door. Thieves aren't wild animals, are they? No, they are not. They have guts like you and us, and their throats crave alcohol like all other ordinary throats. We understand the thieves: next to the three bottles of rakia, we left five sujuk. The thieves can pause, have a drink, have a bite to eat.'

At this point, Dona, the more intelligent of the two bakers, remarked:

'When a man's had a drink and a bite to eat, what else might he want, huh? He wants a woman, of course. That's why I reached into my pockets; Dida is a scrooge and doesn't think things through properly. So I went and bought an inflatable doll. And you? You've been robbed like the simplest creature, let's not use ugly rude words here, excuse us. They set your house on fire and defecated in your living room, but they neither robbed us nor set us on fire, and they didn't do their business in our living room. Our flats are prim and pretty, the thieves have just scratched the front door, but that's nothing. Absolutely nothing. We simply gave it another lick of paint.'

After that exposé, the whole district exclaimed, *Well, well, well, smart ladies!* Some people of course, the ones who are always discontented with something and see the dark side of life first, said, *Why on earth would I buy rakia for the thieves? Should I leave my daughters at their disposal too, huh? A knife in the neck might be a better idea, what do you say?*

'Ignore those grumblers. They're primitive, no tolerance, no proper upbringing,' Dida and Dona remarked. However, only an hour later, it seems that the bastard thieves, not quite understanding the word 'tolerance', slipped into the sisters' flats and pilfered a blanket here, a blouse there, took the toilet bowl, filched vases, the table and chairs and satisfied their calls of nature in the kitchen. They pocketed everything; they tore the two sisters' love letters into pieces and threw them from the south-facing balcony. As for the north-facing balcony, the glazed one, well, they smashed the windows with a meat tenderiser. The police couldn't find the perpetrators; they searched for ten days and left it at that.

The burgled citizens got on with piecing their flats together again.

Since it was March, and the people of Pernik and Sofia had planted saplings on their plots back in autumn, the bandits dug up and took the trees too, leaving the whole slope looking like Swiss cheese.

People in the area were shaking their heads: *The police will catch the wind's galoshes*. And that's what happened. Everyone was hunting for an unknown perpetrator until one day neighbours noticed an expensive ornament from Dida and Dona's flat in Ginger Dimitar's Jeep. The twins had also spotted a TV in Ginger Dimitar's kitchen that strangely resembled their TV – including the scratch from a pin in the left corner, for which Dona's boy had got a serious beating.

Just outside Café Solaris a magnificent motorbike was parked: huge, volcanic, titanic. Not a machine but the god of all two-wheeled vehicles. In fact, the noun 'vehicle' would be a vile insult, spittle on the divine engine of this feat of engineering. Every day at 11 a.m. Ginger Dimitar drank his whisky in Café

Solaris, accompanied by well-roasted peanuts (the old cook in the café would put them in the oven the moment Ginger Dimitar's pinkie rose two centimetres above the tablecloth; it was well known that Ginger preferred his peanuts warm and peeled before his eyes). One day, after he had licked the last drop of whisky from his lips and gorged on the last peanut, Ginger Dimitar left the café and mounted the god of all vehicles. The engine roared and shuddered, the wheels leaving ugly marks on the asphalt. The whole of Solaris shook, the sky ruptured. The motorbike crashed into the nearest telegraph pole. Ginger Dimitar tumbled onto the street and started vomiting before managing to lean on the nearby fountain. His nose sank into the puddle of alcohol mixed with half-chewed peanuts which had been rejected by his stomach. Ginger tried to stand up but slumped into the puddle instead. His hands began to tremble, very slightly to start with. Then they stopped. People gathered around, watched and clicked their tongues, but no one suggested taking him to Elena the Healer to sort him out. On the contrary, two people spat on the motorbike. People dispersed and walked past as if nothing had happened, as if he were a sweet wrapper lying on the street or even something lower than a sweet wrapper.

At one point though, a girl dressed in an oversized coat almost reaching her boots – everyone recognised it because seven or eight of those coats had turned up in Second Hand-Second Chance and sold out as if they were reduced bread rolls in Dida and Dona's bakery – ran to the man on the pavement and started whispering something in his ear. Only when the girl opened Ginger's mouth with a thumb and forefinger did people realise who the kid with the weak faculties was: Damyana, Elena the Healer's granddaughter.

'Oi! Leave him to die!' a passer-by shouted. 'Get away from there before I slap you.'

The girl ignored him, quickly pouring a few drops from an ordinary beer bottle between the ginger teeth. The passer-by and a short woman pulled the fool away, but too late – the bandit started wriggling next to the motorbike-beast with its headlight smashed and mudguard bent.

'You're such a stupid kid,' the passer-by said. 'That one will set your grandmother's house on fire tomorrow.'

'And cut your nose!' the woman screeched.

Ginger Dimitar rose – a man of iron, the strongest in this town and in the district. The woman quickly hid her face in her scarf, and the passer-by pulled his hat to his moustache and buried his face in the collar of his coat.

'C'mere,' Ginger Dimitar shouted at the child. Three Solaris customers, as well as the waitress Mirella, saw that with their own eyes. The child dug her heels into the ground and didn't dare move. Mirella assumed that the child had wet herself because a little puddle appeared under her coat skirts. 'Come here right now!'

The girl went closer, and everyone saw the mini patch of damp Mirella had pointed at.

'Here, take this!' Ginger Dimitar hissed, reaching into his pocket and pulling out a wad of money. A large wad of money. His face resembled a pile of banana peels; he was probably still drunk. 'Put this in your pocket!' he ordered, shoving the wad the colour of hundred-lev notes into the girl's hand.

The girl tossed the money to the ground, pressing the beer bottle to her coat, just where the heart beats.

'Oi, scumbag, take it,' Ginger Dimitar roared.

The girl picked up the money, clutched it to her chest and, like a dog with a broken spine, began retreating towards the town's library, which happened to be shut at the time.

Then, suddenly, the girl pelted off, but the second-chance coat prevented her from running fast. She fell into the snow, began crawling and so, holding firmly to the beer bottle and the money, reached the steep street leading to the cemetery on all fours.

Quite some time passed before Mirella made an angry comment: 'Who's gonna give that kid a proper beating? Who the hell does she think she is, raising that little nose in the air and healing Ginger, huh? Stupid little cow!'

Then Mirella bit her tongue. She had, however, made clear to the clientele who she was going to slap across the face good and proper. *If someone's annoying little ears don't start ringing, then my name isn't Mirella. Never mind that the little one's grandmother is the healer!*

'The kid pocketed a tidy sum, though,' remarked one of the perpetual drinking presences in Solaris before ordering another Kamenara rakia – an honest, honourable moonshine people around here drank with pleasure.

Ginger Dimitar was the only one who ordered whisky at 11 a.m. in Solaris.

* * *

'What have you done, you fool!' The woman with silver-grey hair spoke slowly, with bile, as if the Struma had frozen under her tongue. Her voice – pure ice, white as an antibiotic. It was even sharper than ice, but no voice should be called a cleaver because steel doesn't just chop steaks, it chops off heads too.

'Tell me!' the ice demanded. The girl was always filled with dread when her grandmother spoke to her dad in this tone of voice.

The man just stood there – tall, almost reaching the light bulb or even the ceiling, the girl thought, curled up under the table.

'I gave it away,' the tall man muttered. His hair was brown like a sunset, like a man who had lost everything and God wasn't around to help him.

'How much did you give her?' It wasn't just the table, the whole room froze. The girl was hiding, curled into a ball. Both of her hands were wrapped in bandages, so wide that they covered not only her hands but her arms all the way to her elbows.

The little one had heard her grandmother say that when you mix evil eye drops for someone, even if they are a criminal, even if they are Ginger Dimitar, your hands will wither – even if you bring him back to life after he collides with the telegraph pole. This was why the girl had wrapped her hands in bandages, so no one could see her bones and skin slowly withering.

On a chair next to the table sat a man with silver-grey hair, a very handsome man, quiet, not uttering a word, just staring at his nails, as if he were somewhere else. The stove was lit, the meal simmered in the pot – potatoes and meat from the old goat they had slaughtered. The handsome man cut its throat because after eleven kids, she could have no more. White as aspirin, her milk had no smell; they could make wonderful cheese from it, they had even made butter.

The handsome man hadn't lit a cigarette after slaughtering the goat because as soon as he got married, his wife took all his cigarettes and tore them to pieces. Then she gave him a concoction to drink after which even the slightest thought of tobacco gave him pains beneath his ribs – to the right, where the liver is, and beneath the heart to the left. The man stood by the slaughtered goat as if someone had slaughtered him, then ran into the house. He entered the house without taking his shoes off, something he hadn't done since his only son was born; actually, once since: when he ran in to tell his wife that they had a baby granddaughter, Damyana.

He had just slaughtered the goat and rushed into the house, his boots leaving a dirty trail, like fugitives, but he hadn't noticed. He was probably coming down with something or had lost the plot. The man snatched a bottle from the cupboard in the vestibule; it was full of the rakia they used for massage, the same rakia that the flu feared like the devil fears the gospel.

From an icon on the kitchen wall the Virgin Mary with baby Jesus watched over them. Our Lady had the biggest heart of all, bigger than all the hearts in the world put together. She helped mothers, children, animals, ill and healthy people, and she caressed the souls of the dead too. Beautiful had grabbed the bottle of rakia which no one was allowed to touch without his wife's permission. He hadn't asked permission, but took the bottle to the slaughtered goat, her coat as white as a snowdrop, and poured out the precious liquid, then had a sip himself. His wife – tall, skinny, crow's beak – had seen him from the window. As per usual she didn't say anything to him, but just gave him a hard look. Returning to the house, the man had stood frozen in his boots in the middle of the vestibule, his black tracks – thieves in chains.

'Grandma, please don't scold Daddy,' the girl said. 'He gave Mum money. That's a good thing.'

The bearded man's eyes wandered God knows where, most likely without hearing a word. His father, obscenely handsome for his advanced age, gripped the table. On it, incriminatingly, stood the forgotten-about bottle of rakia. Elena slowly removed it, then lifted her hand – scrawny, almost the handle of a hammer – and tapped the beautiful man on the shoulder. Her fingers only rested there for a second, she did nothing else.

Their son, buried in his beard, didn't even notice them.

Something odd occurred – perhaps the old man's eyes got a little confused, since when you lived with a woman like Elena, wet cheeks were rewarded with ridicule and scorn. Perhaps a little fly had squeezed its way into his eye, but then when you think about it, where would a fly come from in March? How could anyone know what had got into his eyes?

The potatoes and the old goat's ribs simmered on the stove. The girl with the bandaged hands waited under the table. She had used this as a hiding place from a young age, from the day she smashed a very important glass. Her mum and dad had drunk wine from it when they got married at the Radomir registrar. That glass was an excessively expensive crystal object, even more expensive than the house they lived in – that's what the girl thought – and after she broke it, she skulked for the first time under the table. Thick sorrow enveloped her because she had broken such a beautiful thing made of crystal; she tried to mend it with the glue she used to fix her notebooks, but unsuccessfully. As well as hiding under the table, she wrapped her head in her grandad's old shirt. Nowadays she didn't wrap her head in her grandad's old shirt, or with plastic bags for that matter – her grandma had warned her that she could suffocate like that.

'Dad,' the girl whispered, but the beard was silent.

She curled up at the feet of the handsome old man, who they said she had 'taken after, thank God', and observed her grandma, to whom everyone noted that 'she bore no resemblance'.

'How much was it?' the old crow asked the girl's father.

When her grandma spoke with that gravel in her voice, the girl knew that the man about to be treated with skinny Elena's herbs was going to experience a lot of pain. Her grandmother would turn into cast iron so she didn't melt and could cut faster. *When you cut fast, the pain has less time to think, it gets confused and doesn't know where to bite you.* Did Grandma Elena want to cut something from her dad?

'Eight thousand one hundred,' the girl's father said. He was very handsome, but you couldn't see that because of the beard. Not a beard, but a brown bear that had climbed onto her father's face and now lay in wait to eat him.

'You wanted to buy your wife, so she would stay with you?' her grandma intoned evenly. Then she slowly and monotonously ordered the girl to read THREE pages from *Pippi Longstocking*, but the words in this book were long and difficult. Not even the pretty pictures helped. Sometimes her father (she and her father, they both knew they were not supposed to) would read ten pages from *Pippi*, and oh, how wonderful it was.

Pippi was an amazing girl. Damyana, a brave girl herself, had also tried to lift a few animals with her strong, muscly arms. Well, not a horse, but for now the cat Markan would do. Markan had scratched her, then she had seen two chicks that had just hatched. If a girl could lift two chicks, surely one day she would be able to lift a horse – so long as her hands didn't wither.

Her grandma had told her: 'If you don't want your hands to wither, you need to daub them with an extract made of yarrow, coltsfoot and fat Mara.'

'I don't know what fat Mara is,' the girl had cried because she wasn't sure what that herb looked like.

'Your hands will wither then,' her grandma said so slowly and ominously that Damyana had pushed the chair to the cupboard, then, on top of it, put the small stool, the one she sat on to take her shoes off, and climbed up until she reached a very very thick book in which her grandma had placed a photograph of fat Mara. She had picked up the book, searched and searched inside and started to really doubt whether fat Mara was this one or that one.

'Grandma, is this one fat Mara or that one?' she asked, pointing at one picture then another.

'Where were you when I was teaching you what's what?' Grey-hair snapped, so much ice in her words that Damyana shed a tear which she immediately pushed back into her eye or perhaps wiped with the sleeve of her homespun woollen jumper.

Instead of giving in to her tears, the girl had picked up the broom, swept the whole kitchen, then took a rag and washed the floor – twice. Then she dusted the TV, even though it was already spotless, approached her grandma and very quietly – so quietly that her words couldn't even stand on their feet – whispered: 'Please, Grandma, I've swept the kitchen, mopped the floor in the vestibule and dusted the TV. May I please ask you a question?'

'Yes.'

'Please, Grandma, tell me, is this one fat Mara, or that one?'

'That one. See, it says *Hylotelephium spectabile* underneath it,' answered Grey-hair. 'I won't be telling you again.'

'Thank you, Grandma.'

That's why now, quiet under the table, the little girl was certain her hands wouldn't wither, but she wondered why it wasn't her grandmother talking but an early March storm. Her tummy tightened so much it was as if a leech had sneaked into it.

'Did your wife take it?' her grandma asked.

'Yes.'

'All of it? Didn't she leave you anything?' The monotone voice was becoming so, so flat that the leech inside Damyana's stomach gave birth to a snake.

'She left me ten lev… but…'

'But what?'

'I didn't take it,' Damyana's father said.

'That's why she was kissing your tears. For the eight thousand one hundred lev.'

'But if a person drinks tears…' Damyana called from under the table.

Her father was silent in his brown beard and a good thing he had it, thought his daughter, otherwise his neck would wither.

'She drank quite a few of your tears and then went to Ginger Dimitar.'

'I know,' Damyana's father said so quietly that it might have been that little fly talking, the one that gets into people's eyes in March, just after the fresh, icy snow has fallen. Her father's beard was probably very heavy because his head drooped down; it was probably even heavier than the bottles of tetterwort tincture used for blisters and warts.

Just as the beard and the neck were beginning to wither, Damyana's grandad got up. He walked so silently that one always wondered what he stepped on – the floor or the air. Grandad reached for the big bottle of the most expensive rakia that no one was allowed to touch without her grandma's permission, yet Grandad picked it up. He was an intelligent man and knew that arguing didn't help anyone; he lifted the bottle and took a gulp.

'Don't scold our son,' Damyan said quietly under his breath.

Grandma Elena stared at her husband for a long time, then looked away and just said, 'Leave.'

★ ★ ★

Vasko pressed the bell of Crazy Elena the Healer's house. *Good job I have pain under the ribs*, he thought. He really wasn't interested in all the potions, but at least he had an excuse to stand in front of this house. He needed to see Damyana. He had something important to say to her but hadn't yet worked out what it was. He could no longer postpone it. He knew that the moment Damyana opened the door, the words would compose themselves. He had fought a lot of fear to muster the courage to press this bell. The door was locked, no one rustled behind it. He pressed a second time and kept pressing until his finger hurt from the cold.

'Dame-Damyanka,' he called. 'Come out! I've got something for you. No, I don't really, but I've got to tell you something.'

Dame-Damyanka didn't hear him.

'Dame-Damyanka!'

The wind completely lost its mind, began picking up handfuls of snow, throwing them left and right, managing to slap Vasko's face every time. His hat was thin and on top of that it was a girl's hat; it belonged to one of his sisters and was pink like a strawberry, shameful.

'Dame-Damyanka!'

No one answered. He reached for the doorbell one more time and pressed it so hard that if electricity was human, it would've broken his bones. He rang and rang and rang.

'Damyanka,' the boy whispered and slowly, as if he were moving through granite and not air, began walking home, towards Stramna Mogila, the steep rise where their house was. It was a nice house, it was warm inside – even warmer than he liked, as warm as the oven when his mother baked the bread for Christmas Eve or for his Grandad Vasso's birthday. Vasko liked his grandad's birthday. A whole orchestra of friends gathered in their house and got properly drunk. Even though they were completely soaked, they still played music. Hardly able to stand on their feet, they still played. Because once you stop, you die.

If there is no Dame-Damyanka, you die.

Stop that nonsense. You have to be strong and not afraid of the nasty cold, so you can wait for Dame-Damyanka to come back. Doesn't even matter if she's gone to her mother in Sofia.

It's nice in Sofia though. No one comes back from Sofia.

Vasko's sister, the twin who'd been drinking Crazy Elena's potion against tapeworm, was finally showing signs of gaining weight. She had turned all pink, just like the hat Vasko had borrowed (shame and disgrace!). Now his sister's cheeks were looking so healthy that their mother cheered up. She began sipping from their father's rakia bottle, and even took out a very old tambourine – it was her grandmother Valentina's – and played and sang. Old Vasso smacked his hand on the table in surprise. 'Wow! Well done, Valya! I've never heard you play before. You're good!'

And just as his mother was rejoicing in her father-in-law's praise, Vasko came home.

'What's the matter, son?' Vasko's mother threw the tambourine to the floor and put her hand to his forehead. 'My God, you're burning up!'

Valya was a strong woman, although not very tall (that's why she always wore heels as high as possible). She picked Vasko up as if he were the fat tomcat Mousy and dragged him to bed. His father left the rakia, left the grumbling and felt Vasko's neck. 'He's on fire,' he said. 'Forty degrees…'

Vasko didn't remember anything after that. Who came and went, why they were there, was it light or dark, had the snow melted, did the wind carry on dancing around, had April arrived? His mother's face was so odd that it didn't even look like a face: taut like the skin of the kid they slaughtered last year for Saint George's feast. He got scared.

At some point Vasko saw her: Dame-Damyanka! She was sitting next to him.

Vasko lay and the ceiling wobbled above him. The table lamp wobbled; his mother's face wobbled like the skin of that kid goat Vasko liked so much, the one he kept taking pictures of with his grandad's phone as it ran around the garden like a wayward child Wayward but beautiful.

Vasko saw her again – tiny Damyana – and thought, *My brain's gone walkies and I've lost the plot.*

Wherever he looked, he glimpsed Damyana. She was pouring something nasty into a spoon, a vile stink emanating from it. You would want to cut your head off just to avoid smelling it.

'Come on, Vasko, drink this and you'll get better.'

'My brain must've got a cold. I've lost it. You're not really here, Dame-Damyanka, are you?'

'Yes, I am. Drink this now.'

'Don't lie to me,' he muttered, but still propped himself up and swallowed the nasty contents of the spoon; his head fell off and rolled onto the carpet.

'You need to give him one tablespoon every two hours. Tomorrow your boy will be as fresh as a daisy, Valya.' *Look at her*, Vasko thought, *talking just like her grandmother, Crazy Elena the Healer*. Only then did he fall into despair – it wasn't Damyana, it really wasn't, it was her grandmother the healer.

The ceiling and the electric bulb began wobbling again.

'You've called Crazy Elena,' Vasko mumbled. 'Am I really that ill? Am I going to die? Mum... I have half a sujuk... I put it aside for Dame-Damyanka. Give it to her if I die.'

'Shut up!' Crazy Elena cut in in a terrifying voice. 'Shut up or I'm going to smack you across the face. It will hurt. A lot.'

The following morning – or perhaps the one after that or the following evening or even at lunchtime since it smelt like sauerkraut and the nasty medicine that made you want to dig your own grave – Vasko woke and sat up in bed. Neither the ceiling nor the light wobbled. He was hungry, so hungry he thought someone had stolen the contents of his stomach.

'Mum, give me some bread,' he said.

His mum immediately ran to him, his dad did, his Grandad

Vasso did, and all his sisters did too, each carrying a piece of bread as thick as a doorstop.

The ceiling had stopped spinning and his mum's face looked as if she was about to pick up her tambourine again. His three sisters were grinning from ear to ear. The light bulb wasn't wobbling. He just had a little headache when he turned around to examine the room.

'Where's... where's...'

Dame-Damyanka wasn't there.

The earth turned into sky, the sky into earth.

He started hurting all over. Where on earth did his hunger go, where did it hide, leaving a bitter taste in his mouth? So it must be true, Damyanka had gone to stay with her mother in Sofia. Vasko got frightened. His brain clouded.

'Damyana will be here in a minute!' his mother cried, but Vasko thought, *I'm just dreaming, Mum's talking nonsense.*

The ceiling leant towards him, the light bulb, apparently small, suddenly became huge, the size of a haystack. The bed sank beneath him, and the house was about to collapse. The roof tiles were about to bury him when his mother shook him and shouted: 'Hey, look!'

His eyelids weighed more than the asphalt on the street, but his mother wasn't going to shout 'Look!' if there was nothing to see. Vasko prised his eyelids open.

Then he saw her.

Damyanka. Dame-Damyanka.

'Damyanka,' he said. 'I've kept a sujuk for you.' Then he gathered his strength and promised, 'I'll get better. Honest.'

The girl, as tiny as a purse full of yellow stotinki, dressed in ten tops against the icy winds, stood by his pillow. She was numb, not even breathing, just watching him.

'I'm OK,' Vasko lied.

Damyana didn't move, but slowly, white and light as the colour of mirabelle plum blossom at the beginning of March, smiled.

'I'm hungry,' Vasko rejoiced. Then he fell asleep.

★ ★ ★

It was drizzling. The wind blew. The white house looked like a palace from a fairy tale, but there were no fairy tales in this town. No one believed in fairy tales any more. People got used to the news at seven, then eight, then ten. Yet another grandmother robbed by a phone scammer, having transferred all her money so she could save her son who had been in an accident. Another young man beaten up outside a nightclub now in critical condition in hospital. Schoolboys from an elite grammar school played truant and robbed older women. Sales of apartments and garages. Fluctuating prices. That's what everyone heard at seven, eight, and then ten, so not even little children believed in fairy tales any more. But they knew their rights and understood the term 'demographic crisis'. When you see a kid wearing an ankle-length oversized coat from Second Hand-Second Chance, it makes you not want to have children after all.

'Clear off!' a young man with ginger hair shouted. Of course, he was entirely clad in *orange* – orange socks, orange sweatshirt, orange jeans – everything singing and dancing in orange. It was not a man but a lit fireplace standing outside the white house. 'I'll shoot you in the head,' the man said. The woman before him was tall and skinny, drowning in her coat.

'Ginger Dimitar, the only reason you're walking this earth is because I had horsetail. Your kidneys were infected, you were in a lot of pain.' The skinny woman spoke in a clear, loud voice. 'The only reason you can see me now is because I turned up with an eyebright tincture. You were about to go blind. If the cure had been delayed by only ten seconds, you would've gone blind. A person who shoots their healer keeps the next bullet for their own head.'

'You're a witch,' Ginger said.

'That's what you call me. Your mother calls me "Elena". Twice now I've walked her only son back from the grave.'

'Twice now you've walked me back from the grave, and twice now I've failed to kill you, so we're quits.'

'I want to talk to Siyana.'

'You can't talk to Siyana. If you're trying to get Christo's money from her, you can go whistle. If you want to plead and kiss Siyana's shoes, I'll bring you a pair. If not, move on.'

It started raining heavily, enough to soak you through your coat.

'I know Siyana very well; she was my daughter-in-law for seven years. She might be mean, but she's not a coward. She won't hide behind your back.'

'Well, you do know me very well.' The door opened. A young woman with brown hair and beautiful eyes (despite the heavy make-up) stepped forward and said to Ginger, 'Let her in. I'll deal with this one.'

'You sure? I don't want "oh" and "ah" afterwards,' muttered the orange fireplace. 'I'd enjoy smearing that one across the tiles.'

'You'll get the opportunity,' the woman reassured him kindly, yet her face was a galaxy away from a smile. In this part of the world people understood cosmic affairs: in Café Solaris they sold the brownish rakia Galaxy. If you're one galaxy away, that meant you have twenty lev. You order a drink full of stars. The stars have no scent, no taste, just proof. You drink them. Before you collapse, you mumble something which even the old doctor in the Radomir hospital wouldn't understand. That's the language of Galaxy.

Solaris was rife with belote tournaments, but to take part you have to put your hand in your pocket for fifty lev. You could win around five hundred, but during the tournament you'd drink three hundred. If you talk in a manner that terrifies the doctor and he needs to call the ambulance, that means you've drunk seven Galaxies.

The woman with beautiful brown eyes wore a gold necklace whose weight exceeded her own. But who would have appreciated it in this ugly province? Her watch was Swiss. Ginger Dimitar had his own trade channels. Her trousers were some killer label known only to teenagers. Her top, revealing just enough of her skin's beauty, was Dolce & Gabbana or possibly Versace, but did it really matter what gabbana the top was when her body glistened with as much gold as was in the coffers of the Bulgarian National Bank?

'What do you want?' the bejewelled woman asked.

'I want to talk to you,' replied the healer with the coat that hung to her ankles and smelt of twenty second chances.

'I'm busy,' the beautiful eyes declared.

'You're very pretty,' uttered the skinny woman and stretched out her hand. Brown, thin, bony. Fingernails clipped.

Siyana offered her hand. She genuinely looked very good in that gabbana. She had grown, not in height but in beauty. She was wearing knee-high stiletto boots.

'I won't give you even one lev,' the beauty announced from the height of boots that probably cost as much as the white house.

'You're developing fast,' Elena remarked. 'You never used to adorn yourself with necklaces before. I used to like you. Now I don't.'

'Not a single lev.' A smile emerged on the perfect lips and the scent of an expensive perfume wafted from the smooth skin. Evidently Ginger Dimitar had channels for scents too. People say that when he was a dancer in Amsterdam, he would smear something on himself that made the ladies cry. Ginger Dimitar had channels for things like that too. 'In fact, if you could beg a little…' The young woman's smile was a cosmos away from this room. 'You know how I treat requests. The beggar must kiss my slippers. Actually Elena, wait. I don't have slippers; you could bend and kiss my boots – Alexander McQueen!'

'So, if I kiss your boots, I can brag that I've kissed Aliksander Maksomething-or-other,' Grey-hair concluded. Then raised her head.

'How much money are you begging for?' the young woman asked.

At that moment something snapped in the air. Behind the window the rain was bashing the street, bringing freezing cold and wind. Just like Ginger Dimitar thrashed the Radomir district, and Aliksander thrashed the catwalk.

'Eight thousand one hundred lev. That's how much my son gave you,' the ankle-length coat said.

'Don't you want me to treat you to a coffee too?' the young woman asked. The brown eyes appeared jolly.

'Eight thousand one hundred.'

'I'll call Ginger,' the galaxies smiled. 'I was thinking of giving you five hundred, if you bent over Alexander McQueen, but you…'

'I wouldn't call Ginger if I were you,' Elena said. 'If you give me the money now, it won't hurt a lot and there'll be no scars.'

'Hurt? What are you on about? I doubt anything will hurt.'

'Doubt all you want, but be quick about it because in two minutes you'll be on fire,' the tall woman said. 'You do remember we shook hands? Smell your hand now.'

'Urghh, what's that stench?'

Outside, the rain was dancing with the wind. Rain that dances to the tune of the wind quickly turns into ice.

'Are you calling, my love?' a voice like diesel echoed in the hallway. All you needed to do was put a match to it.

'No. Wait there,' the young, brown-eyed fairy said.

'You'll get a rash all over your body. There'll be blisters. It won't only hurt, it'll itch too. There'll be scars. It won't be pretty.'

'You're lying.'

'Yes, I am,' Elena said calmly. 'Eight thousand one hundred lev. That's my son's money. It's for your daughter.'

'You're lying. It's impossible with just one handshake.'

The tall woman stepped towards the door. Without hurry. That broom was never in a hurry. She reached for the door handle.

'Wait!'

The brown hand in the twenty-second-chances sleeve didn't let go of the knob.

'Wait!'

Scraggy's coat dragged behind her galoshes.

'Eight thousand and one hundred.' The young woman bit the air, the gold on her chest fluttered. 'Here, take it. Where's the antidote?'

Elena turned, took the money. A wad of hundred-lev banknotes – Aleko Konstantinov's face staring out as if he didn't care about the value of the banknote he adorned.

'Do you know whose face is decorating the hundred lev?' the tall woman asked. From the inner pocket of her dark-green coat – Italian, a thin garment but good for the wind – she took out a bottle, flat as a chopping board, poured something onto her palm, took the hand of the woman with the ordinary eyes, which were now not so ordinary as they anxiously watched the brown hand rubbing the white skin exactly where the golden bracelets shone.

'If you know whose face is printed on the hundred-lev banknote, I'll leave you one so you can treat yourself,' Elena said.

'You're smearing water on me,' hissed the admirer of Aliksander Maksomething, who took care of her feet's comfort. 'You're cheating.'

'Shall I stop?'

Elena had stopped rubbing the hand a minute ago, or maybe half a minute, who knows how quickly the time passes around the heels of Aliksander Maksomething.

'Carry on!' the young woman ordered.

'The face on the banknote is that of our famous writer Aleko Konstantinov, the creator of Bai Ganyo,' the tall woman announced. 'Shame you didn't know. I was going to leave you a hundred lev so you could buy a textbook on Bulgarian literature.'

The healer didn't hurry to put the money into her inside pocket, just under the heart.

'Won't you see me off?' she asked. Then, wrapped in her coat of many chances, she opened the door sharply. Ginger nearly crashed into the room, obviously eavesdropping.

The old woman took a step back, observed him for a while and said: 'You seem a little yellow, Dimitar. Take a sip of water…' Her brown hand, thin as the handle of an umbrella, reached into her outer pocket, took out the same flat bottle, no thicker than a chopping board, and handed it to him.

'Drink!'

The ginger man gave her a nasty look. 'You drink, Elena,' he snapped. 'You were smearing Siyana's hand with this vile stuff.'

Elena took a sip, swallowed and drank again. 'Ginger Dimitar,' she said, 'if you get in trouble again, I'll have to really think about whether or not I'll be bringing you back from the grave.'

The young woman grabbed the bottle, which was as disinterested as the badly paved street under the rain outside.

'The water's good,' Elena remarked. 'Pure. From the tap. I'll leave you the bottle, Siyana. You can rub some on your hand again. Ginger Dimitar will return it at some point.'

The skinny woman walked out of the room.

'Should I beat her up?' Ginger Dimitar asked, but he didn't hear the bejewelled woman's answer.

Elena carried on, walking slowly along the path, without turning back, without even pulling up her coat's collar. When she was out of the gate of this snow-white house, the skinny one stopped, looked around. Ginger Dimitar and the young lady, who looked stunning with Aliksander Maksomething on her legs, stood by the window.

Elena nodded at them and continued down the street.

Everything was wet: earth and heaven, beast and nature, even Aliksander Maksomething.

★ ★ ★

He was standing on his own. A tall man with a brown beard waiting outside the white house. The rain sank into his dark hair, his beard was soaked, the raindrops lashed him, yet he wasn't moving, only staring at his shoes. His coat pockets were bulging under the weight of a wad of money, most likely hundreds, because you could see the face of Bai Ganyo's creator on one of them. And so what if he had created him? They shot the poor man, young and green as grass. Who cares if his image now adorns the front and the back of the hundred-lev notes?

The man who, as well as having a wet beard, also had money – a rarity in this part of the world – was not interested in the rain or in the money or in Bai Ganyo. There were hardly any people out walking because it was cold, two in the afternoon. He was likely to catch something, perhaps pneumonia. At one point, another man came out of the house clad in an orange jacket, orange hoodie, orange shoes and orange trousers. Bloodless orange matter.

Orange walked closer to Beard and clenched his fist. The blow landed – whether in the stomach or in the brown beard, it hardly matters, though it probably does since there was no blood. The rain lifted from the man's head for a few seconds. Beard didn't crumple under the orange fist. He straightened up and reached for the wad of money. He had no gloves. His fingers were blue from the cold.

The blue fingers pulled out the wad and handed it to the bloodless orange matter, but Orange didn't take it. Another embarrassingly light blow landed somewhere, perhaps into the coat, which didn't reach the ankles and didn't have the distinct second-hand smell. It was a perfectly ordinary coat, a coat that could take many more punches.

The man swivelled inside it, the wad of money with one hundred and sixty-two portraits of Aleko Konstantinov didn't fall to the smashed paving stones, it returned to one of the pockets. An orange boot dug into his ankles. Unlikely that any blood came out, but even if it did, it was very little. The bloodless orange matter turned his orange jacket away, lifted his head high and continued down the street.

It kept raining; the weatherman said that a cyclone or maybe an anticyclone would roll around these parts for a whole week; it would cause rivers to overflow. Climate change, damn it; we were walking around in T-shirts in January! Then in March the polar bears turned up to break our necks. The wind whipped and whistled. At one point it started howling so strongly that the rain hid in the sky, and you couldn't work out if it was raindrops or sky falling before your eyes. A camel coat came out of the house. The horoscopes said that this colour was favourable in all aspects of life this week.

The wind picked up the coat, the woman inside it shivered in the heavy rain, or perhaps in the sky because it wasn't clear where the raindrops began and where the cloud above them ended. The expensive coat – which surely hadn't set foot in such a scruffy town until now – came to its senses and carefully, step by step, reached the brown beard huddled under the deluge.

'Are you sick?' the woman asked and shook her head. 'I'm not coming back to you.'

The man didn't say a word; the blue fingers reached into his pocket, pulled out all the Aleko Konstantinovs and handed them to the beautiful coat.

'Mother took your money the other day,' the man said. 'But I was saving it for you. Keep an eye on the girl from time to time. If you can, don't forget me from time to time.'

The woman took the money, went to put the wad in a safe place inside her coat (which surely had many safe places) but, perhaps because a whole dam was pouring over her head, split it in two and put one part in the safest of safe places in her coat and dropped the other part, the smaller one, into the pocket with the blue fingers.

'Are you going to die?' the woman asked, or maybe that was the torrent talking, which in that moment was more like sky than rain.

'No,' the man said. 'I wanted to see you. I'm leaving for Spain tomorrow.'

'Fine, but I'm not coming back to you.'

The man nodded. The woman seemed to change her mind because she went closer to him and kissed him. But in reality that was impossible. She kissed the beard and the rain. Her thumb and index finger found the second, thinner wad of money, considered for a moment, but didn't take it. Another safe place for Aleko Konstantinov – the inside pocket of the camel coat — remained empty. The woman's knee-high boots were some awesome brand, but the raindrops were indifferent.

She walked back towards the house. She obviously thought of something, because she went back and tentatively searched for the blue fingers. The wet black coat didn't emanate that smell that kills parasites. Even the seams on the sleeves weren't worn out. Beard must've bought the coat from an ordinary shop.

The man suddenly hugged her, though it wasn't really a hug, since it was just a second long. The fool even started crying, but that wasn't certain either — who could be sure what went on in that vicious rain.

'I'm leaving tomorrow,' he whispered and kissed her. That is certain, because the woman wiped her face with her pretty glove, turned and left him there, staring at her back — magic in a camel coat so expensive anyone's back would look incredible in it.

'Siyana,' the man said. The rain played with her name, tossing it towards the road. 'Siyana,' the man whispered, so quietly only the wind next to his lips heard him; the torrent didn't pay any attention. She returned to the house. The man in an orange top and orange trousers came out for a moment, just to bring in the knee-high boots, a killer brand, then presumably locked the door on the inside; click.

The brown beard remained on the street — a freshly dug molehill in March's rainy heart. The man forgot to pull his coat collar up. The rain trickled down his neck. A child appeared on the street — a hat with ear flaps swamping her entire face; a scarf wrapped around her neck, with the tassels on one side sweeping the pavement and on the other side sliding into her boot.

'Dad, let's go home,' the child said.

The man didn't even notice her. He was staring at the silky white home which had swallowed the woman in a camel coat. Fool. Who on earth stares at houses in the freezing cold?

The girl saw her father's blue fingers, took her scarf and wrapped it around his hand. 'Come on,' she repeated.

The man freed his hand from the scarf and stroked her enormous hat.

'Please, listen to me,' she pleaded. 'Mum's not coming home. The wind's howling. It's cold.'

'I'm leaving for Spain tomorrow, Damyanka.'

'OK. Let's go home now.'

'I'm leaving tomorrow.'

'You said the same yesterday,' she murmured uncertainly. 'Better you had left. It's warm in Spain.'

The man didn't say a word. He shook his head.

'Dad, I'm cold.'

The man came to his senses. Still said nothing. He embraced the girl, lifted her into the air and carried her away. The street was deserted.

'Don't get angry,' the girl said quietly. 'Mum's fine. Ginger Dimitar's house is warm.'

The beard nodded.

The man and his daughter were struggling through the rain towards a single-storey house huddled under the torrent.

'Dad, buy me some watercolours, please. I'll paint you smiling. Then you'll look happy.'

* * *

'Damyana, get in here!' The girl was wearing a thick green jumper knitted from homespun wool. The sleeves were long and her hands were completely invisible. She stood before her grandma, her gaze buried in the floor. A few days ago, they had covered the floor with new rugs, woven by Elena's mother; until now, they had kept them rolled into bundles in the chest in the narrow room which smelt of mothballs both summer and winter. The rugs were colourful and covered in different patterns. Here, in the Radomir region, people called rugs *puteki*, paths, because they look like paths through a meadow. 'Look at me. Not like that. Look me straight in the eyes.'

'Ginger Dimitar punched Dad,' the girl said. 'I saw him.'

'If I were your dad, he wouldn't have hit me,' snapped the woman also dressed in a thick green jumper knitted from homespun wool. 'What's that in your hand?'

'A bottle,' the girl mumbled, and her sleeve hung even heavier towards the floor.

Grey-hair barked: 'Give it.'

Slowly, like a duckling hatching from an egg, a bottle emerged from the girl's sleeves. Elena took it and opened the cap, though she already knew what it was. These were the bottles for storing yarrow tincture, used for healing infected wounds, stubborn dark skin spots, and even snakebites.

Elena also knew that she hadn't made yarrow tincture this year. She lifted the bottle and smelt it. 'When did you make this?' she asked.

The girl's eyes drowned in the rug. 'When it's supposed to be made. You know, when…'

'I know when it's supposed to be made. But I'm asking when you boiled it,' the old woman growled.

'When the Chinese dates were ripe but not too ripe – when you bite into them and your tongue hurts,' the child replied.

'Look at me.'

Titch's eyes weren't blue like her father's, or green like her grandad's, but grey-green like the glass of the bottle.

'Why didn't you tell me you've been making this?' Her grandma was staring daggers.

'I've not taken any of your herbs, Grandma,' mumbled the little one. 'I picked my own. I dried them on my own and...'

'Why didn't you tell me?' the old woman interrupted with an icy voice. 'Don't you have enough money? Were you planning to sell this? Have you been left hungry?'

'No!' the girl shrieked 'No.'

Her grandma's eyes became a storm. She lifted her brown hand. The brown fingers drew a semicircle but didn't touch the girl's cheek.

'Was it you who poured hellebore in Ginger Dimitar's water?'

The girl was silent.

'Was it you who poured the hellebore?' The brown fingers trembled.

'In the coffee,' the little one cried out. 'Half a drop. He cut the cherry... He cut my cherry tree.' The brown hand didn't touch the small face.

The old woman was silent.

'The police didn't catch him. He... Don't look at me like that. Don't...'

'Why have you taken this bottle now?' Grey-hair's hands were calm now. She lifted her head – a woman tall and dangerous, like the night.

The girl lifted her gaze from the floor. Tears glistened in her eyes, but she raised her oversized sleeve of dark green wool, wiped them away and quietly, bitterly and very clearly, without sobbing said:

'Ginger Dimitar hates Dad.'

'Damyana, a cure should *cure*,' said the woman with the big black eyes.

It was no longer snowing or raining. The cold wind sliced the earth in two – one half bare and naked, the other half frozen under the snow.

'Everyone knew about my cherry tree. No one told the police,' whispered the little girl. 'He hates you too, Grandma.' The girl's eyes were quiet and grey like death's footsteps. 'A cure should cure. But it wasn't going to cure him. It was going to hurt him.'

'Damyana!' shouted the tall thin woman. 'Listen to me.'

* * *

The snow began wilting under the sun, which rose timidly over the naked treetops – like a schoolboy turning up late for his maths test. But that was enough. Water ran everywhere; the landslide woke up.

A child was buried under it.

Thank God the twins Dida and Dona noticed something stirring under the silt and began screaming. No one in the Radomir district screams uglier that these two women. If you happen to hear them, you dream of it for three nights; young children wet their pants, and men comment: *It's obvious why these two bake their own bread and spend their money alone at the seaside in Greece. Their husbands left them on the same day. Bravo.*

This time the screaming turned out to be useful. People gathered and saw the child. A young Roma girl, as small as a basketball. Two men trudged through the silt and pulled her out. One of the rescuer's boots remained in the mud.

'How did you end up here, in the landslide?' they asked her, but the child just chattered her teeth, unable to say a single meaningful word.

An unknown child.

Crazy Elena ran over with her tinctures, her granddaughter trotting behind – both carried bottles.

'Here, child, drink this,' Elena said.

'And this, child, drink this too,' the granddaughter said.

Look at those two – the little one had learnt to stand up just like the old crow, weaving the same words. She plants them, lines them up next to each other, as if she were threading scotch bonnets on a hemp string. It wasn't the old crow that stroked the child's head, but her granddaughter.

'Go one, swallow this. It's not bitter, honest.' The girl believed the caress and drank the whole bottle the granddaughter gave her. She stood up from the mud. Even though she was covered in filth and sludge, she pressed her little body to Damyana's.

'Big sis, I'm hungry.'

'Go fetch bread and butter,' the crow ordered.

After the girl had scoffed almost half a loaf, Crazy Elena said: 'Stop eating or you'll die.'

The girl carried on chewing.

Young Crazy Elena stroked her muddy head again and said: 'Please, don't eat any more. Your little belly will burst. Then it's going to hurt a lot.'

The child stopped eating.

'How did you end up in the landslide?' old Elena asked, and the child began to cry.

Did the kid get frightened by Elena's black eyes which fixed her balefully, burning her? Or perhaps Elena looked scary because she was so tall.

Young Crazy Elena stroked the girl's cheek and she came clean: 'I was caught stealing,' she whispered. 'But I wasn't stealing, I was just eating. The smell of banichka was so delicious, I wanted to cut my nose off so I wouldn't smell it. They were all watching the football, well I was watching the football too – I go for CSKA – but I sneaked in and started eating the banichka. And he got me. Ginger…'

'And?' old Crazy Elena asked sharply. 'What happened next?'

'He threw me into the mud. Could've at least let me finish eating.'

What happened next became the talk of Radomir for two days and two nights, and for the whole of Radomir to talk about something for two days and two nights at least two people had to have died. Old Crazy Elena said: 'Wait here.' She sprinted off somewhere on her long legs. As well as 'Crazy Elena' they also called her '*Zhiten Begach*' after those grasshoppers that neither die nor sleep but – right up till November – jump and sing the moment you get close to their hole in the ground.

So the Zhiten Begach flew away. When it returned, it carried a hundred lev, a handsome hundred-lev banknote, the image of a man drawn on it – he must be an important man if he strolls around with the big money.

'Here, little one, take this money. Give it to your mum, Kerana. I know her.' The tall woman looked around and her eyes as black as a landslide paused on each face. 'Don't you dare steal this girl's money. Don't you dare so much as touch this child.'

'And this is from me,' Damyana said. Young Crazy Elena untied a long – practically endless – home-knit tasselled scarf from her neck and wrapped it around the girl's muddy one. 'Run home so your mum can change your clothes,' she said.

'You see how the old crow teaches her,' people murmured. 'Of course she does, she's got money. Do you really think that when she cures this one and that one, they don't give her a bit of cash, huh?' 'It doesn't matter how much they give her; I take my hat off to this woman.' 'Me too.' 'I don't; she's got the money so it doesn't hurt her to give.'

On the fringe of the group that had gathered around the little Roma girl stood a boy – a thistle with a home-knit hat in all colours of the rainbow; his mother had most probably made it from the left-over wool she kept in the basket under the bed in the kitchen. The boy looked like a scarecrow with that hat and the huge accordion – battered on all sides, stained and splashed with mud – hanging from his neck like stone on a rope. The boy, a Roma, began playing.

And what a song that was; he was picking it up here, dropping it there – it was not a song at all but a street with potholes, a house with broken roof tiles – yet the boy carried on playing.

'What're you doing here, Vasko?' asked one of the men who had rescued the girl from the landslide. 'Have you decided to earn money here, huh?'

Vasko didn't even hear him. His fingers, frozen by that deranged March, ran and danced on the accordion. It moaned and groaned. There was no melody in that instrument, skinned like a rabbit. There was howling and shrieking. There was fire. A whole garrison of soldiers marching, a whole army attacking; the sound that came out made people duck for cover.

The more sensitive folk were struggling to cope, but those who understood fire took a few stotinki, ones and twos – the richer ones among them even fifties – and dropped them on the ground at the boy's feet.

But this boy, in a hat as colourful as a dragon, didn't see the stotinki at all.

He didn't even notice them.

He played and played that horrific molten song for one person only.

For the girl with the thick homespun wool jumper, who was now without a scarf, without tassels, just a bare neck in the freezing cold. Vasko was torturing the song but with such gusto that if a heart could fly, his would land on the sun.

Did the girl with the bare neck guess that the dragon-hat was playing just for her?

'Dame-Damyanka!' the boy whispered, but his horrific accordion, with its moans and groans, drowned out his words and no one heard him.

* * *

It was still snowing in the middle of March, on Saint Theodore's Day, but no one was frightened of a few snowflakes. There was a feast, which meant barbecues, market stalls, sturdy local folk, and people from the neighbouring villages, even from Pernik – everyone who was born in this region, so rich in rocks and fights. They came to sip warm, sweet rakia, to eat sausages and pork steaks, to see what had been stolen and what was left after the robbery, though today that wasn't really so important.

Because it was the day that some people celebrated – sometimes in advance, sometimes belatedly – the birthday of a father called Thodor, a mother called Thodora, a girlfriend Theodora. Those without a Thodor or Thodora celebrated the fact that they hadn't married as early as their stupid friend. But the most important thing of the day was the horo, the folk dance as wild as the Rila and Pirin mountains. Men and women were inclined to have a sip or two of fiery Kamenara rakia, which you could only make from the damsons in the Radomir region – stubborn, wild damsons that withstood cold and howling winds, flood and drought – and which, if you drank a glass every day, made your heart as strong as iron, your nerves steel, your fist a volcano. After a few glasses of this fiery rakia the horo took on a life of its own, so vigorous that the paving stones were stomped two centimetres down. Grannies forgot they had arthritis; toddlers took their first steps.

That was the only day that no one stole anything, no one touched anything that didn't belong to them until 4 p.m. and no one got into a fight until 10 p.m. The horo sucked away their anger, the only thing anyone could do was tip a glass or two more of the fiery rakia, smile like a pumpkin and embrace their wife – a rare occasion for married couples over thirty.

'Grandma, please, let's practise the quick horo,' said the little girl who for once wasn't wearing the chunky homespun wool jumper. She had on a blue cotton top, almost new.

'Stop bothering me,' snapped the skinny woman, who was crushing roasted snail shells into a pot. She was making a potion for inflamed joints, but just like everyone in Radomir, she too turned an eye towards the street.

'Come on, Grandma. Everyone's going to laugh at me,' the girl insisted.

At that moment, her grandad dropped the newspaper he mostly argued with rather than read, picked up the little girl, lifting her almost to the ceiling, and said:

'Do you know how much I struggled until I managed to teach your Grandma Elena the Graovo horo? It pains me just thinking about it.' His beautiful face beamed, and he looked like a silly child.

'Tell me, tell me! I'll iron your shirt straight away if you tell me,' the girl exclaimed.

'Your grandma was much skinnier back then,' began Damyan. '"Go on, Elena," I said, "let me teach you how to dance the Graovo horo," and she said, "No! Everyone's going to see me and take the micky out of me until the end of my days." "Show me how you dance it," I asked her.

And so she did. I had to bite my lip so I didn't burst out laughing. She was jumping up and down like a cockerel with his legs tied, trampling on her own toes, kicking the paving slabs. I couldn't hold it any longer and fell about laughing; your grandma got so upset, her face twisted as if she'd been given bitter lemon. I didn't know what to do.

"I'm not laughing at you," I said, yet her face twisted even more.

"Come on, Dushichke Lenche, we'll go to Golo Bardo, and I'll teach you. No one will see us there and no one will laugh at you. But I have to tell you, Elena, it's really funny."

Your grandma's nose dropped like an abandoned hoe, she wouldn't look at me, so I didn't repeat myself and say, "Come on, Elena." Because you know what your grandma's like once she's decided something, she's as stubborn as ten donkeys on ten bridges. Doesn't budge. Then, without asking, I picked her up, lifted her in the air — nowadays she's as thin as a thread, back then she was even thinner, almost transparent like water. I picked her up and she began kicking — not as if she was trying to break my bones, but as if she was trying not to hurt me. I know her very well, I do.'

'That's not true. I kicked hard,' Grandma Elena protested over the wooden bowl where she was crushing the poor snails' shells.

'You weren't kicking hard. Anyway, I carried her across the street. Everyone saw us and said, "Hey, Damyan, where're you carrying that spindle of a girl, are you going to bump her off?" I didn't respond. You know where Golo Bardo is, Dame-Damyanka, don't you? It's a long way, I carried her for two hours. At one point your grandma said to me, "Put me down, Damyan, you'll get tired. I feel sorry for you." And I, the idiot, put her down. Of course, she did a runner, flew like a kite with those long legs of hers. I had held and carried her for two hours so I wasn't taking any of those shenanigans. I managed to grab hold of her again and pelted up to the peak of Golo Bardo. Just before we got there, I ran out of strength and said to her, "Elena, please, I'm knackered, walk for a bit yourself so I can rest a little."

Do you know what she did? "OK," she said.

I let her down and she tried to pick me up.

Well, she did pick me up, but she only managed to carry me for half a step.

Then we had a rest, and I began teaching her how to dance the Graovo horo. I would agree to carry your grandma to

Golo Bardo again, but I don't ever again want to teach her to dance the Graovo horo.'

'Liar!' the snail shells called out sharply, but Grandad Damyan had never lied before. So he probably wasn't lying now.

'Come on, Dame-Damyanka, let me teach you the horo. I just hope you're not like your grandma!'

He began whistling and gently, as if he had a breeze rather than feet, picked up the steps. He stepped and jumped and squatted; the one-storey house was amazed and began swaying to his rhythm. Damyana followed suit – jumped and stepped and squatted and flew towards the ceiling.

'Well, well! You're not at all like your grandma,' Grandad Damyan exclaimed in amazement. 'You're like a jay! You can dance the Radomir horo. Who taught you?'

'Grandma told me to dance if I didn't want to read.'

'It's evident how much you were reading!' remarked the grim (but not really grumpy), skinny woman.

On the day of Saint Theodore, Elena didn't wear clothes from Second Chance. She put on her nice clothes and dressed the child in new jeans, new boots, a new coat from last year. They waited for Grandad Damyan to dress up. He simply brushed his hair, slung on a pair of trousers and a jacket, and that was it. When they stepped onto the street, all eyes turned to him – there was so much beauty in that old face.

Only on Saint Theodore day did Damyana see her grandma tipple two consecutive glasses of fiery Kamenara rakia. Her grandad tippled three glasses, but Elena didn't comment, as if she hadn't noticed. Everyone around them – neighbours, newcomers from Pernik and Sofia who had abandoned their cars by the town square – were tippling the Kamenara, grinning like radishes. Everyone was jolly as if they were about to break into song.

Suddenly, beautiful music rang out.

The accordion – like an aeroplane, was none other than Grandad Vasso's brother; the drum – as big as the mayor's Citroën, was Grandad Vasso himself, olive-skinned, terrifying, the tallest man in Radomir; the trumpet – ah, what a trumpet! A trumpet like this had not been born before. Imagine who it is – a woman! God, where are you? Come quickly to see her: tall, olive skin, beautiful like the fields around Radomir, as majestic as Golo Bardo. Valya – Grandad Vasso's daughter-in-law, Vasko's mother – played with God, in fact beyond the realm of God; everyone stopped sipping Kamenara to look at her. What a horo this trumpet played, from here to the heavens and God, to the mother of Christ, the most cherished, most beloved Virgin Mary and back to the people. A golden horo, strong and powerful.

People grabbed hands, left their glasses right there on the pavement; rain drizzled into them, but no one cared. Vasso, the tallest man in Radomir, not a man but a forest, pounded the drum as if his heart were the earth, the sky and the rocks all at the same time. His brother was stretching the accordion from here to Greece. The accordion roared and played, but the most beautiful thing was Valya's wild, golden trumpet that knew where to emphasise, where to go gently, where to fly and where to kick.

An amazing horo snaked around the square, as if all one hundred people were just one person with one heart and one pair of feet, as if God had joined the horo too, though He was not leading it. It was led by a man so handsome that everyone exclaimed: 'Gosh, you're amazing!' This was Damyan, Elena the Healer's husband, known as 'Beautiful' around here, but he was even better known for his skill at dancing every folk dance from the Thracian Valley, from the Danube region by the border to the north, and from Pirin Mountain to the south – all of them!

And since on this holy day it was Damyan leading the horo in honour of the Virgin Mary and all the mothers she protected, everyone knew many children would be born here. Healthy children, beautiful children. And there would be bread for all of them, despite the robberies and bandits. There would be faces like these – beaming with joy. Because the horo is the biggest kick in the teeth to evil. The infamous saying is *Hold on, Mother Earth, Shopi people are trampling on you!* But these were no Shopi, but rather Graovtse. Here, around Radomir, grew the largest peas – *grao* – not peas but cannon-balls. Their leaves were green, green like the eyes of most of the Graovtse, and beautiful like Valya's amazing trumpet, like Valya, who never studied music but only listened to her father, the radio and her father-in-law, and who began playing herself, better than her father, the radio and her father-in-law together.

On the horo's tail came the teenage boys and girls, and behind them the little children like commas, dots and dashes, all dressed warmly in their best clothes. Their new boots thumped and slapped the pavement, the water and the rain evaporated in despair. Everything was so beautiful, so sweet that one of the children, the last one at the tail – a child in new boots like all the other children, a girl in a new jacket from last year – reached for the clouds, arranged her steps, jumped and squatted and didn't know if it was the start of the horo or its tail, her face beaming and beaming like the morning star.

Somewhere near the end of the horo a tall, skinny woman in a long coat was kicking and tossing her feet, sometimes in tune with the music, sometimes not, but mostly out of rhythm; no one paid much attention to her.

'Go on, Elena!' someone shouted. Good job the woman didn't hear them, otherwise she would've tangled her legs and frozen to the spot.

A tall, slim boy dressed in a beautiful new jacket – not from three years ago, not from last year, not even from five months ago – stood without dancing. That boy hadn't put on the hat Valya, his mother, had knitted for him with all the colours of left-over wool from the basket under the bed in the kitchen.

That boy had strapped an enormous accordion across his chest – it was not his Grandad Vasso's accordion, nor his uncle's, it was his Great-grandad Vasil's, from the Second Radomir Infantry Regiment. Great-grandad Vasil had been wounded at the Drava river, but the accordion remained unscathed, together with the Order of Bravery that Vasko's father had nailed to the kitchen wall. Vasko had inherited this battered accordion.

The boy was now stretching and pulling it, as much as he possibly could and even more than he could.

How he managed to play and sing and smile all at the same time, no one could work out.

Only the huge, wild, endless Graovo horo!

* * *

She had danced at the horo, on the end. A pea, that was my daughter, dressed in the cheapest pair of trousers, the cheapest boots. At least she had inherited those deep eyes from her father, his delicate bones, his face. Her face is white, dainty. When she's not by my side I sometimes think she's never existed. That warm face got its beauty from her grandfather – Beautiful Damyan, as weak-kneed as fresh cheese. For so many years he's walked by Crazy Elena's side, obeying her like the sheep obey the shepherd. Bringing her water, buying her bread. If he weren't so daft, I might have shed a tear of pity for him.

Around here there are so many illiterates that if you know what the square root of sixteen is, you're anointed Galileo Galilei. Hence the abundance of geniuses in the Radomir region – geniuses that step on each other's feet, steal whatever they can find, rummage through the bins. If you drop your guard for just a moment your car keys vanish, or the strap of your handbag is sliced with lightning speed by some unparalleled innovator.

Who am I leaving my child to? To Elena with the gravel brain. They say the little one is learning how to mix potions from the priestess herself. The kid had saved some bandit or other, otherwise he would've gone blind. Look at my eye! As if! Ginger stuffed more euros into my daughter's pocket than her grandma, the old tapeworm, has earned in ten years. Apparently the kid can make compresses and ointments on her own and because she's beautiful like her father – and not a *maladroit specimen* like me – barren ladies go to see her, begging her to make them juice or porridge. What juice anyway, didn't they chop down all the trees and shrubs in the garden of my headstrong mother-in-law, the healer?

Damyana mixes ointments, the barren Graces watch her, stroke her hair and then miraculously conceive. Conceive, my arse! My daughter always wanders around on her own; that one, the crazy one, has stuffed her in a long coat and strapped a scarf around her neck – most likely picked up from some dead granny. When I think about this town I imagine ditches along a dirt track. My daughter walks on that track with boots from the era before Christ, pink trousers that really couldn't be any uglier, a jacket, hat and tights – all frayed.

That boy, the clown, luxuriates in the same fashion range from head to toe. That awful hat, an accordion bigger than he is, shoes two sizes too big. By God, when he starts squeaking on that damn instrument… sitting on the bench under the mulberry tree opposite the healer's house like that! Actually, it's not her house; it belongs to Damyan, destitute of character, meek grandad. Just look at that vandal sitting under the mulberry tree, stretching his accordion and singing, in other words: coughing. No lyrics, no melody, just bog swamp and chaos in a croaky throat. From time to time, he yells 'Dame-Damyanka'.

I lost my temper one day.

'Listen to me,' I said, 'I don't care who you are, I don't care how many cousins you've got and who your dad and grandad are!' The idiot looks at me menacingly. 'You're making a noise. I'll call the police. In fact, not the police, if you yell my daughter's name one more time, you'll meet Ginger Dimitar.'

'Damyanka's no longer your daughter,' the little vandal behind the accordion barked. 'You walked out on her.'

'Maybe I did,' I said. I picked up his ugly hat and tossed it into a nearby puddle. Then it occurred to me that there was a better way to bring this juvenile rural Don Juan, the face of Second Chance, to his senses. 'Wait a minute,' I said, quietly so as not to alarm him. I opened my handbag and found it straight away – my nail file.

The weather was lovely.

The nail file pierced the accordion. A high-pitched whistle flew out. That idiot stared at me as if I had gutted him. I noticed tears glistening on his cheeks.

'Now, if you please, explain to me how exactly I deserted Damyana.'

'You're nasty,' the audacious weed screamed. For a moment I thought he would hit me.

When I'm in Radomir, I don't step onto the street without a spray against stray dogs and that device 'Tranquillity' – a miniature electric shock baton, more expensive than my gold opal ring. The ring and Tranquillity are presents from Ginger. I could only regret that the gypsy didn't try to hit me. I took out my phone instead, an expensive item yet to attract an assassination attempt from the local experts, a fact that never ceases to amaze me.

'A boy from the minorities is attacking me, my love.' I spoke slowly and clearly. 'Please hurry, he could kill me.' I watched the tiny rivulets of tears glisten on Snotty's face, the moisture sinking into the dirty accordion. Carefully, I closed the phone. The gadget was probably more expensive than the house opposite me. I turned to face the young villain, 'If I hear you pronouncing – you don't know what "pronounce" means, but anyway – if I hear you saying my daughter's name one more time, you'll be severely punished. Understood?'

'You're nasty,' the savage repeated, but when Ginger's Jeep – a vehicle as spacious as the house in front of me, including the adjacent barn – growled into the street and pulled up next to the kerb, I ordered the little snot:

'Kneel.'

He stood there, a toad clutching a lifeless accordion, fixing his dark gaze on me, face smeared with tears.

'You were told to kneel, you piece of shit,' Ginger shouted, and I realised I've always needed a specimen like this in my life. A man capable of defending me against snails, mosquitoes and impertinents.

The kid didn't kneel; instead, he lifted his head. The nape of his neck shone — he had a bad haircut, most likely performed with shears by his sisters or his mother, who sold fidelity tokens to add a handful of coins to her family's earnings. Ginger Dimitar is not inclined to use humane methods of persuasion. He slapped the neck of the arrogant brat; the maggot groaned, but not very loudly. As big and powerful as Ginger is, he knows how to judge a punch — by the sounds emitted, he can tell whether he's broken a bone or not.

'Kneel,' he shouted. 'Next to my left trainer. Or I'll slice off a piece of your ear.'

The nit obeyed. He knelt, slowly, until he resembled a molehill.

'If you say anything to this woman, ever again, I'll douse you with petrol. Just like that.' To my amazement (Ginger often surprises me, and I find this very pleasing) he poured something, which I personally don't think smelt like petrol but who knows, over the kid's badly cut head and pulled out a lighter. 'If I see you squatting here under this tree ever again, you'll be on fire. Do you understand me? I'll ask one more time — do you understand?'

The small obtuse creature remained silent. He tried to straighten up again.

'Did you hear me, you filth?' Ginger clicked the lighter. For a moment I was worried that Ginger would set the peasant alight before my eyes and I'd be in trouble.

The nit mumbled something. He had mud spread on his cheeks and forehead. Tears welled in his eyes.

'That's how I like you,' Ginger said, 'you're cool like this.' Then he pushed him. The filth collapsed over his accordion, but by the time you could count to five, he had risen again. I thought he'd run away, but obviously he hadn't been cured of his audacity. He stood up, completely covered in mud, accordion strapped over his scrawny bones, and walked away slowly, very slowly, his nose in the air, that ugly hat in his hand. Ginger also has a keen eye for stuck-up noses. He hit the juvenile annoyance on the back of the head, then ran over to me. That man is in perfect condition. He picked me up as if I were a Valentine's card.

In one step he carried me to the Jeep. It's clear what we did. It's clear where we did it – in front of the house of the unparalleled Elena, my magnificent mother-in-law.

'Ginge, move the car a bit to the left, towards madam's window, you know who.'

This is what I highly value in Ginger: he responds swiftly to my ideas. Not only that, but he also develops them further – an expression I wouldn't normally use to refer to people who have lived in this forgotten crease of geography for years.

'Shall I ring the old crow?' Ginger asked and winked. He has beautiful blue eyes. All the men in my life have the same eyes. If they haven't got beautiful blue eyes, they haven't got a chance. I kissed Ginger, and of course I enjoyed it. The colossus had a voice as deep as a gorge, which excites my senses.

'Elena, come over. I need you for something. Yes, you!' Ginger called. He enunciated each word, and as they say in this magical region, he 'broke the sink'.

That one, the weirdo, came out wrapped in her coat from the fifth century BC. We were doing it just as she appeared at the gate. Let Elena watch. Hopefully she'll learn something. Let her kiss the pavement under the tyres of the Jeep in gratitude.

She was stiff as a plank, watching us with no interest, as if her ears resounded with information about the level of the Danube. Not blood but mucus ran in the old turtle's arteries.

'Ginger Dimitar, what do you need me for?'

After this question Ginger's love deflated. Crazy Elena had no consideration for his condition. She was looking at me.

'Christo left,' she said. Her voice held no special emphasis. 'For Spain.'

What a voice – gravel over a friend's grave.

*   *   *

I'm writing you a letter.

I'm writing it in my head, Siyana. I remember you saying, 'I'm giving you this equation as a present,' and then asking me to solve it. Apparently, it was simple.

$-3y + 4x = 11$

$y + 2x = 13$

'This is our equation of happiness,' you smiled. I kept postponing finding the solution.

Pop in to see our child. The little one asked me to buy her watercolours and a drawing pad. I didn't. I left in a hurry. Please, buy them for her. That's the end of my letter. I'm falling asleep, Siyana.

He would write to her in his sleep and while he was digging. They had to dig big trenches to lay the pipes. It was very humid. Payment wasn't regular; with the last of his money, he left for Brussels. He had a friend there: Berisha, Albanian. The Albanian didn't pay regularly either, but at least he put him up in his garage for a while; then he kicked him out of it. But Berisha had a good heart and said:

'Come, brother. You can live in the loft; pay me just two hundred euros. There's electricity and a toilet. Try to wash there.'

Berisha gave him an old mattress, old blankets and some old shirts. The shirts were too big; Christo had lost weight. Sometimes he would pop into Café Ciel in Evere. It was warm there in the evenings. The coffee was good and cheap. Christo would repair the coffee machine, the odd old chair, sweep and clean the toilet. Often they would treat him to a lukewarm tea, Berisha would give him four or five sachets of honey for free.

Christo would breakfast and lunch on bread and honey; even when he could barely keep his eyes open, he was writing her a letter for which he had no paper or hands – his hands were always full of something for Berisha's garage. It drizzled constantly in Brussels, but the rain was no bother, it fell softly even in strong winds. Brussels' rain was a fog that fell and didn't want to hurt you.

Siyana, I'm writing to you in my head.

The moment I saw you, I knew I had to save you.

I would ask myself: do we live just for profit? Happiness is profit: when you see summer in the eyes of the person without whom you don't care if tomorrow comes, or if the year has gone by and there won't be another one after it. What does a year mean if you're not awaited by eyes that desire you? You walk. You breathe. That's it. Scientists must've explained it — a complex chemical reaction: the receptors for sorrow kick in and you're sick without that person.

I wanted to transform your receptors for sorrow into receptors for joy. I told you the story everyone in Radomir learns at a young age; I told it to our daughter Damyana too — what to do with someone's tears so you can turn them into your own blood for life. There must be something wrong with this story. It's old and worn-out from telling and retelling, but I've lived all my life in Staro Selo, Radomir's most godforsaken neighbourhood. I never looked for other stories. You knew the story differently — you don't drink someone's tears but their money. Then you become their blood.

I couldn't live without the girl who had quarrelled with her mother and come to our house. 'Money,' your mother pointed out, 'means a house, a family, a child. Money is life. If you don't have a wallet, you're not alive. That's it!' But that girl trusted me.

I wanted to rescue you from money, Siyana.

In Radomir we believe that if someone gifts you a smile, they gift you a summer. You made all the streets smile at me.

When you went to Ginger you must've looked even more beautiful. I saw you kissing. But the girl kissing him wasn't the girl I loved. It wasn't the girl who gave me the sky. It wasn't the girl who gave birth to my daughter and taught her to recite 'I am Bulgarian', Vazov's ode to the Bulgarian people and their fight for freedom, when she was still a tiny titch.

'Damyana doesn't know what "homeland" means,' your mother said flatly. 'No one needs to learn those things nowadays.' For me Bulgaria is our street, covered with ice in winter, then mud, then dust; the corner where I met you.

You were in the last year in school and had the most beautiful brown hair – it was like sunset. You were crying. I told you something stupid, the stupidest thing I've ever prattled on about.

You said: 'What a stupid thing to say!' but you smiled. Since that day, I've loved our beautiful, quiet street. I had no money then, not a penny, and eight days left until my pay cheque. I was on my way home for lunch – Mum had cooked bean soup – and I was saving to buy a used car.

I wanted to go to Greece. When I was young my father used to talk about Greece. I thought the sky there was big and generous, and if I went there, I was bound to see Zeus and Athena Pallas. I was so crazed by the idea that I vowed if I ever had a daughter, I would call her Athena. I still want to go to Greece, hoping to meet her someplace – in a car park, in the clouds, on the motorway. Athena Pallas, the Wise. Anyway, I didn't have money to invite you for a coffee, and being an idiot, I admitted it.

'I don't have any money,' I blurted out. What a muppet! 'Wait for me, I'll be ten minutes. I'll borrow some and I'll take you out for coffee.'

You didn't wait. I ran home to Mum. Fool! I told her I had seen a girl I fancied and I wanted to buy her coffee. Mum didn't say a word but gave me ten lev.

'Pay it back when you can,' she said.

I came back, but you weren't on the bench where you were supposed to wait for me. I was clutching the ten lev, an absolute moron. I sat on the bench and wished I could rip off my head. I turned around and began walking home and as I was walking, a girl even more beautiful than the one who had been crying, with a smile stretching from me to the train station in Pernik, tapped me on the shoulder. You. I'm not sure what I liked better – your grumpy face or your smile.

'Let me see what this fool will do,' you said to me, Siyana. 'I had decided to dump you. A man like a pine tree yet counting his pennies.

Blue eyes, thick beard but no money. Why do I need a man like this? He's probably been begging from his mum...'

'I'll pay her back,' I interrupted you.

'If only you knew what you looked like — a wilted cabbage. And now you bow that head of yours as if trying to hide it inside your shoes.'

'I fancy you,' I mumbled. Idiot. But it was the truth.

To this day I'm no good at spinning and twisting tales. If you don't know what to say, keep quiet, my father used to say, and he's a decent man. He's never been in a fight, and he's never been beaten — no one else in Radomir can boast that. Then I thought, that's it, I've lost her.

That's when I kissed you. Just like that, as you were standing next to me. Your whole smile — stretching from me to the train station — landed on my lips. I understood. My eyes don't see beautiful faces, but they can see happiness. I saw it in you. I bought you a coffee. It was bad, weak coffee; you know how they make it in Solaris ever since Ginger Dimitar took possession of it. I had nowhere to take you, we didn't have an allotment with a shed I could invite you to, and I hadn't saved enough for a car so I couldn't even take you for a drive. It's a good thing it was so hot at the end of that May, you would've thought it was the end of August.

'I've got nowhere to take you,' I blurted out. How thick was I? If you don't know what to say, keep your mouth shut — but I never learnt! 'I don't have a car to take you anywhe—' and while I was saying 'anywhere' your kiss drank the word and all my worries, then drank my unhappiness over not yet having saved enough money. 'But we've repaired the barn, I bought bricks and tiles for the roof, we even repaired Dad's sawmill, we bought a new fridge because the old one was giving up the ghost.'

'You have a beautiful face,' you said. *'Blue eyes. Sad eyes. Come on, smile. Forget the old fridge and your dad's sawmill for*

a moment. Come.' You took my hand, and we went behind the community hall.

There, among the elders and the wild pears, was a bench. I had never been there before. Dad and I ploughed the fields of the cooperative, then harvested the crops. The rest of the time I went to construction sites in Sofia; I wanted to learn how to fix the engines of the combine harvester and the tractor, you know. Then you said:

'I've been waiting for such a long time for you to approach me. You had no eyes for me. You're such a silly boy, Christo. I know you are.' You were kissing my forehead, eyes, nose, beard, and I understood – my eyes have seen the truth – you are happiness. That's how I see you in my thoughts, Siyana. The girl who was crying on the street, so dusty as if it were August, not May.

I wasn't sad when you went to Ginger because that wasn't my girl. That wasn't my crying girl with the brightest chestnut-brown eyes, eyes like a sunset, like an autumn which will never leave me. November will always be my home. Ginger took another woman, not you. I wasn't interested in that other woman whose fingers were swathed in gold. I stood by Ginger's house so I could catch a glimpse of my girl, the girl who'd kissed me on that old, crooked bench among the elders and the wild pear trees. That was when love had walked into my life for the first time; you had begun crying again.

'Why?' I asked you.

'Because I'm happy... No one has ever been so good to me.'

'Silly girl,' I said. 'You sweet, silly girl.' Then I drank your tears, one by one; they were salty and light like nimble fingers that cure the most terrible of illnesses – loneliness. I told you that old Radomir story, about the tears and the special friend.

You said: 'I have no eyes in my thoughts, Christo. I have eyes in my fingers. They see that I'll never meet a better man than you.'

What a stupid thing you said. Nowadays if you're 'good' it means that you're sick and good for nothing. I didn't have anything to give you. We drank two coffees and paid three lev in Café Solaris. I had seven more lev from the money I borrowed from Mum.

'Here,' I said, 'take this seven lev. That's all I have, but in eight days when I get my pay cheque, I'll have seven hundred.'

You took the money and said: 'Let each lev you give me bring you one hundred years of life.'

Then we both laughed and I walked you to your house, then we turned around and you walked me to my house, then back to yours and back to mine. We ate an ice cream – the best one I've ever eaten. They don't make it any more, but it shooed away my fear and the thought that I was penniless for the whole of seven days.

I'm writing you this letter. I'm constantly writing to you in my thoughts, my eyes are always fixed there, nothing has changed. I can only see happiness. You are happiness. Not that woman in an expensive coat which Ginger bought.

'You are the most beautiful boy,' you had said back then. But that didn't matter.

Siyana, please buy the little one watercolours and a drawing pad. Please.

* * *

'Listen, Elena, I've always been exceptionally honest and open with you. You are my only in-law, Siyana is my only child, a beautiful daughter.' The woman talking would catch the eye – slender, a white face glowing like cream cheese under the thin, but impeccably done, black hair; you could tell she had dyed it just before her visit.

'Marietta, a man suffering from shortness of breath is waiting for me to prepare a potion from eleven herbs. So, if you please: if you would like something from me, tell me right away and I'll consider whether I'll give it to you.'

It was exactly 11:15 a.m. The lady with the carefully dyed hair was exceptionally punctual. She had called to say that she was going to arrive at 11:15 a.m. and that her visit would last exactly ten minutes.

'Why do you always think I'm going to ask for something?' She smiled, but her voice stumbled and didn't follow her lips. 'Perhaps I've come to give you something.'

The tall woman stared at a small pile of dried herbs. Her fingers were moving with lightning speed from leaf to leaf – little snakes driving their venomous fangs into someone. Her face, olive-skinned, unblemished, didn't move, as if the face belonged to one person and the fingers to another.

'If your daughter Siyana has sent something for me, then hand it over. As you can see, I'm very busy.'

Without a word, without putting a full stop on her smile, which made her face look like a glowing light bulb, the visitor took something out of her handbag – a pair of knee-high boots. The brand, a connoisseur's idea of perfection: Alexander McQueen.

'Siyana said you'd guess why she sent them to you.' The smile swelled so much that it could no longer be contained on the lips carefully treated with lipstick; it jumped to the light brown eyes and transformed them into appetising roast peanuts, bursting with pleasure. 'In fact, Elena, I would like to remind you: you promised Siyana to kiss a pair of boots.'

The olive-skinned face didn't twitch, didn't tighten, didn't twist; it was as if it was carved from an ox bone.

'Very well,' replied Elena. 'Give me her boots, thank you.'

'My daughter gave me a hundred and twenty lev. If I decide, I am to give it to you,' the woman with the impeccable hair said. 'If I conclude that you and the child have no need for money, I can pop over to the boutique Harmony and buy myself a red jacket. You must've seen it in the shop window; it's ever so chic. As I see it, you're making that potion for the man with the breathing difficulties – and probably a lot of locals are tormented by breathlessness – so I can conclude: Elena is financially stable. I do not need to give her financial resources. I'd better buy myself that red jacket.'

'You'd better buy it,' the tall, slim woman said. 'I'm just about to go out. Thank you for bringing the boots. I'll probably kiss them, what do you think? Before you leave, I should tell you: Damyana's developing well. She's over her flu.'

The white face smiled from ear to ear, which meant that both the nose and teeth gleamed with a special sparkle.

'Actually, Elena, my daughter mentioned that one of her possessions was here... she wants you to give it back. You know that Siyana's busy – she's taking part in a show on one of the big TV channels. I doubt you're interested in which one I'm talking about.'

Elena must have crushed and ground the herbs not into powder but into atoms, though only she knew this. She carefully opened a tall, dark blue jar, scooped out a spoonful of something that looked like mud and started stirring again.

'That looks disgusting,' remarked the visitor. 'I understand you're in a hurry. You didn't even offer me a coffee; it's a little disappointing, though.' Her white teeth carried on smiling; apart from chewing, that was the only thing they were capable of. The smile was the same, chewed up. 'Back to the question, Elena. I know you're a business-minded woman...

You had offered my daughter a ring with the face of some saint on it, made of gold. When Siyana married your son, you gave her that ring. You told her that you had received it personally from your mother-in-law, old Christina.' Elena didn't respond, dropped a few more leaves into the dark mixture, pressed them and sprinkled some brown powder over them. The scent of cinnamon spread around the room. 'So I won't waste your time any more, Elena, give me that ring. My daughter wants it.'

The tall woman straightened. Her eyes, as black as the mixture into which she pulverised the leaves, did not leave the guest's white face. Still staring at the precisely painted eyebrows, she covered the wooden bowl, then washed her hands in the sink, walked to the door, opened it and left the room. You could see her slow, measured movements as she put on her coat which reached almost to her ankles, then walked along the garden path. She opened the gate and stepped onto the street.

The woman with the immaculately dyed hair looked around, poked into the wooden bowl, sniffed the contents, stood up, carefully examined the glasses in the dresser, opened the cupboard under the sink and attentively studied everything there. Then she pulled open the drawer in the table and counted the cutlery – five spoons, five forks, one large knife, probably for steaks, and not a single serviette, only old-fashioned cloth napkins. This lack told the visitor more than five volumes of specialised literature. Such backwardness. The table was covered with an oilcloth of faded roses. As dull as dull gets. Her teeth radiated a glow of pearly whiteness. *That tall one is trying village tricks on me. She's so simple.*

The lady with the impeccable black hair and white face was prepared. She knew you couldn't fell a tree with a single blow. She reached into her pocket; she had written a note in advance, in clear block capitals: DEAR ELENA, TOMORROW I WILL COME BY AGAIN FOR THE RING. WITH LOVE, YOUR IN-LAW MARIETTA.

A little girl in a long green coat was waiting for her on the street.

'Damyana, you're dressed like a beggar,' pronounced the woman's white face. 'I'm embarrassed that you're my granddaughter.'

The girl's long coat stiffened. After a little while it came to its senses.

'If you had asked me for Mum's ring, I would've given you tea to drink,' the girl said slowly. 'Your hand would have begun to tremble. And when the nails started oozing pus, it would have hurt a lot.'

* * *

Just behind the old church of Saint Nikolas was the start of a narrow path that dived into the pine forest. Someone had been logging here; only a few pines remained sticking out of the earth like an old granny's teeth. Between them had grown European dodder, wild roses and hawthorn. The area was overgrown. Two kids were struggling to get through the thorny bushes. They were sticking to the edge of the forest where young pines waved their necks, as thin as cats' tails. No one would think of chopping down those young saplings.

'Look, I've saved this for you, Dame-Damyanka,' the boy said. That stupid colourful hat was adorning his head again. The boy reached into the pocket of his jeans – a new pair, though bought in Second Chance where you could buy new things too, for only one lev fifty stotinki, so long as you kept your eyes peeled, and Vasko peeled his eyes so hard they hurt.

After seven days of singing – and not just anywhere, but on the bridge over the Struma in Pernik – he had saved a bit of money. You catch the early train in Radomir and at eight o'clock you crouch on the bridge. The town centre is deserted – no cats, no people around, no one to listen to your music. So Vasko just sits there waiting for the ladies who work in the town hall to start their day. He's all dressed up in his new jeans, he's taken off the colourful hat because in Pernik if they see something colourful, they avoid you.

The plumper twin sister had cut his hair, then the slimmer one found three hundred faults, so she took over the shearing, then his cousin had a go. Now, with the big accordion strapped to his chest, Vasko was ready for his performance. He had glued it together himself after Dame-Damyanka's mother pierced it. If he had told his mum about it… she would've probably gone to rip out the lady's hair, then Ginger would've burned their house down. Vasko bought one-minute glue and the accordion ended up stronger than the ones they sold in the shop; the only problem was it gave out a funny roar.

Vasko only played if it wasn't raining and if one of the ladies from the town hall walked nearby. He recognised them by their nice coats. Vasko would watch TV and as soon as he heard a song he liked, he poured its melody over the Struma bridge the following day. If he got ten lev in a day, he was happy. He carried his food in a plastic bag; he made himself smaller on the train by squeezing into a corner and, because he was so skinny, the conductor thought he was younger and didn't charge him. The boy got rich, but the other day he had been starving and bought himself five kebapche from the stall. Before he knew it, he had scoffed the lot. Only four lev remained from his treasure.

'That's for you, Dame-Damyanka. Buy yourself something from me for your birthday.'

'Vasko, my birthday's long come and gone,' the girl reminded him, then smiled. 'I like your jeans,' she said.

'Never mind the jeans. You had a birthday; it doesn't matter if it's gone.'

'Yeah, but you gave me a little ring then.'

'I did, but that was when I was collecting scrap metal, and the ring was from Second Chance; it only cost seventy stotinki.'

I really like it, Damyana wanted to say, but how could she tell Vasko how her grandma had reacted when she saw it?

'What's that ugly thing? Someone's thrown it away. Don't pick up other people's rubbish.' Her grandma had grabbed Vasko's ring and thrown it into the wheely bin. Damyana went rummaging through the bin, the dog Gasho is her witness; she dug in there for two hours but didn't find the ring. Her grandma caught her sifting through it, outside on the street in front of passers-by so that everyone could see her and call her a loser and make fun of her.

'I want my ring,' Damyana had cried. 'Vasko gave it to me for my birthday.'

'He stole it,' snapped her grandma, and because all the neighbouring housewives had seen Damyana going through the bin, she sent her to bed without dinner and without watching kids' shows for three days. It had been a sad birthday.

'Let's go to the shop,' the girl said.

Precisely at that moment the boy with the colourful hat *totally* – that's what everyone said on TV – *totally* remembered that he was not to be seen with Dame-Damyanka. That's why when the children got closer to the door of Second Chance – the best thing in Staro Selo – they walked separately. This shop, which was as dark as good stout inside, had given people here the sweetest happiness. Everyone can find something on its shelves, almost new, almost never worn, just for one lev, maximum one lev fifty stotinki; then you proudly stroll the streets looking gorgeous. Beside the path that velveted like a cat towards the church of Saint Nikolas, the children took each other by the hand and suddenly, as if possessed – well, they were infected with stupidity – ran down the narrow, sneaky path between the hawthorns and rose hips. It's a shame the path quickly gave up walking with them and vanished.

They reached the little road disfigured by potholes, and then the self-important, haughty road laid with paving stones where, if you didn't watch your step, you'd end up prostrate, kissing the granite. It was exactly that granite that led to Second Chance, Staro Selo's most generous place.

The girl with the long green coat – not green like a boastful young pea and not green like sorrel, which is so full of vitamins that it keeps you awake during the afternoon nap even though your grandma's ordered you to sleep and threatened to leave you without dinner, but a calm green and a little sad, probably because the coat was so long and wide that the child swam like a wild carp in it. The kid lost in the carp coat clutched four lev, two lonely coins, in her hand. She was holding them so tightly that they began sweating and were at risk of melting.

'Come here,' the girl said and smiled. The boy with the colourful hat smiled too and forgot where he was going.

'What is it, Dame-Damyanka?'
'Vasko, come here!'

The titch in the large coat longer than the Struma and wider than the forest with the felled pines picked up a jacket from the rails – a very grown-up denim jacket for a skinny boy with a colourful hat.

'Put this jacket on, Vasko.'
'Why?'
'Just put it on.'

Wow, how well that jacket fit the boy! Not a boy, but a wind in trendy, almost-new jeans and a gorgeous jacket. He was glowing!

'You're the most beautiful boy I've ever seen, Vasko,' said the titch.

'I think not! Look how they sheared me like a sheep.'
'That's not true.'

'How much is this jacket, please?' Damyana asked Granny Sara, who's been the shop assistant in Second Chance for as long as the Struma has flowed by Staro Selo.

'Four lev and eighty stotinki,' she replied. 'It's very nice, isn't it? Almost new.'

Then a kid and green sleeves began rummaging; in one pocket they found four stotinki, in the other, twenty. Fifty had sunk into the inside pocket, and in the pocket of her top, the girl found another six stotinki. Plus the four lev. Hooray!

'Granny Sara, give me this jacket. I'm buying it.'

'What!?' shouted the boy with the colourful hat, so loudly that his hat jumped to the floor.

'Don't wrap it up. He'll wear it straight away.'

Granny Sara, as old as the river, maybe even older, said: 'Enjoy wearing it, Vasko!'

'It's his present for my birthday,' said the girl with the longest, widest green coat in the neighbourhood of Staro Selo.

'Dame-Damyanka, you're mad,' Vasko rattled, but she – that silly little thing with long hair made of summer – put her hand to his lips and pressed really, really hard. Where on earth did this tiny titch get so much power?

'That's the best present for my birthday, Vasko!'

The spring, like a tomcat, very quietly and cunningly sneaked into the shop and everything became so illuminated that even Granny Sara, the oldest person in Staro Selo, smiled. She looked a hundred years younger, honestly!

* * *

The man was sitting in the narrowest room in their house, the one overlooking the garden with young fruit trees, as thin as ice cream cones, still bare, sticks about to perform a miracle (and performing miracles is a habitual act when it comes to unfurling each new leaf). But the man wasn't looking out of the window, he wasn't interested in the thin treetops, or the weather – cold and raining as usual. The Struma was swollen and sported a new fringe, brown and murky, wild, but the man wasn't even thinking about the river.

'Thank you, thanks very much, Elena,' he said. He was shorter than the skinny woman; he had broad, heavy shoulders that just about squeezed into his tight jumper. It was made of homespun red wool, which you could still find here because there were still people around stupid enough to rear sheep. The man bent, picked up Elena's brown hand and kissed it. He held it a little longer and mumbled, 'Huge thanks!'

He straightened up, a broad, strong man, his hair still black. He was clutching money in his hand.

'I'll pay it back,' he said. 'Even if it kills me, I'll pay it back.'

'Let's hope the boy's well,' Elena replied. 'He will be,' she added firmly.

'Your daughter-in-law ruined your son,' the man said. 'I saw him walking, staring at the sky, an unlit cigarette stuffed between his lips. I thought to myself, *that one has driven him to madness*. Good job he went to Spain.'

'...'

'You're a good woman,' the man blurted, clutching the money even tighter. 'Sometimes I bang my head against the wall. Why didn't I take you? Why did I play stupid and turn my back on you? We would've lived well together.'

'Your son will be OK. Pay where you must,' Elena said.

'I can't believe he chopped down all the trees in your garden. But the neighbours keep telling me, "We saw him. Vova cut them down." I told him, "Steal where you want, don't touch her property." The bail is so expensive, it hurts. If I don't pay it, they won't let him out. I didn't know who to ask for a loan. It's no good me coming to you, Elena. I still remember… and even now I'm banging my head against the wall over it. Where were my eyes, where was my slow brain? My dad only said, "She's taller than you. You'll turn into a laughing stock." Why couldn't he say, "She's two hundred times cleverer than you"?'

'That's water under the bridge now.'

'It wasn't meant to be,' the man sighed. 'But I was pleased when Damyan took you. My father was saying, "That one's gonna be a spinster. She's gonna walk around, begging men, just like she begged you." And he, Damyan the Beautiful, took you. Women were crying after him. When he took you, I sighed with relief. A weight left my shoulders... I always thought I had ruined your life.'

The man spoke quickly, with many words, acted with a lightning speed. He ran over to Elena, hugged her, and even though he was shorter, kissed her long and foolishly. He realised he was out of order, stepped back, wiped his mouth, then her cheek where he had planted the kiss and said:

'I'm sorry. I insulted you, but... I've been thinking about it until now. What an idiot. So I thought, I'm gonna tell you, Elena, because that's a sin before Him above, before God, if He exists at all – if He doesn't, it's a sin on my soul. Even if I haven't got a soul, it's still a sin... I'm sorry, Elena. Elena, don't worry, I'll pay you back. I could sell the calf when it's born, if it's a bull. If it's a cow, I won't sell it. I'll wait for Gabriella to calf again and then I'll sell the calf... I'll pay you back. If you got pregnant back then, my father could've said whatever he wanted, I had decided: I'll put my head in the sack. I'll marry her. Now, I'm kicking myself. I messed up... pulled out like a snake. Idiot... I'll pay you back. I swear. The wife doesn't know I've come to you. She hates you; she hates you from long ago. Because I'm a fool, I told her about you. The neighbours had told her about you too. I'll pay you back. Honest.'

'Whenever you can,' the tall woman said. 'If you can, get your son away from stealing.'

'If Vova was a girl, he would've been called Elena,' the stocky man said. 'That's another sin before God, if He exists someplace, it's a sin on my soul too. I spoilt Vova. He was such a clever, beautiful child. I would say to him, "Vova, son, we'll get you to study to be a vet. I want to breed horses, Vova. Since I was a kid, I've been wanting to have horses. The horse is a bigger man than man himself. A horse has a soul, a man doesn't." When I was a boy, you know, Elena, I kept pushing myself to jump over Munish. The brook had overflowed, grown deep, like the Black Sea. I was riding our Dorcho, the chestnut. You know I wasn't really a show-off. Well, just as I was jumping over Munish, I fell. Dorcho was about to trample me, his hoof was heading for my forehead. I thought to myself, *that's it, finished. I'm dead.* But Dorcho, I've no idea what he did, he twisted, turned his hoof to the other side, jumped over me and here I am, still kicking. When Dorcho got old, I didn't let my dad take him to the abattoir – I got ill. He died a peaceful death, of old age. I still remember him. That's why I wanted Vova to become a vet. I kept giving him money, time and again. I ruined him. He got it into his head that someone should always give him money. He began believing that money was like last year's leaves, that it falls down on its own... Sorry, I'm blabbering all these things to you, Elena. Thanks. Thanks very much and merci. You're great. I screwed myself. I didn't catch you. Dimwit!' He turned around again, made a few steps and kissed her on the forehead, for one second. 'You're saving my child. I hope there's a God someplace out there to keep an eye on you. To guard you. Perhaps there is one, but not around here.'

The man strode out with powerful steps. Before closing the door behind him, he turned again, waved, still clutching the money, and said:

'Ta very much, Elena.' Then he bent down. Perhaps that was meant to be a bow, but his jumper, knit from thick homespun red wool, was squeezing him like a cast.

The coat he held in his hand dropped onto the tiny rug in the vestibule.

'I'm such an idiot,' he blathered. 'Goodbye, Elena. I hope God is someplace nearby to keep an eye on you.' He forgot to close the door behind him.

The tall woman waited until he had gone, got up, closed the door, then took out some horseradish root and started cutting it precisely, as if she was cutting a baby's nails, into miniature cubes, no bigger than a pea. It was late morning, cold and damp, just the time to prepare a paste for sick kidneys. That paste was difficult to make. You had to wait forty-three days for it to mature. But if you didn't cube the horseradish, you'd be sitting there forty-three days waiting for nothing. The following day – in fact why not the same afternoon – you could mix the paste for knee pain, that balm only needs twenty-three days, and the drops for a sick tummy, which take only two days. Like this, every other day, you've got something to be checking on, something waiting for you; you're free, you're not the one waiting.

'What was Simeon doing here? Why was he kissing you? When did you go to him? Tell me!' Damyan, wet from head to toe but looking beautiful even in his overalls from the docks, was staring at her. His face was glowing as if he had coals instead of skin. His blue eyes swam with blood.

'I lent him money. They've caught his son. He'd been stealing again,' Elena said. 'I gave him money to pay the bail.'

'You've turned very chatty, eh,' whispered Damyan. 'You've never talked that much. I'm not asking about the money. Tell me. Why was that one kissing you? You're my wife. Mine. When have you been to him? Why didn't you marry him then?'

It was drizzling. The air brightened like a smiling face, the horseradish cubes lay in the wooden bowl, waiting to grow, to mature and cure many sick kidneys. People in the region suffered from sick kidneys. Elena walked to the dresser, took out a small jar filled with a thick, oily liquid and poured it into the wooden bowl.

'Tell me!' shouted the handsome man, who even in his anger remained as beautiful as an icon. Even smeared with hatred, his colours were still beautiful, it's a shame that anger drained his brain. 'Have you been lying to me?'

'Simeon and I studied together. He never finished college. He was expelled for the theft of two rolls of wire. No one paid attention to me. He used to sit next to me in maths. He never studied. Just copied. One day, after they'd already expelled him, he called me. He asked for money. I gave him some. He kissed me. I was eighteen. No one came to pick me up for the end-of-year ball. My classmates were getting married. I didn't have anyone. I went to Simeon's house. Thursdays, when his mum and dad would go and water their allotment. They had a well and a pump. I went to Simeon. I wanted to see what it was like. Not that I really fancied him. I wanted a child. If it happened, I would've gone to Sofia. I would've raised the little one there. It didn't happen. I thought I was barren. A dried-up root. Then you asked me, "Will you marry me?" and I turned you down. I thought I wouldn't be able to have children. I didn't want to smear your name. When I got pregnant, I called you. That was only fair. If you hadn't taken me, I would've gone to Sofia. Shame though that the herbs are here, in Staro Selo. There are no herbs in Sofia. But for the sake of the child…'

The rain carried on, the sky wasn't blue, but white as if someone had sifted flour over its face. Fog, light as a kite, descended. The home-made rugs on the floor were large and colourful. Damyan's mother, Granny Christina, had told Elena when she first walked into her house:

'I don't have a daughter. Where on earth did Damyan find this plank? Simeon kicked you out because you're barren, now you turn up on my threshold.' Five, maybe seven years later, Granny Christina – blue-eyed, with bones as delicate as a spider's web, a woman who walked so softly even the chickens didn't run away from her, not even when she went to catch them for slaughter, with a face that stayed smooth until she was ninety – had walked over to Elena.

Elena was bent over the table at the time, mixing tetterwort leaves with black buttercup blossom. It was then, when Granny Christina, who liked a tipple from the Kamenara rakia she hid in a flask in the garden among the ivy, approached Elena, touched her daughter-in-law's black hair, stroked her olive-skinned face and said: 'Forgive me for saying those words. I was stupid back then, Elena.'

'I still remember them,' Elena had answered. 'I'm trying to forget them, but I can't.'

Now it was Damyan, Granny Christina's only child, who approached his wife. He lifted his hands – heavy from work in the locomotive depot, brown, smeared in grease and engine oil, with skin like sandpaper. Those strong hands now went to Elena's face. She didn't tremble, didn't move. She was like that. Granite.

The two heavy hands cupped the tall woman's face, held it gently and clumsily.

'I'm such a moron, Elena. I spoke out of place.'

Elena remained still, neither trembled nor moved. She was like that. Stubborn.

Only her face became a little quieter, as if it relaxed, but not because a white sky had spread out above Staro Selo on that Thursday.

The olive-skinned, still, calm face smiled. It brightened, just a tiny bit. You had to have known Elena for thirty-seven years to know she was smiling.

Damyan knew.

'Shhh,' Elena whispered. 'Don't say anything.'

* * *

Early one morning, just before the frost crept in, they found a Roma boy – Vasko, Vasso the musician's grandson – beaten to a pulp, dumped on an old, crooked bench next to the rose hips and hawthorns behind the communal hall. His back was black and blue, his belly was black and blue. People said they needed to take him to Pernik, maybe even Sofia. His mother Valya carried him in her arms. That boy was as tall as stinging nettles. The woman ran, clutching him to her chest, one of his spindly legs dangling disturbingly.

Vasko was Valya's youngest child. She was holding on to him, running in the middle of the street, howling. Her wails were black, hollow. The sky was so clear, you couldn't look at it. You couldn't look at that woman either. One bare foot, the other one in a galosh. She wasn't seeing the cars on the street; she wasn't seeing the absence of rain.

'Elena! Elena!' the woman in the brown cardigan, knitted with rough wool which scratched more than a rope on the gallows, screamed and charged onwards. 'Elena!'

The one-storey house Vasko's mother ran towards was surrounded by a drystone wall, the bricks arranged in a strange fashion – with gaps so the garden could be seen. Elena's husband – they called him Beautiful – had built it like this so you could see the flowers in bloom. He, believe it or not, grew roses and tulips, daisies and daffodils, hyacinths and all sorts of other flowers, although no hyacinths or daffodils were in bloom yet. Valya couldn't talk any more, her throat produced only grunts, not even that, just gasps.

'Elena, Elena!'

A tall thorn of a woman, brown hands and brown face, flew out of the house with the odd wall that didn't hide anything. It was unbelievable how fast the skinny pole ran.

'Valya,' the woman as dark as the earth around here shouted, 'I'm coming, Valya!'

The women met in the middle of the street, the asphalt cool under the twisted, wicked sun.

'Put him down.'

'Mud will get into his wounds,' Valya said, her hair as long as her fear.

Elena quickly took off her coat, threw it onto the ground and then, carefully, they laid the boy on it.

He groaned.

'He's breathing well,' Elena said calmly and clearly, as if she had punched the nastiest ailment on earth and knocked it out. 'Vasko,' she whispered gently, 'Vasko, son, spit. Spit into my hand.'

The boy managed to spit after three attempts. Very lightly, as if touching the most expensive pearl on earth, Elena stretched her arm towards him. She touched Vasko and shook him ever so gently, then a little more and a little more.

'Does it hurt a lot, Vasko?'

'No, no,' the boy whispered.

'Only one broken leg, Valya. The other one is fine.' The tall woman carefully circled the skinny body, listening to the boy's breathing, whether his sighs were quiet or piercing, choking or just normal.

'I think three of his right-hand fingers are broken.'

'The people who found him said we need to take him to Pernik. They said to take him to Sofia.'

'OK, Valya. We'll take him. But first let's bring him inside; he could have a broken rib. Did he pee or vomit blood, do you know?'

'No, I don't know.'

'Valya, tell your husband to slaughter a sheep. He can buy it from Dida and Dona. I'll pay for it. But he needs to hurry up. I need the fleece. We'll wrap Vasko's chest. Send one of your girls to tell Damyan. I'll wash the boy with tetterwort. Go fetch Dr Varbanov.' Then, the willowy woman bent down, embraced the boy and lifted him. He screamed.

'It's OK, Vasko, it's OK, son. You'll be fine,' Elena said gently. Without turning towards his mother, and with a firm, flat tone, she ordered: 'One of his sisters should come to my house. Don't fret. If he's not vomiting blood, if he's not peeing blood…'

A little further down, in the middle of the street, lay her coat – faded and old. She had forgotten it.

★ ★ ★

I'm thinking about you, Siyana, and I feel much lighter. You might have forgotten me by now, but I doubt it. Even if you have, I haven't forgotten you. You taught me what it means to be happy, to be alive. I'm happy to be alive. When it's cold, when it's raining, I can hear you telling me that story about your crazy maths teacher, Mrs Gerova. How she used to write equations on the blackboard, dust clouds circling around her head, how the class watched if she was going to slip on the wooden dais, and how she never noticed because she was too excited. 'Everyone,' you told me, 'hated maths, but no one hated Gerova. "Green heads, far too green," Gerova would say, and write and write. If she could, she would've used a whole box of chalk just to get those green heads to ripen.' You used to tell me, Siyana, that you loved two people – Mrs Gerova and me. And I would ask you:

'Do you love little Damyana?'

'Damyana is my blood, she's like my own arm, my own lungs. A daughter. She is me, don't you understand?'

'And what am I?' I would ask.

'You're stupid. A green head. How could you be my lungs? My body would reject you.' You told me what Mrs Gerova meant to you: 'Mrs Gerova was the first person to show me what I'm worth, Christo. She announced it in front of all the stuck-up noses in that all too serious mathematics school I went to. She said, "Look at her! Just look!" And I? A village girl. Do you understand, Christo? Mother was an accountant, a teacher, a manager, you name it; my father, I couldn't tell you, Mother's second husband lasted two years, husband number three – only one.

"Your intellect is a laser beam, Siyana," Gerova told me. No one had ever even noticed my intellect before her. I wonder how she saw it.

She would give us an equation, the class, all those kids from Pernik, from the centre of Radomir – there was even a boy from Sofia – sat there, reading the equation, drawing. While they were still reading, I thought to myself: Are these people blind? Can't they see that the equation is sewn together with white strings? White ropes! Gerova hadn't yet adjusted her glasses and I put my hand up, holding it high like a flag, and sang the answer.

One day Gerova praised me in front of all the kids from Pernik – in front of the daughter of Dr Zaharinova, the dentist who only works with American products, in front of the daughter of the boss of the Pernik Theatre, in front of the daughter of Pelev, who was the go-to moneylender in town and in the surrounding villages, in front of all those clever clogs who were driven to school in Mercedes Benzes and had private tutors from Sofia coming to their houses, in front of all the elite girls and boys from "noble" families, those ravens (I called them ravens because of the noises they made when they spoke) whose jeans cost as much as four months of Mum's salary... Gerova, arm dirty to the elbow with chalk dust, stood in front of all those people and waxed lyrical:

"Chapeau Siyana! You have a brilliant mind." Then the mathematician paused before carrying on, "It takes more than a brilliant mind. You have a gift, girl. You can't buy that. A person without the gift can have private tuition all they want. They can hire the President of the Bulgarian Academy of Sciences or a Nobel laureate in mathematics as a tutor. If they don't kill themselves, if they don't get depressed and take a glass of poison, that student will only achieve about as much as you do when you wake up, turn on the TV to see who's been robbed, what's the latest stupidity some manager or other has committed, and open your maths textbook to solve equations for pleasure."'

'And why do you love me?' I asked, but you weren't seeing me then. You were seeing Mrs Gerova. You leant towards me and I thought you would kiss me; you bit me. You bit me so hard I bled. I have a scar now and I love it very much. Honestly.

'Do not interrupt me when I'm talking about Mrs Gerova!' you ordered. 'That woman, our maths teacher, had a son and a grandchild. Her son, poor thing, was struggling with an engineering degree at the Technical University; in mathematics he was one of those who, no *matter how much they tried, could only get the minimum pass grade – and he could barely do that.*

Gerova's husband was long dead, and she said to me: "Listen, Siyana, I'm going to sell... you know I have this old Ford. I'm going to sell it so you can go to the Paris Olympiad. You've won your place fair and square."

My mother said: "So what if you go to Paris? You'll come back here to us, the simpletons."

"I would win a stipend."

"You would win carnation stems. The stipends have already been distributed to those... selected. I couldn't possibly repay the loan to that cuckoo Gerova."

That cuckoo Gerova died before she could sell her old Ford, but even if she had managed to sell it... I go to the cemetery.'

'I don't know when All Souls' Day is, Christo,' you would say to me.

'For me, every time I had five lev in my pocket, it was All Souls' Day. I never bought flowers because Gerova always said: "I don't want flowers, students. Bring me a tree instead, both cost five lev. Together we'll plant the tree in the school playground." Have you noticed, Christo, how many apple trees there were alongside the school of mathematics in Pernik, along the Struma? Four. They were puny. We gave them as presents to that cuckoo Gerova. I, the bigger cuckoo, would water them. She died. She never complained. For a long time, I would go to Pernik just for those four apple trees. I staked them, tied them up, dragged water from the tap in the toilet to them. And what happened? Someone cut down all four. But do you think I threw up my hands and quit? You don't know me, Christo. I planted five trees in the same place. Oaks. Bandits don't eat acorns. To me, that's Gerova's grave. Two of the oaks are still standing. When I had more money, I would go to her grave in Pernik. I only weeded once. That woman was a big cuckoo... I love her.'

'And me?' I asked quietly, very quietly so I didn't make you angry. It was as if you were returning from a faraway place, as if you were returning to me from across the water.

'You're a good man,' you said. *'I've never met anyone like you.'*

Then you returned for longer, squeezed my cheek and said a very stupid thing, but I remember it: *'You are beautiful.'*

★ ★ ★

They found Dimitar Dimitriev, otherwise known as Ginger Dimitar, lying flat on his back near Café Solaris. His face was yellow, like those hard envelopes in the post office, like all poor souls that have drunk one too many, or rather like one who's sniffed a lot of things one after the other. His eyelids weren't swollen or green. His face appeared far too pale under the ginger hair, as if instead of cheeks someone had glued pieces of yellow wallpaper beneath his eyes. A large swarm of onlookers quickly gathered around the prostrate gentleman.

He was the owner of Café Solaris; his name was the heaviest stone in this neck of the woods. When you heard 'Ginger Dimitar', you shut up even if you didn't know him. If you did know him, you obediently stepped out of his way and observed your shoes, wondering if they were clean enough. Word went around that he would get annoyed if you looked at him, but if you didn't look at him, he would still get annoyed. The recommended thing was to cast a timid eye, like a fish, and immediately step aside; if possible, your lips should form a smile. Like this you wouldn't have any problems. But if you wanted to, you could stick your nose in the air. Your skull is your own at the end of the day.

That man was now lying seven metres away from his own café. Two years ago, the former owner of Solaris was beaten to a bloody pulp; it never became clear who exactly did the deed, naturally it remained 'a deed by a person unknown', like most deeds around here. Some long tongues suggested that this unknown perpetrator was red in the head, but soon these imbeciles found themselves with one or two fractured ribs and things calmed down. Well, how much they calmed down... Maybe under the layer of meekness, another, darker, layer was buried. Even if you are red in the head, someone from above sees *everything* (that was the only hope people had left) and you find yourself prostrate on the pavement, whether you've smoked or sniffed a bit much, entirely your business. Over the scarlet hair stood many faces, each of whom had been an unknown perpetrator not long ago.

A young, slim woman with ordinary brown hair, like most women south of Vitosha, approached Café Solaris. Well, there was something uncommon for these parts – shoes which immediately caught the eye and wouldn't let it continue on its way. Her coat most probably cost more than the annual salary of old Dr Varbanov in Radomir. A remarkable garment for Staro Selo, a place as far from fashion as a village privy is from the palace throne.

Why did this coat and these shoes gallop as if they didn't cost the annual salary of Dr Varbanov, and where were they headed? The woman with the ordinary hair – or perhaps not so ordinary because it was lush, with the kind of shine that costs a lot of money – raced towards a one-storey house surrounded by a drystone wall without a single flower blooming behind it.

'Elena!' the woman screamed. 'An unconscious man is lying outside Solaris.'

The tall, paper-thin woman was nowhere to be seen or heard. A small voice muttered; the answer slunk like a thief under the closed gate.

'Elena's not at home.'

The lady with the gleaming coat shoved open the gate from behind which the voice emanated. Next to the drystone wall stood a girl in grey trousers.

'Damyana!' the woman barked, grabbing the small hand. 'Lift your head. Look me in the eye.'

'I don't want to look you in the eye, Mum.'

'Damyana! Where's your grandmother? You're chicken-hearted, but you're not stupid.' The woman in the magnificent coat spoke slowly, leaving space between the words. And they weighed heavily.

'I haven't done anything to Ginger this time. And I'm not chicken-hearted,' the girl said. Her gaze hardened and she lifted her head. 'If I have to, I'll tie Grandma down so she can't come. Ginger beat up Vasko, Mum. His leg is broken.'

'Run to Dimitar. Immediately. Help him!'

'Vasko's leg is bro—'

'Now!'

The girl lay on the ground. A woman and a coat bent down and picked her up with ease, as if she were a shoebox.

'I'll tell the police that you're an evil child.'

'Vasko can't walk.' The girl wiped her nose with her coat sleeve.

'Damyana, go help Ginger Dimitar.' The voice was sinewy, that dry voice of Elena the Healer.

'I should've boiled hellebore today!' the girl shouted. 'Ginger Dimitar beat up Vasko! You said Vasko won't heal, Grandma.'

'No, he will.'

'Do you promise?'

'Yes, I do,' said the sinewy voice.

The girl rose angrily, like a badly wounded soldier who won't throw the regiment flag to the enemy, like a faithful old dog.

'Damyana, I do not want to see you with that scumbag Vasko. Ever again!' said the magnificent coat. 'Do you hear me, Damyana?'

The girl froze on the spot.

'You will see me with Vasko,' she spat out. 'Vasko's the best.'

It was cold. Perhaps a downpour was on its way. This year spring was confused and didn't know which way to go.

'Is that so?' her mother asked. 'Anything else?'

'Yes. Vasko is my special friend.'

For a moment the woman froze inside her glorious coat. She regained her senses quickly though. People who wear garments like that always come to their senses quickly. She went to say something but decided not to. The sky tore apart. Hail pounded down from the wounded clouds.

'You. Are. A. Very. Stupid. Child. Damyana,' the woman pronounced slowly.

The clouds ruptured. Hailstones the size of hazelnuts covered everything – houses, fields, granite. It was very cold.

'Vasko,' the girl whispered, but almost silently, and no one, not even the glorious coat, heard her.

★ ★ ★

Do not allow life's misery to bring you to your knees. Let a smile conceal your failures in love, because what is love if not a reason to wave goodbye to misery? You are my daughter, Siyana. I'm honest with you.

When I split up with someone from the stronger sex – strong! Haha, please pinch me so I won't burst out laughing – I cry. I insist that the strong one sees and counts my tears. I do not stand before him like a cheap fishing rod, like you do, Siyana. Do not forget that a fishing rod is thrown into a corner and only picked up when the man is dumb enough to look for fun catching trout. Do not be a trout either.

You are not a genius mathematician, despite what that senile cuckoo Gerova tried to drum into your head. I used to get a headache whenever I met her. She drove a seventeen-year-old car, for heaven's sake. You are not as beautiful as me, Siyana. I have an explanation for your fixation with theorems: you have limited natural beauty, the One above – I love You, Lord! – has deprived you of my green eyes and given you olive skin, the colour of stagnant water in the fountain outside the local watering hole, Frog Bar.

I married your father. I didn't study axioms like you, darling. First, I walked around Pernik to identify a beautiful residential building. Then I selected a young man who lived there. He was the son of a certain party member. In those days their mouths were large, but so were their wallets. Your father had private tutors in mathematics, Bulgarian literature, English and swimming, in total four private tutors at his disposal. He was nothing special, but he wasn't ugly either.

I liked his family home, a fourth-floor, five-bedroom apartment with a view towards Golo Bardo. Your father invited me for a coffee. The reason he invited me was because I had given myself backache from hanging outside the miserable café in front of Block 36 entrance B, reading *War and*

Peace. I was hoping his mother would notice my literary inclinations. She did. Such philistines! The thicker the book the more respect they give you. I developed the methodology *War and Peace* on the principle of trial and error, but in my case, errors amount to zero, because I learnt from life. I wasn't mouldering, like you, Siyana, over insane stereometry equations that no normal person looks at without getting a migraine.

'I've always worshipped you,' I told your moron father, who believed he was the emperor of this rusty can of a town. It is very difficult to survive among agricultural faces who can only spit, swig, swear, snuffle and stuff themselves (the 'five big S's' – gosh, how terribly boring life is in a provincial town!). If you stand out, God help you. Intelligent people are the first to end up on the gallows of gossip. If you're stupid enough to work your socks off, no one notices you.

After divorcing your father, I acquired his apartment. He, your parent, was an elementary particle; the sound of his voice evoked thoughts of a creaking cart. My methodology, born from one of my happy strokes of genius, turned out to be successful in Sofia too. I liked a residential building behind Sofia University: a lovely quiet place, bearded types always hanging out in the café… You were born, your father, of course, got drunk and remained drunk from joy for three weeks. As I already mentioned, he was too simple to invent something more original.

I enrolled to study straight away, but not mathematics like you. Have you ever seen an attractive mathematician, Siyana? No, you haven't. Usually, they are fat and their husbands cheat on them. In this light, even if the rat you married – I mean that shallow-minded Christo – cheats on you, even if he were a philandering husband, you wouldn't notice; that's how insignificant he is. Fortunately, you eventually realised that and signed his passport to go hang himself in Spain – or was it Italy? – where the rope is cheaper, because he is a fool par excellence.

You were still a baby, Siyana, but I left you to my mother-in-law, an old basket who did nothing but wipe her dull son's snot and mourn his misfortune in marrying that... I don't want to even mention the noun she used to refer to me, it's too vulgar. The wretched woman had gone as far as to investigate with whom I had... hmm... 'conversed' (let's not use vulgar verbs here) while I was still married to her darling son. Why did she need to spend money? She could've just asked me.

You were five months old when I realised that my marriage to your father was irreparably broken.

I had already noted a residential building behind the university and a gentleman who lived there – a long-bearded specimen with a Roman nose, lost in reverie, a space cadet who offered me his hand. You have told me in the past, Siyana, that the gentleman in question was good to you. Please don't make laugh! When exactly did he tell you fairy tales? He was a good-for-nothing and couldn't even tie his shoelaces. You were overly fat as a child and that idiot's mother didn't stop pitying you.

'My sweet meatball,' she would say to you, 'you're such an ugly little thing.' But despite everything, the old cow gave you two gilded Viennese dinner sets and a necklace, also from Vienna. After the bearded moron's dog died, he took you for a walk to the art gallery at Shipka 6. He was as much an artist as I am Galileo Galilei's wife. Well, OK, Siyana, I cannot deny that he treated you well sometimes, but please don't make me laugh by telling me he told you bedtime stories. He was far too simple to remember them. One thing I am grateful to him for: he introduced me to Georgi.

Georgi lived in an even lovelier neighbourhood in the capital. When Mr Space Cadet and I divorced, his mother, the one who called you 'meatball', died. The long-haired snob moved into her apartment, and I, my dear Siyana, appropriated his apartment. I didn't take it by force; he gave it to me. Even after I married Georgi, he would come over to have a glass of wine with me because apparently he loved contemplating my visage. You loved hovering around him. You were stupid even then. Why otherwise would you have such a penchant for mathematics, Siyana? The equation of happiness – x plus and y squared. Don't force me to resort to cynicism and profanity. That type of vocabulary doesn't fit into my spiritual makeup.

I lived with Georgi, perhaps the smartest and most charming man I've known – and with a sense of humour – in a wonderful apartment on Tsar Boris street, number 116. For the duration of my cantata with Georgi, you, dear child, were very annoying. You didn't stop crying and insisted on stuffing your face with chocolate. Thank God that long-haired ex-husband of mine, the artist (don't make me burst out laughing! What an insult to the word 'artist'!), came to pick you up for walks. When you returned home, you would cry for him. You would tear your lungs crying. But this turned out to be good practice: he gave you, one after the other, the rings of that old badger, his mother – all nine of them.

I remember one, a magnificent ring in the shape of a mussel with three inlaid rubies. You, stupid girl, sobbed: 'I don't want rings! I want to be your daughter!'

But why would you want to be his daughter? Little by little he gave you everything of value anyway – the mirror set in silver, the large gold coin with Arabic inscriptions. His apartment was slowly stripped bare like a beggar's.

'Marietta, may I adopt Siyana?' the audacious impertinent asked once. I have no idea what he saw in you. You were fat and mediocre; I must admit it. When I was certain he had nothing left to give you, I called the police. I told them he was molesting you, whatever that means. I didn't let him anywhere near our building. People say he got ill, stopped showering and got up to all sorts of nonsense. He is an independent person for whose behaviour I bear no responsibility. Is that not so?

Siyana, please tell me – why did you despise Georgi? He was a busy man who had no time for you. I understood that. He was a director of some academic publishing house, constantly bringing home maths textbooks. You were such a daft child; at times I wondered if you suffered from mental disorders. You didn't run around with other kids, you were deeply sunk in your own lard and instead of playing checkers or flirting with boys or writing little love notes, you swam in fat and solved mathematical equations, for God's sake!

You would come to me with a textbook just as fat as you and say: 'Mum, it's flowing into one pipe and out of another…'

Give me a break! The authors of those textbooks suffered from a congenital mental deficiency. You would go to Georgi, but he was a very busy man. If I've ever had happiness in love, that happiness would be called Georgi. You know what my idea of happiness is. It always has a financial dimension: in other words the thickness of the pile of banknotes accumulated diligently in my bank account.

Georgi was extremely busy in his high-ranking post; I eagerly anticipated his return — wait a moment, please! I would begin caressing him at the door. Oh, today's youth are so vulgar! You would describe our worshipping with ugly and vulgar words — worshipping is what I call the act of our nirvana in the corridor. I performed the act of worshipping in all three corridors of his apartment, on the floor, et cetera. I liked him. I liked him to a degree I thought myself incapable of liking a man, but he was terribly unprepared for me.

Who was looking after you back then? Oh yes, I remember — Georgi's mother, a greedy tights merchant who huffed and puffed every time I worshipped her son. She would curse me openly whenever she saw me exchanging ideas with one of Georgi's colleagues in Costa Coffee. The merchant would grab you by the hand and drag you to me; in the best-case scenario, she would abandon you to your equations and wish me a speedy acquaintance with the worst of the three-letter diseases. She wished me a number of such acquaintances, but I always thought positively, Siyana.

From Georgi, I gained respect for tall men and his villa in Boyana, a genuinely dignified building which I inherited due to my partner's innate generosity. Georgi's friend, that boy in the tracksuits — after Georgi, I've never lowered myself to so much as even look at a short specimen from the male sex — anyway, that tracksuit turned out to be the boss of a building company. His boys spruced up the villa in Boyana. I can't remember where you lived at the time, Siyana. I remember that the tracksuit had a brother, as fat as you. I suspect that was the time you exchanged your first kiss.

You were not impressed with it, Siyana. After the fat boy kissed you, you vomited for three days and calmed down only after I bought you two more thick maths textbooks. I considered whether you were developing a predilection for girls, which of course is absolutely fine, but except your own obesity, you developed nothing else.

The tracksuit turned out to be a bland emotional menu. A simpleton. He gave me his mother's gold bracelet, which apparently dated back to the Romans or the Ottomans and had belonged to the wife of a famous local dignitary. I immediately consulted a jeweller. Yes, the bracelet had some value, but other than that, the tracksuit's mother didn't own anything significant. Perhaps the Iranian scarf which he gave me as a present, but as I've already mentioned, he suffered from an emotional deficiency even though he was physically very well built. The tracksuit's mother had the desire to bring you closer to her fat young son. I didn't mind that, but you came out in a rash every time that fatty slipped a hand onto your thigh under the table.

This fact contributed to my decision to become closely acquainted with a philosophy professor at Sofia University, about whom I'd harboured certain suspicions. How, in the presence of so much tender flesh – students, PhD candidates and so on – had he remained an old bachelor?

His mother greeted me enthusiastically. What a pity, Siyana, that you haven't inherited my green eyes! I admit your ankles are as elegant as a doe's, but come on, who's seen a doe except in the form of steaks for sixty-five lev per kilo? My own ankles are heavy but that hasn't stopped anyone from adoring them, has it? The professor's mother was called Siyana, like you. She saw in this fact the hand of providence.

She started dragging you to the Natural History Museum, talking to you about philosophy. Poor child! You only ever smiled over your maths books. The philosopher was afraid of you. He was a timid potato sack with glasses who experienced certain problems with intimacy, but of course such difficulties do not disconcert me. The professor followed me in body and spirit with the eyes of a hungry calf. He dedicated his book on Western and European philosophy of the nineteenth century to me, though that hardly filled my wallet. He bought me my first ever car.

The professor's mother gave you her herbaria and her collections of postage stamps and butterflies, which you regarded, transfixed, for hours. When the old bag died, I inherited her small one-bedroom apartment – I rented it immediately at a good price. Toncho, the man who moved into this dwelling, turned out to have a dark past, a shady present and an extraordinary future. He bought me a Jeep.

My, how the professor cried when I left his life! The ambulance came to collect him and took him to hospital, or maybe it was the psychiatric unit. But could I possibly be responsible for every psychologically unstable specimen? From Toncho, the tenant of the small apartment, I received a number of nirvanas and gained experience in handling foreign currency.

Toncho asked for my hand, but I worried that he was an individual with an educational deficiency. At the end of the day, the professor had set the intelligence bar quite high. From Toncho came the only ingot of gold I own and this scar, here – Yavorov himself, a poet I adore, writes *and on the left breast, a moon of velvet.*

Toncho's mother looked after you. I think it was in one of those villages, Divotino or Malo Buchino, not sure. As a result, you learnt to sing that awful song 'Dine Rado'. I was embarrassed by you. The badgered granny forced you to plant peppers, onions and God knows what other vegetables. I think you lost weight while staying with her because of the fresh air. The old farmer saved me a lot of money on nutritionists. However, instead of using proper language in your speech, you began rattling in dialect. The shame of it! I think, around the same time, I noticed how you pined after the neighbour's boy – an insignificant greasy pubescent – and decided that you weren't developing a penchant for girls, though I regarded such tendencies with tolerance in the spirit of our modern times.

Siyana, in this light, I would like to ask you, 'When are you intending to collect the ring your mother-in-law, Elena the Healer, promised you?' You shouldn't behave as if you're suffering from amnesia. Go and collect your jewellery, Siyana. If she didn't want to give it to you, why would she have promised it to you, this village woman with pseudo-scientific inclinations? Sometimes I regret saying 'goodbye' to Toncho (who is still my tenant, by the way). He's someone who would've broken the healer's brazen neck, but… I just cannot stand specimens with an educational deficiency, Siyana. I'm far too sensitive to poetry, darn it.

Siyana, I still cannot get over you marrying that peasant Christo, your so-called husband. Intellectually negligible. A beautiful face without a single thought under the cranium. Thank God your daughter inherited his looks and not yours. You've been ugly since you were little. Goodnight, Siyana. I love you.

In three days I'm leaving for Baden-Baden on a short break with a very well-brought-up lawyer, a high-ranking professional.

Are you going somewhere? Of course not.

Draw your own conclusions.
Kisses, Mum.

* * *

You asked me back then, Elena: 'Do you smoke, Damyan?'
I answered: 'I smoke.'
And you said: 'Give me your cigarettes.'
I handed them over. You pulled them one by one out of the packet. Then you tore the first cigarette into two, then into four. Then the second one, first into two then into four.
'Elena, I've paid money for that,' I couldn't resist saying.
'I'm worth more,' you said.
'Give them back,' I requested, but very quietly, because I heard something that wasn't contained in the words. You've got that habit, Elena, of making people hear things that are not in your words.
Sometimes that thing is a good one, and I want to pick you up and carry you all the way to Golo Bardo, and at other times I want to pick you up and tear your head off. Just then, I wanted to tear your head off like you were tearing my cigarettes apart – just like that, I wanted to tear you into four pieces, but I didn't. It was a Thursday. You had told me that on Thursdays your folks went to the neighbouring village to water their allotment; your mother, God bless her soul, produced good crops, and I thought you were going to take me around to yours. I had seen your house from a distance; afterwards, because of you, I would walk along your street, thinking, *Let's see if I can get a glimpse of her*, and I did. You were always digging something in the garden. My mum was the same, God give her soul a bright passage, that's

why from a young age I have trusted people who dig in the garden.

She'll take me around to hers, I kept thinking while you were tearing my cigarettes, the tobacco falling like snow onto the grass. When you tore the last one, you didn't turn towards your house. Your house sticks out, the last house in Staro Selo, beyond it was just a thicket – hawthorn, wild roses and dogwood and above that pines and butter mushrooms. No one would see you taking me to yours. People said that you had a hundred flowerpots; I couldn't care less about the flowerpots, honestly. But you didn't take the road to your house.

That crazy woman, where's she off to now? That's what they called you in Staro Selo – 'crazy'. They saw you drying herbs and roots, and gossiped, 'Her grandmother, a healer and sorceress, has driven her crazy and twisted the poor child's brain.'

You were very funny, you and your grandmother. You – tall like a telegraph pole; she – round like a goose. I remember your Grandma Elena. When I was young, the truck that collected the bins, the yellow one from Clean Streets, went past our house. The thunder rolling from it, blimey! Mum always said that afterwards I began to stutter and wet myself. Apparently, the moment the Clean Streets truck approached on our street corner, I would hide under the bed and cry or squeeze between Dad's legs and not move for an hour. Mum took me to your grandmother – not really a goose though, she was so short and fat that she looked more like a round rakia glass.

'Do you drink rakia?' you asked me.

'I do,' I admitted.

'You're going to stop,' you told me, Elena.

Anyway, Mum took me to your grandmother, she was so ancient you would think she was barely alive, but you'd be wrong. The old goat ran around like a spring lamb.

Your grandma said: 'Wow! What a pretty child. Wow!'

She sprinkled flour all over me and I choked; I thought I was dying. I had heard that grannies like her put spells on you. She didn't put a spell on me. She sang a children's song and gave me a slice of buttered bread. Then she asked Dad for twenty stotinki and buried them in the ground, that's all.

After, she said to me: 'Damyan, over there, in the garden, son, you'll find a white stone. Go cough on it.'

What garden, what stone? Every inch around us was covered by vegetable plots planted thickly, not with tomatoes and peppers like in ordinary people's gardens, but with grasses, herbs and prickly blackthorn.

'There's no white stone,' I called out.

She went to a drawer and took something out of it – an ordinary piece of marble – and ordered: 'There. Put it on the ground and cough.' I didn't feel like coughing, my throat wasn't scratchy. She drew water from the tap in the garden and said: 'Drink! All at once.'

Only after that could I manage to cough. I coughed like thunder on that stone.

'Now, Christina, take your child.'

'How much do we owe you, Aunty Elena?'

'You'll make a guvetch, vegetables and veal,' your grandmother said without beating around the bush. 'Put plenty of oil in it. I like it a bit fatty. You'll bring it to me only if Damyan stops stuttering and wetting himself. Do you understand? Make sure to put lots of parsley and mint in the guvetch too, that's how I like it.'

Three days later Mum made guvetch in a huge oven tray, as if she were going to feed all the workers in the brickworks. She picked two additional bunches of mint and parsley, but your grandma didn't take them.

'I told you only guvetch, Christina. I don't want your herbs; I've got enough to feed a whole garrison. Take them back.'

Ever since I haven't wet my pants or stuttered, but I love guvetch, Elena. I learnt how to cook it and I can even cook it better than you. You always serve it a little underdone.

Back then you didn't turn towards your house, empty because your parents had gone to water their plot. So I thought, *Maybe she'll take me to her Grandma Elena's summer hut.* But you didn't take that path either. You took me to the Sklon and I said to myself, *People are right to call her Crazy Elena.* That's what you were. Forgive me for saying it. The Sklon is cursed, a steep and ferocious hill; even when we were young boys, we didn't dare ski on it.

If you want to train a nasty dog and get rid of the malice in its character, you climb the Sklon but from the Struma, not from the other side, and you chase the dog down. If it doesn't break its muzzle on the slope and manages to squeeze unscathed through the blackthorn, the dog loses all his malice and anger, becomes loving, runs around you and licks your hands. It was hot that day, earth and sky, beast and nature sweated and sighed in the heat. *What's that one going to do here, why is she going among these rocks; haven't her parents gone out?* I thought and then you said to me:

'Damyan, run up to the top. I want to see if you can run after puffing on all those cigarettes and tippling all those glasses of rakia with that pretty face of yours that makes everyone sigh when they see it.'

'What!!' I stared at you in disbelief. 'It's true, you're totally mad, Elena.'

You didn't say a word. As thin as my belt, you turned your back and pelted off towards the houses in Staro Selo.

'Wait, wait!' I ran after you, just about managing to catch up. 'Fine then, I'll run to the top of the Sklon.'

Again, you didn't say a word. Your girlfriend, actually hold on – you had no girlfriends – but that girl Katya, who sat next to you in college, told me that you didn't like chit-chat. I was finally convinced by my own ears that you weren't very skilled in the talking department.

You started walking in front of me. At the time we had a young ram called Radko. He had been such a wayward creature, you couldn't make him do anything, and he too was always running in front of me. One day I had taken all the weaned lambs to pasture on the banks of the Struma, near the Yamata – you know the one, the deepest pool. There I sat peacefully, munching on wild strawberries until suddenly that crazy ram Radko sprang and pushed me with his horns. I fell into the Yamata and got wet like a pile of washing, but I managed to get a stick and hit him between his horns. After this he stopped pushing and butting, we became friends. He grew into a huge ram. So, when it came to you, I thought, *Shall I find a big stick and hit her between the horns? She doesn't have horns though, but God's given her plenty of obstinacy.* You were marching so fast in front of me that my head began to spin. You brought me to the foot of the hill and said: 'Go on.'

I, that's how shallow-brained I am, pelted up the steep hill through the cool, murky gorge. I ran, struggling to breathe, and when I turned back, what did I see? You, light-footed as a grasshopper.

'Phew! That's enough,' I said. It was as if I had said, *You're a brainless, crazy woman.*

You turned your back and ran down. 'Fine, fine. We'll carry on.' I scrambled and scrambled, first like a goat, then more like a lizard, and finally managed to get to the top. That poisonous Sklon! I turned around and saw you right behind me on those legs thin as saplings. Hop-hop, no panting, no breathlessness. I had to gather my breath like a puzzle, barely piecing it together. You laughed at me; not even sweating under that horrible, frying sun. And I had to stop three times before reaching the top! When I got there in the end, the fields, the hills, the strip of Munish, the houses of Staro Selo laying quiet as mice in the evil heat, were spread before my eyes. At first, I couldn't see anything, that's how exhausted I was. I was left with no eyes, no breath, no ears. The only thing I could see was the slope beneath me. I had only just caught my breath when you kissed me.

I stopped breathing again.

It was then, on the Sklon, Elena, that I understood what it meant to say: 'This is my girl.' That means saying: 'This sky is mine. This wind is mine. For this girl I would swim in the sky, I would eat stones, I would bring the sea to her in my pockets.' Elena, Elena, I'm glad you took me to the Sklon. I'm glad you agreed to stay with me and make a home for me, to be around so long as God keeps me on this earth.

I hear my granddaughter's voice at some point: 'He's delirious. Grandma, Grandad's delirious, but I think his temperature's dropped.'

I feel a small hand, as cold as a stalactite, on my forehead.

'Grandad, Grandad! You've not been coughing. Only seven times. Your temperature's dropping.'

'Dame-Damyanka,' the man, wrapped in two duvets, sighed. He had got soaked to the bone in the rain. 'Dame-Damyanka, mesechinke moya,' the man babbled.

The girl's grandmother came over holding a glass of something so disgusting, the moment you set eyes on it, your bones began hurting.

'Drink that. All at once,' the woman said, and the grandad obeyed.

He paused for a moment and said: 'That's a nasty tea, Dame-Damyanka.'

Grandad Damyan had invented his granddaughter's nickname – Dame-Damyanka.

It's a wonder where Vasko, the boy with the accordion, heard it, but he started calling her that too.

* * *

God, when I'm poorly, my head is a bell, perhaps that's why I can't hear You. Lean forward a bit. Mum said You've moved in with us, to revive me. Could You please finish me off, so the pain can die with me and then put me back on my feet after the pain's gone? I'm Vasko, I still can't play the accordion well, or the trumpet for that matter, but if only You knew the things I hear in my head – songs, only songs. You can do everything, can't You, God? Then get into my head then so You can hear them too. The most beautiful song, but really the most beautiful one, the one that flies and swims and runs and beats you up if you lie – that song is for Dame-Damyanka.

I haven't created one for You yet, God, but I have an idea. My Grandad Vasso's played the accordion and the trumpet for years now, he could teach You too. Just take me away while the pain pains me. Sometimes I think I'm dead. Mum says that when a man dies, he becomes the wind; when a woman dies, she becomes the dew.

When they're alive, people don't have money to go to Africa, they just see it on TV. Mum says that You know Africa because You created the earth. Africa is big, very big, because Your heart, God, is big and everything You've created, You've given a big brain, but You gave me a small brain – I can't play well and I don't sing, which is a shame for all the songs that come into my head. Before my ribs were broken and when the nights were warm, I would put on my best thing – a denim jacket.

Dame-Damyanka bought it for me for her birthday. That was back when Dad got sick again and You came to our kitchen. You helped him come to You. Why didn't You stay with him on earth? You could've sipped his grape rakia together. Dad was like me, he couldn't sing well so he couldn't have taught You how to sing, but he danced, God. You've never seen a man creating steps like that, not even in Africa where people are masters at dancing without even bending a leg.

When the sky thunders, I know Dad is with You and You're dancing the Radomir horo. Mum said that You don't drink rakia, but don't worry, Dad will teach You. He might've become the wind already, so he can fly to me. I would be the goalkeeper and he would score penalties. I could only ever save two out of five, but when I took the penalties, he would save five out of five. At first, I was very angry, God, but then, much later – I always notice the good things late – I saw him grin as if he had eaten a whole roast lamb. Then I thought, *Good job he saved all five penalties, he's smiling as wide from happiness as the road to Pernik.*

I've seen You; they stretched You on a cross, God. Mum takes me to Saint Nicolas' church. When she was a girl, she helped build You a house – the church is Your own bedroom, so You have a roof above Your head. In the summer it's all fine, it's warm here, but in the winter there's not much bread around, the frost bites, so it's better if You come to Saint Nicolas.

I watched You nailed to the cross and thought, *I'll beat them up!*

You made them the whole world, created an accordion, forged a trumpet and made it so that Dame-Damyanka was born right here, in Staro Selo, so close to our house. And they, they've gone and nailed You to that cross, the bastards. Your mother, the Virgin Mary, she looks like my mum. When You were small, did she cuddle You and hug You so that You could grow big, and so that Your broken ribs wouldn't hurt any more? Thank You. Thank You that my pain has shrunk a bit. When I breathe, it bites again, but it's the same when you fall off your bike. I'll be fine in ten days. Mum's sure of it.

God, I really want You to be here when Grandad Vasso comes with his accordion. He cures me when he plays for me, but not 'Djelem, Djelem', not the Danube horo or the Graovo horo. It's a song that has never entered my head before. I listen to it and I see the Struma and all the fish in it. Big fish! I think to myself, *Why am I not a fish? I'd swim along the river all the way up to Vitosha, near Chuypetlovo where the living water springs. Then I'd return here, to Dad's grave and Mum's kitchen. And afterwards*

I'd go to Greece. Perhaps You know what Greece is, not sure if Mum's told You about it. Right now Mum goes to look after an old granny in Sofia and that's why she doesn't have a lot of time to explain things. But Mum loves You very much, God. As much as she loves me, I think. Greece is a warm field. There are Greeks and olives there.

'Dame-Damyanka,' I asked Damyanka one day, 'do you want a trough? It's made of wood and it's huge. Mum used to wash clothes in it, but we're rich now and bought a washing machine, so the trough is mine. We'll go to Greece with it, we'll pick olives and then return to Staro Selo.'

'You're a very clever boy,' Dame-Damyanka said to me, but I'm not really that clever.

We dragged the trough to the Struma, by that hole, Yamata. You, since You've created this earth, You must know where Yamata is. It's as deep as a dumper truck; Doncho the Blacksmith's dumper truck sank into it and they had to pull it out with a crane. At Yamata, Dame-Damyanka and I lowered the trough into the water and jumped into it. And that turned out to be my biggest disgrace, God. I'm rightly in pain with these broken ribs now. The trough sank into the deep pool. I was supposedly swimming, but only like a frog. What's worse, Dame-Damyanka can't swim even like a frog. She'd drown. But then I thought, *I've only got one friend, actually two – Dame-Damyanka and the accordion, but I'd let the accordion drown even though it's the only thing that can hear the songs singing themselves in my head. The only reason I hear these songs is Dame-Damyanka. If she's not here, why do I need songs and an accordion?*

You, God, You probably hear songs just like I do and because You're big, You could make one more world, You could put up one more sky there so it would rain and make the tomatoes in the gardens happy. Dame-Damyanka was drowning, God. Not like a frog, I swam like a dog or a bear or a cat. Even like a worm. I kicked with my legs and hit the water with one hand. I caught Dame-Damyanka's hair and pulled and pulled and pulled. Good job the hair didn't tear away and her head didn't come off. I touched the shore and only then I realised – Dame-Damyanka wasn't dead, but wet. She had no energy left in her to even walk.

I said to her: 'Don't worry, Dame-Damyanka, I'll carry you.' I picked her up and carried her two paces. Then both of us fell into the dust. God, when You created this world, You dropped a lot of dust in Staro Selo! If You want me to, when I grow up, I'll make pots with all that dust, I could make bricks too if You prefer, like this You could build yourself a bakery in the clouds.

We dragged ourselves to Mum and she shouted: 'You're crazy, both of you!' Then she slapped us across the face – first me, then Damyanka. Then she slapped the table. 'Since you didn't drown, why didn't you bring the trough back home, huh? That trough has seen me through four children, including you, Vasko, you dimwit! You grew up in it. Nowadays there are bathtubs for babies – light as an ice cream wafer – but back then there were none, you stupid Vasko and you Damyana, just as stupid! Birds of a feather! Dimwits!'

Then she got over it, kissed my wet head, then Damyanka's. She gave us dry clothes to change into and told us she would treat us to bean soup. Very tasty beans, as if they were made of gold.

The following day Granny Elena punished Damyanka, leaving her without lunch and dinner because she could've drowned.

God, please, never let Dame-Damyanka drown! I want to play Go Fish with her because I always win and then I make her do ten star jumps. But now that she brings me the syrup for broken ribs, I won't make her jump. She's cut her hair so she looks like me and scares my pain away. Do You know what I'm gonna do, God?

I'm not good at singing, Mum says that my throat is all twisted and that's why I'm all tied up by songs – 'Of course you can't sing, you always ate the fish heads and it's a well-known fact that fish don't sing. God has made it so.' I think You've got this wrong, God. I'm sure fish want to sing; I've eaten a thousand carp heads and I know what carp think, I'm probably a carp myself by now. I'm waiting for the scales to appear on my back. Though, when I die, I'm going to try to turn into a wind, like that I could go everywhere in the world. But what's a world without Dame-Damyanka? When she comes, I'm gonna drink that disgusting syrup for broken ribs and sing her that song which even Grandad Vasso, the cleverest man in the world, hasn't thought of yet.

Thank You that the pain has become as small as a just-hatched duckling. Come listen to that song of mine. I'll be grateful to You for a hundred years, until I turn into a wind and then another hundred. When You're hot, I'll blow close to Your brow to cool You down, God.

Ten minutes later, but who knows how long ten minutes are – for the pain it might be a second, for the boy with broken ribs it's a century, and for the girl who carried the weird bottle full of something green and nasty under her arm, those ten minutes might be exactly three heartbeats. At one point, outside the bare brick house, which nonetheless had a TV aerial with three hundred and twenty-nine channels from the whole world, you could hear a song.

It had no lyrics. But the melody! Oh, the melody! It was gentle and sweet like a child who has just drunk their milk and whose mother kissed their forehead, like those beans of gold the two kids ate after they nearly drowned and swam like frogs and dogs, like worms and ducks to the shore. It was lovely – a melody like departing pain. Even lovelier, like the girl sitting by the bed of the sick boy, staring at him with enormous eyes. That's why September walked into the room and didn't want to leave.

'Vasko, you're a genius,' said the girl who carried September in her eyes.

The boy attempted to get up, but the medicine for broken ribs hadn't taken effect yet. It was a very idle medicine – let us not say lazy – but it was powerful. As powerful as a truck waiting for the driver to start the engine.

'Genius how?' the boy asked and tried not to sigh. His rib remembered again that it was broken and summoned the pain with all its might, because if a rib doesn't hurt, then it's not broken.

'It means that you created the best song for Staro Selo,' Damyana explained.

The boy, despite the pain which had stuck its nose up in the air to show who was boss around here, propped himself up and said: 'That song's not for Staro Selo. It's for you.' The girl didn't believe him though. 'Dame-Damyanka,' Vasko said, 'thank you for cutting your hair so you look like me. You're very pretty like this.'

It was only then that the medicine for broken ribs took effect. The pain thinned out, became a grasshopper and jumped all the way to another hill, to a tractor driver who had a splinter in his finger.

★ ★ ★

The car that stopped outside Ginger Dimitar's house – as white as a towel – drew the eyes of everyone in Staro Selo. A dozen amazed faces stuck their noses out of Café Solaris. Young girls smoking outside the bar dropped their cigarettes. Boys playing football in the school grounds forgot which way they were supposed to kick the ball, all staring at the car.

It was a giant. Silver, with huge tyres. Everyone, even the pensioners clutching half a loaf of bread and a pot of yoghurt in their bags, knew what a vehicle was. But that monster wasn't a vehicle, it was a space shuttle. It shone so brightly the town square warped and the air fled. The wind fell apart.

Pines and elms in front of the town hall doubled over. The car's number plate was foreign. A teenager who had stopped kicking the ball and was observing the situation carefully managed to decipher the writing – not that he excelled in English – and was the first one to read: *USA*. That meant a whole ocean stood between the space shuttle that had found itself in Staro Selo and the factory in America where they had screwed the bolts and installed the electronics. Wow!

Look at Ginger Dimitar's business partners! Wow! He'll be a minister before you know it. Hmm, a minister, don't make me laugh! Ginger's put them all in his pocket and now he's shaking them out, one by one. Ginger Dimitar had already bought all the arable fields around Staro Selo, the banks of the river by the neighbouring villages, all the fields by Opalovo village and the dam in Debeli Lag. Ginger would show them where the frogs hibernate. He bought the old houses for pennies and helped ten neighbourhoods become deserted. Ginger was an expert. When Ginger likes a girl, all he needs to do is sit next to her in Solaris. The young lady knows exactly what she needs to do. If she happens to be unaware, someone who's already been there will instruct her. The female population in the valley – Staro Selo, Opalovo and beyond – are well informed about the details of Ginger Dimitar's preferences. He doesn't even need to sit next to a girl. Lifting his index finger is enough. There's a rumour going around that lately he will sit next to young boys too. Nothing wrong with that. But people are spiteful.

Ginger Dimitar bought the old chapel and transformed it into a private church so his sins could be forgiven by a private priest. He bought the polyclinic so he could be treated by a private doctor. He bought the mineral spring so he could drink private mineral water and be bathed by private boys and girls. Ah, why can't a private punch find its way into his private gob?

Dimitar, in an orange jacket, orange jumper and hair the colour of fresh carrot juice, came out of his house. Since Siyana (the vicious teacher 'Sit down, muppet!' at the mathematics school) left, since that savage teacher 'Sit down, muppet!' who only knew how to fail her students (who all apparently wanted to skin her alive but wouldn't dare) picked up her bags and left Staro Selo, Ginger Dimitar frequently lifted his index finger in various bars and restaurants. All types sat on the chair next to him. He bought the pub Sausages; acquired the diner Hunger; privatised the tavern Hashove and renamed it Siyana; bought the community centre and the empty kindergarten, renovated them and turned them into a marvellous gaming club. Bought the brickworks. Bought the sky over Staro Selo. Clearly, he had bought this space shuttle with four explosive wheels. Wow!

A slim lady, with dazzling white skin, dazzling black hair and dazzling shoes with skyscraper heels, got out of the car.

'Hello, Mitya!' the white skin greeted Ginger.

'Marietta?' Ginger frowned.

'Call me Josephine,' the lady corrected, her smile beaming. 'I sent you an email.'

'Marietta, where's Siyana? Where's your daughter?' bellowed Ginger Dimitar. It was a miracle Josephine's head didn't leave her body amid all that thunder. 'I'm no longer interested in your cow,' the ginger voice added coldly. 'Kindly pay back the money your daughter pocketed.'

'I believe she received a respectable amount for certain skills she introduced you to, Mitya.'

'I'm introduced to plenty of skills like that from the rags in the district.'

'Do not forget that Siyana's not a rag but a mathematical genius,' the woman reminded him, an even brighter smile revealing her teeth – implants, fitted by Professor Georgiev, though it's doubtful if anyone in this miserable province has heard about the professor's golden hands or his astronomical fees.

'Yeah right!' Ginger shouted and spat next to his visitor's skyscraper heels. This action didn't darken her dazzling smile. That woman's mouth was infinite.

'Do you remember that verse?' she asked softly. '*And on the left breast, a moon of velvet… and a tiara gracing the moon*. Do you remember, Ginger, darling, my first literature lesson with you? How old were you, fifteen? You haven't forgotten, I hope... You wanted to commit suicide, my darling boy, when I met an artist from Sofia.'

Ginger grinned. His teeth were implants too; he had managed to convince Dr Yordanchev from Kyustendil to voluntarily pull the ruins out of his mouth and stick new teeth into the gaping caverns left behind. Now Ginger's bite was indeed beauty itself.

'Do you remember who the poet was who wrote about the loveliness of the tiara above the moon of velvet?'

'I stole my mother's wages and bought ten literature textbooks. Do you know what I did to Yavorov? I cut out his face. I poked out his eyes. I stuck his blind image on all the school windows. Mum had seen people buy books, so she lifted her foot to get the golden horseshoe on it and went and bought three fat volumes. Total rubbish, five hundred pages each. Then, Marietta, I showed Mother what's what. I gathered all the books from our house, every single one of them. I burned them, page after page. With hatred. Slowly. My father – you know him, the idiot and drunkard. When he got drunk, he couldn't beat Mother, because she learnt to run to the neighbours whenever she saw him swinging. Anyway, my father read Zahari Stoyanov's book about the uprisings against the Ottomans. A fat book. He only read when he didn't have enough booze. But I, Marietta, I burned Zahari.'

'Well, it's not a big loss, Mitya.' The woman's implants shone even brighter. 'We're talking about a different thing, about the thing between us, as in my favourite verse, my darling boy.'

'Dad hit me then. With a cement pole. Broke my ankle. If he had hit my head... "See," he said, "you miserable worm, see what heroes we had back then. What traitors we had and what we are now. Sludge. You are sludge, since you burned Zahari." If I had found you then, Marietta, I would've poked your eyes out.'

'Ah, you – volcano, passion and fervour. But I have come to you for something else. I have come to collect a golden bracelet with the inscription *AMOR VINCIT OMNIA*.'

'Huh!'

'And a ring with the seal of Emperor Octavian which my daughter has seen in your house, my darling boy. You are thick and unable to appreciate the value of such artefacts.'

Ginger Dimitar shook inside his orange jacket and lifted his fist towards the lady.

'This futuristic vehicle in front of your house is mine, sweetie. It's worth three Octavians and one thousand two hundred and twenty-four *AMOR VINCIT OMNIA*,' the lady explained. Her radiant smile climbed even higher, almost to her eyebrows. 'In translation the inscription on the bracelet means "Love conquers all". And speaking of love, at the age of fifteen you achieved three on the six-point system, Mitya. I am not surprised that you sit next to some frightened-to-death country partridges and expect oral reflections on matters devoid of philosophy.'

Ginger Dimitar straightened – a pile of corn husks someone had inadvertently put a match to. Burning. Crackling. Hissing.

'But that's not the only reason my daughter Siyana... hmm, how shall I express myself so that you understand me? You have delayed gnostic reflexes, which is not to say you're a person of limited capabilities all round, though Siyana did sign your indefinite leave after you wrote her: "I's appy with you".'

'You filthy…'

'At this moment – well, only the novels of incompetent writers contain the phrase "at this moment" but you, Mitya, don't read. Against the backdrop of your mental landscape, a man who knows how to write all thirty letters of the Bulgarian alphabet would shine with the greatness of Homer. Have you heard of Homer, my love? No, you haven't. I believe you. As I was saying, at this moment, look, mon amour, look who's getting out of my car.'

A young woman appeared from the space shuttle. Tall and slim like the schoolgirls, waitresses and shop assistants Ginger Dimitar communicated with on a physiological level. When he felt bored he drove them away with his hand, but they wouldn't dare move since they were never sure if their withdrawal would be read as absence without leave. He often broke teeth, they say.

The young woman who alighted the vehicle was wearing Armani, but even if she had been wearing a rag from the flea market, Ginger Dimitar wouldn't have noticed it.

'Siyana!' he choked.

'Mitya, no need to accompany her. She can collect Octavian and Love that Conquers All herself. Love – look at my eye! My darling, I like seeing you all fresh. After all, I was the first to introduce you to the universe of velvet moons. I adore poetry and have excellent perceptions of it – oh, of course you're thick and have no idea what "perceptions" or indeed "poetry" mean.'

The woman in Armani flew past Ginger Dimitar like the flicker of a candle. She didn't look at him. She glided forward with ease as if there had never been Staro Selo or velvet moons in her life.

'Oi!' Ginger's face was bloodshot. 'Oi!' he whispered.

A tall gentleman came out of the spaceship then. Head-spinning Ermenegildo Zegna outfit. An unfortunate ensemble that had found itself slung on algae.

Ginger Dimitar bowed his head. His arms hung by his side. The orange-clad man ran his fingers through his curls then spat on his right hand and wiped his face with it. 'Good day... please,' his throat gurgled. 'Please! How kind...'

The deep-sea specimen didn't register the orange presence. Didn't account for it. He hurried with stiff steps after the woman. 'Siyana!' the alga exclaimed.

'Excuse me! Can I have a minute... please... ten seconds... five?' the orange jeans twisted.

Ginger Dimitar walked past the woman in Armani, flew over the steps and slunk into the white house, which was, like him, longing for the scent of *jorgovani* – of lilac blossom – to return, like in that Yugoslav song. Eight seconds later he flew back out clutching a box. Whether it was ivory or some other bone, who could tell you in this godforsaken suburb which wasn't even called a town but bore the agricultural name Staro Selo. Something rattled in the box. The deep-sea specimen cast his eye towards the source of the noise as Ginger Dimitar pulled out a few objects from the box, things that shone as befits necklaces, rings and coins.

'Siyana! Siyana, here, choose!'

'She's not Siyana to you,' snapped the sea creature, without as much as a glance.

'Excuse me... please... you're welcome.' The words poured out as ginger lava. The gentleman's knee, encased in Ermenegildo Zegna, crashed into the low-bent ginger forehead. 'Merci... please. Tennku sir... Tennku.'

This was the limit of Ginger Dimitar's knowledge of English.

The gentleman took the whole box, which rattled with a dozen Octavians and seven or eight AMOR VINCIT OMNIA, and completely ignored the orange apparition stuck to the marble path. Word went around that the marble came from Italy.

'Siyana! This is for you,' said the deep-sea gentleman with a voice as soft as goat's cheese.

The woman didn't look at the box – its lid was inscribed with signs in Arabic or Hebrew or perhaps Old Aramaic – but simply put it in her handbag without trepidation or fanfare. Not a very large item; it could fit in a paper bag from Dida and Dona's shop.

'Gudby, sir,' Ginger Dimitar whispered even softer than goat's cheese. 'I wish you good health, sir... happiness... luck.'

The Ermenegildo Zegna trouser leg didn't flinch, not even the hem.

At this moment ('only the novels of incompetent writers contain the phrase "at this moment", my darling Mitya') the older lady in Chanel approached Ginger, cupped his face in her soft, perfumed hands, but didn't kiss the lips.

'You and I will organise a nirvana soon, Mitya. And I don't mean just a velvet moon,' clarified the lady with a smile more radiant than the sun. 'Ask a teacher what "nirvana" means.'

'OK,' Ginger Dimitar whispered. The woman shook his face without losing her smile even for a moment. She clearly played tennis – her fingers were strong and pinched maliciously. 'Yes, ma'am,' Ginger Dimitar said. The woman freed his face. He bent down and down; perhaps this was his way of expressing his adoration of her charm.

'My name is Josephine,' the lady reminded. 'I don't like it when you talk about my daughter. Think only of me.'

'Yes, ma'am,' Ginger whispered. 'Yes, Josephine…' He wanted to kiss her somewhere, perhaps on the knee, but the perfume emanating from her hands and then her hands themselves stopped him.

'Till tomorrow at five, young man,' the lady said radiantly. We'll have time for everything.'

* * *

His Grandad Vasso played at a wedding, and what a wedding it was! Some guy called Nikola, from Pernik, an old man of forty, had finally plucked up the courage to get married. Vasso's entire orchestra – drums, accordion, trumpet – played for three days and nights until the groom's friends finally sobered up. Grandad Vasso knocked back a few drinks too, but the alcohol only gave him additional heart, delivering the whole sky into his hands, together with the moon, the stars and the rest of the cosmos. Grandad Vasso played a song for the bride too; even he didn't know how he managed to come up with it. He looked at the girl. Though she was no longer a spring chicken, it was obvious she could still bear children. When he saw the way she looked at Nikola, it became as clear as daylight to him that she was already carrying Nikola's son. Maybe that's why Grandad Vasso clutched the trumpet, ran over to the bride, who was from Radomir and who suddenly – to Grandad Vasso – resembled his wife, Todora, in her youth.

Todora hadn't changed in old age; she was still a thorny, prickly goat. If there was a storm raging when she opened her mouth, it knew to cease. If the clouds had wrapped themselves into a ball in the sky and Todora happened to be in one of her moods, the clouds would be swiftly on their way on to Sofia. That's how Todora was, though she was as pretty as a lamb. When Vasso first met her, he hadn't yet grown a beard. To lure her, he played the accordion and the trumpet as if he weren't twenty-one but a grown man with a wife and a cluster of children, all of them girls as beautiful as the pools in the Struma.

Vasso thought that old Nikola's bride also resembled his daughter-in-law, Valya – the most beautiful girl in Staro Selo. Valya sang and played the accordion, and when she was young, she was the stand-out of the school choir. She gave birth to twin girls, then another gorgeous girl, all three as beautiful as chrysanthemums. Finally, his daughter-in-law performed most generously – she gave birth to his grandson, Vasko. All his life Grandad Vasso had dreamt of a boy like this, with a brain for the accordion. Through the veins of the boy flowed not blood but the Radomir horo. How was such a boy born? It's clear. During her pregnancy, his mother Valya had sung day and night from happiness. God grant Gichka, the midwife of Radomir, good health and long life! No wonder people called her 'Queen of Birth, Mother Earth'; when she had listened to the baby she said, 'I can definitely hear a boy's heartbeat.'

'Is that true, Gichka?' Grandad Vasso kept asking, trembling. He made a special trip to the Queen of Birth's house to ask, 'Did you really hear a boy's heartbeat?'

'Listen to me, Vasso: If I say I've heard a boy's heartbeat, that means I have. When your daughter-in-law was pregnant with twins and then with her third daughter, did I say, "I can hear a boy's heartbeat?" No, I didn't. I said, "I can hear a girl's heartbeat." This baby is a boy, and if Valya doesn't deliver your grandson, I'll stand outside Dida and Dona's bakery and let whoever passes spit on me.'

This Gichka had a sharp tongue and knew no mercy when she got going. But Grandad Vasso forgave her.

'Oh, my dear Queen of Birth,' he said gratefully, 'I'll come to play the trumpet every afternoon for your granddaughters, I promise!'

'My granddaughters don't like music much, they drool over their phones like just-washed tank tops. That's what they listen to – phones!' complained the Queen of Birth. 'Play me a gentle concerto for the soul now. Like this, I too can find beauty in this backwater.' Then Vasso, as he stood in her garden right beside the hospital, struck up a tune. Everyone, especially the pregnant folk, rushed to listen to him. When you listen to something gentle, even if there are a few sharp edges in the concerto, you give birth to a beautiful, healthy child. Two women, Elena the crazy healer and Gichka, the Queen of Birth, kept the townsfolk as strong as steel. Gichka was made of steel herself, she was heavy and large in every direction, so how was Vasso to find something tender to play for her? But this was craftsmanship – to play the corners and still soothe the soul.

Suddenly from Vasso's trumpet tenderness flowed! He blew with great force. Vasso certainly didn't know what he was doing, maybe he was channelling his joy that at last his daughter-in-law Valya was going to give birth to a grandson. Let's hope, God! Most likely he was also imagining how Valya was going to sing all the time once she was carrying his grandson below her heart. Grandad Vasso was also channelling his wife Todora's fierce heart through his music. She was a brawler and a she-wolf, but also a sweet cherry jam, a supposedly quiet sparrow who screamed louder than twenty-seven little goats. All this poured into the music for Gichka, the Queen of Birth, Mother Earth, who herself was a sparrow and a she-wolf, a little goat and a brawler.

Bai Vasso was born simple and was going to land simple on God's cloud, but he revered his wife Todora – though she was a brawler, she cooked well. All his joy and thoughts about his wife went into that song. When he finished, the Queen of Birth was in tears. It was rare to see this large woman with eyes like the concrete stairs outside the town hall after they'd been washed in July – wet and glowing, radiating beauty. You'd think this midwife didn't come from Radomir but Paris or London, so beautiful were those eyes. The Queen of Birth grabbed Vasso's hand and kissed it. She had slapped lipstick on earlier – there was more lipstick than mouth, and anyway, putting lipstick on an old woman like her was like putting a brooch on a tank – and she smeared it over Vasso's hand. Vasso didn't notice, he was overwhelmed with such joy that he could have picked Radomir up on his shoulders and taken it to Paris, or even better, climbed the Sklon.

'Let's pray that the little one, when he's born, plays like you,' the Queen of Birth had said from the bottom of her heart. That's why God gave Vasso a grandson – Vasko, a boy as beautiful as a cockerel, as Vasso's faithful dog Gavril! Such a smart boy and so gorgeous! He had begun to walk when he was ten months old and when they gathered to celebrate his first steps as was the custom, they followed the rituals to the letter: they put money on the little table, so when he grew up he would be as quick as a banker; a pen, so he would write well; a knife, so he might open a butcher's shop; and beside them, Grandad Vasso secretly placed a tiny trumpet. The boy, as thin as spaghetti, the poor thing, walked around the table a few times and picked up the trumpet.

That's when Vasso's eyes had turned wet like the concrete steps outside the town hall when they wash them in July, making them shine and glisten brighter than the banks in Sofia. Vasso immediately bought an accordion and a small drum for the boy.

Now then, about the wedding of that Nikola, who stupidly waited to the ripe old age of forty before taking a bride: that was when Vasso bought a real trumpet for his grandson.

Vasko's father left this world as young as a spring chicken. He had indulged in eating fatty meat and wasn't good at playing music. You could play something to him, but he couldn't follow the rhythm to save his life, let alone birth new music that no one had heard yet. Besides that though, he was a decent chap, God bless his soul! He took care of his children. When the mine went bankrupt, he went to the brickworks in Pernik, then worked on the trains. They had bread on the table. He looked after his wife, Vasso's daughter-in-law, not as if she were one painted egg but a whole box of them, and as if he couldn't breathe without her. But all that fatty meat cut his head off. High blood pressure, stroke, gone.

Enough of this now, we're at the wedding. That silly man Nikola finally mustered the courage to get married, it's no time to be thinking dark thoughts and bringing the guests to tears. No! At a wedding one needs to think about how Vasso gave Todora a bracelet that cost fifty lev, how Todora picked it up as if it cost fifty million. Then Vasso thought to himself, *This woman is for me. She will shine above me when the sun goes on a drinking spree and forgets to rise at six o'clock.* The old man remembered that day, the day when his son, as proud as the full moon, said to him, 'Hello, Dad, you have a grandson. His name is Vasko, like you.' His son had big ears, but bless him, poor thing, he couldn't hear music with them. And then the fat destroyed him... He was a good son, God bless his soul... Vasso played glorious music at the wedding of that deluded Nikola – and how could he not be deluded, where was he that he didn't get married earlier? Moron! At his age I had a fifteen-year-old daughter. Never mind. He finally got hitched and wouldn't end up singing the cuckoo song, perched somewhere on a scraggy hedge all on his own.

The music became even more beautiful, because a blind Sunday (as they call a Sunday wedding in these parts) is the best thing for a man – it brings Todora home. You look at her all your life and it's not enough. You argue with her all your life and that's not enough either. When Vasso stopped playing, old Nikola's bride was crying – tears the size of orange pips, actually no, bigger than peas, bigger than beans even. Then Nikola, tall and lanky, famous for his stupidity, jumped from his chair, grabbed Grandad Vasso and hoisted him into the air. He lifted him so high that Vasso's trainers touched the light bulb in the bar.

'Ah, you're amazing! The best!' the groom said, and when he dropped Vasso to the floor, his bride got up and planted a kiss on Vasso's cheek. When, after three days and three nights, the wedding finally ended, Nikola, though he had paid an advance, gave Vasso a cap full of money.

'Go buy yourself a new trumpet.'

'I'll buy one for the grandson,' Vasso said and on the spur of the moment, before he'd even sobered up properly, he went and bought a second-hand, almost new, slightly bashed trumpet. The moment you saw that trumpet, you could hear the music it was going to make. Vasso bought it from Dimo Zagoryaloto, an old tinker and musician from the village of Divotino, near Pernik.

This Dimo was a master of the trumpet, a superb musician, even greater than Vasso, just as a house is greater than a brick.

When Dimo Zagoryaloto played, tulips sprouted behind him, children's faces shone like gold coins, and mountains bowed down to listen. That's what Dimo Zagoryaloto was like, but then he had a stroke and could no longer play or walk quickly. It's a good thing his wife was there. The doctors had told her and his children, 'He has two months at most.'

His wife said: 'We'll see about that.'

She fed Dimo with a syringe, Vasso saw it with his own eyes. She had made a meat bouillon and fed it to him. And here we are now – the man was still alive five years on. He needed a walking stick, but he could walk.

At one point Dimo Zagoryaloto had told his wife: 'Give me poison so I won't suffer any more.'

'If I hear you spout this nonsense one more time, I'm going to smack you and you'll die on the spot,' she had barked at him.

That's what Dimo's wife was like, and what he was like – and if you heard him play the trumpet, you'd forget where you were and be left wondering whether you'd landed on a beautiful star or outside the town hall in Radomir. Vasso would occasionally go to play for Dimo in the evening. Dimo's wife would pour them rakia, but Vasso wouldn't touch the glass until he had played a song for his friend. When he found out about Dimo's stroke, dark and murky tunes descended into Vasso's head.

He played a strange song, all about a man who gets dealt a nasty blow, but the blow hasn't yet met his wife. Cool! Clever! Feeds him with a syringe. However did she think of that? At first the man couldn't even swallow, but then slowly, slowly he learnt to drink the broth like a goose, before slowly rising to his feet, whereupon death said to herself, *Look at that woman, how can I take her husband? Let them both live.*

Vasso had played this refrain to his friend Zagoryaloto, bowing deeply for him with this melody. If someone had told him that if he took his friend to the peak Cherni Vrah, the nasty stroke would clear off, Vasso would've done it even though Zagoryaloto was a big, heavy man. With the money from Nikola's wedding in his pocket, Vasso went to his friend and said: 'Take this money for your trumpet, Dimo.'

'You can have it for free for your grandson,' Zagoryaloto said. 'I told you that a long time ago.'

'Yeah, but with this money, Simka can buy you chicken,' Vasso said.

'Nope!' protested Zagoryaloto. After the stroke he spoke very slowly, his words moving like slugs, but even slower. 'I want you to come here with the boy and let him play for me. I never hear any of my family play music. They are scattered all over England and the ones here can't play.'

And so the battered trumpet, the most powerful trumpet in Pernik, which could make the river change course and flow back to its source, arrived in Vasso's house.

The first week Vasso wanted to cut his ears off and give them to Gavril, his faithful wolfdog. The boy was a disaster. The trumpet lowed like an ox, loud enough to move the constellations in the sky. It choked on every tune, squatted there, as motionless as Vasso was when his wife Todora told him off for stomping on one of her flowers without seeing it in his haste.

'You're such a moron, boy!' Vasso cried. 'This is how it's done,' he said, showing the boy how to play. Vasko tried and failed, tormented and sweating, his face burning embers from all his efforts. 'You're a moron,' Vasso said. 'But you'll stop being one. Go hide somewhere where no one can hear you and practise. If you manage to cook up a melody, come and get me. Otherwise, don't torture Dimo's trumpet, you'll kill the poor man. And the brass has feelings. It hears you.'

The boy turned out to be amenable and took his grandad's advice. He took Dimo's trumpet and went to lose himself somewhere, perhaps in the forest with the thin young pines, or down by the Struma where the rocks live.

'If something happens to that boy, I'll break your neck,' Todora threatened. Vasso couldn't remember Todora ever not keeping her word or changing her mind.

'It's going to be fine, wife,' he said. 'Can't you see he's playing? Can't you hear him hauling music from the silt, digging paths in the snow?'

'If something happens… your neck…'

'Todora, why don't you stop growing flowers, huh? You can't eat flowers, can you? But if you stop, you'll die, and then what am I gonna do without you? He's like you, but he's got songs instead of meat wrapped around his bones. Do you understand?'

His wife of thirty-eight years picked up the rolling pin, but slowly put it back down. Then, without a word, though her tongue was heavier than the rolling pin, she went to the dresser. Vasso knew what she kept there – the bonbons he and Vasko had eaten the day before. But no, Todora didn't reach for those. Instead, she pulled out a box of Turkish delight, delicious!

'Eat, Vasse, eat,' she said. It wasn't often she called him 'Vasse'. Only once when he gave her that bracelet worth fifty lev when their grandson was born. What had got into this woman? Was she getting old like everyone else?

Vasso picked up two slices of Turkish delight, which spurred Todora to snatch the box from his hand and say: 'Vasso, pull yourself together. It's not exactly Christmas, so don't be a pig.'

Vasso sighed with relief. This woman would never grow old.

* * *

Siyana, I've moved to Brussels. It rains a lot here, but it's not cold. I buy fruit and meat from the Arab market, it's fresh and three times cheaper than at the corner shop. I've got enough money, and I've saved around eight hundred euros, maybe more, maybe less. I live in a loft, it's clean, there's a sink and running water, it's cheap, though it's a little far from work. I think there are people here who would notice your brains. Maths is difficult for everyone. I find it very difficult.

I don't know if you remember, perhaps you've already lost me from your thoughts. It was your birthday. I, as usual, didn't have a lot of money, but I had been saving for your birthday for four months, putting the money into a box where I kept a pair of summer shoes. I would put a little there when I could; I didn't spend it and I didn't count it. Maybe that's why I've got no luck. Money wants you to count it, to think about it, it wants to occupy your entire head, but in my head there's no place for it. Just a few days before your birthday, you came with a wad of five-lev notes and said to me: 'Christo, what's this money for? Why're you hiding it from me?'

'It's for your birthday,' I said.

You laughed so much that I began laughing too, we laughed like mad. That's what happiness is – your girl finding the money you've been saving for her. It wasn't a lot and I deserved you laughing at me, but you took the money and said: 'That's the best present.'

I no longer write you letters, not even in my head. I call Mum and ask, 'How's Siyana?' Mum's silent. Doesn't say anything, not a word. I'm not going to talk to you about her. And yet, back then on your birthday, I bought you a present with money I borrowed from Dad. You would've asked me where I got it from and if I had borrowed it from Mum; I would've admitted it. You don't like her so I took it from Dad. I didn't tell him why I needed it, but he figured it out. You can't hide anything from him because he's clever. He only said, 'I hope she likes her present.' I went to Sofia, to the Sofia University bookshop, and bought you a maths book. I can't remember the title. My highest grade in maths was a four out of six, and the teacher awarded me more than I deserved. I would sit quietly during lessons, trying to pay attention, I would look at her stupidly.

One day she had even asked me: 'Christo, do you want me to test you so you can get grade five?'

My knowledge was just about sufficient to get a three, so I said, 'No, Miss, even four is too much for me.'

'Look at how dumb you are,' my classmates said. 'So stupid, you're glowing.'

You bought Damyana a dress with the money I had saved for you. I gave you that maths book, the most expensive one in the bookshop. I'll never forget it – you took the book and started to cry. You didn't say a word. When someone cries, they don't talk, but women in the films sob and hiccup. You cried only with your eyes. When I was young, I planted a pear tree. It bears fruit in June – pears larger than the moon, yellow, the same as when children draw them with a yellow felt-tip pen. Your eyes grieved. As if someone had taken your early pear and the moon wouldn't rise.

'Why are you crying?' I asked you. 'Mathematics hasn't run away. You haven't run away from mathematics either. Study. That way there'll be someone to help Damyana with equations.'

Your smile tried to find its way into your eyes but failed. It withered. I said: 'I'm no good at maths, Siyana. Perhaps another man would've been better for you. Perhaps your equation of happiness is for someone else. But I remember it:

$-3y + 4x = 11$

$y + 2x = 13$.'

For you, I... Words don't come easily to me. I scraped an honourable and honest five in Bulgarian language, but I'm tongue-tied. I hugged you and lifted you up, up, up, even higher than the maths book. You were in a school with students who hated your lessons, yet you could wow the world... I've seen you, Siyana. When you were sad and I asked you, 'Do you want me to make you laugh?' you would just shake your head. Damyana taught me how to make you laugh. When Damyana started crying, even when she was a tiny titch, I would cradle her and she would stop. I tried the same with you and swayed slightly with you in my arms. But it didn't work. The sorrow only ever left when you opened the cupboard. I'm happy I managed to at least buy you that oak cupboard, solid and heavy. You would open the cupboard and take out a book full of numbers and Damyana and I would be quiet, watching your face brighten.

I called Dad. I asked him about you. He said, 'I don't know.' But his voice was saying something else. It was a broken voice.

'You taught me to be brave, Dad. Tell me.'

'Well... she... well... Ginger Dimitar...'

'You taught me to be a man. I've earned eight hundred euros. Maybe a little more. I'll spend it all on tickets. She doesn't call me. *The number you've dialled is incorrect*, her phone tells me. What's going on with Siyana, Dad?'

'Well... Damyanka is well... Your mother and I are well,' Dad tells me.

'Is Siyana ill?' I had no more energy to keep asking. We had panelled a hotel that day, with fine rosewood. 'I'm very tired, Dad. Tell me.'

'She... Siyana... Her mother came... You know her, she's all dolled up and that... She left three hundred lev on the table. "Buy Damyana something for her birthday," she said. "But that's in July," I reminded her. "Does it matter?" she asked, all dressed in pink, with a necklace longer than she was. A circus...'

'And Siyana?'

'Well... a man, thin as a reed, came out from the car... It wasn't a car really; it was a whole train, that thing... Anyway,

Siyana sent the little one two thousand lev, post office transfer... Ginger Dimitar drinks in his pub. He's boozing all day long, and if he meets someone on the street while still sober, he beats them up. He couldn't beat me up, though. I pushed him to the ground. Others don't dare do that. I, out of stupidity... pushed him. Don't think about her... her mathematics and that... The reed brought her here. Your mother... well... you know what she's like... Well... the reed and Siyana wanted to come in. You know what your mother's like. Well, she picked up the... No, not the cleaver. The knife. I've no idea why your mother named that knife Vasso... but I think I know. Bai Vasso, the musician, you know him... Your mother named this knife after him, because his music slices through your heart, you know...'

'How's Siyana?' I asked Dad, my heart as tight as a rusty screw. I know those kinds of screws, it's hard to undo them. 'How is she, Dad?'

'Well... your mother picked up the knife, Vasso. You know what she does when she gets wound up. She said, "You, reed, you can land here with a rocket if you like. I'm going to count to five. If you haven't left, I'll cut your head off. You, Siyana, for you, I'll count to three. I'm not going to say what I'll do to you because it's too vulgar and I don't want my husband to hear vulgar words leave my mouth." Your mother was talking heavy, as if hailstones were hitting a tin roof. Ice hitting metal makes hell of a noise and it frightens you. But you know Siyana, Christo. You know her better than I do.'

'What happened to Siyana?' I asked. I no longer had even a rusty screw in my chest. I had nothing any more.

'Well... then... well, it's dirty. I don't want you to hear these dirty things come out of my mouth, but... before our eyes, she, Siyana... you understand... she began... well... she began kissing the reed.'

My dad had a gentle voice; he never hit me or punished me when I was a child. When I was young and got tired, he would hug me and carry me. I was happy then. I used to think, *Dad and I are strong*; I fooled myself that while he carried me, my strength became equal to his. That's why when I thought you were sad, Siyana, I would take you in my arms. I hoped you could fool yourself that your strength was equal to mine. Mathematics and the books in the cupboard have taught you other things, but if, when I picked you up, you thought you were a small girl again, then maybe you would believe... My father's voice, which I was sure brought my fever down when I was ill as a little boy, that voice vanished as if it were a woollen thread and the moths had gnawed it. Besides, I didn't want to hear those dirty words leaving his mouth. When the moths in the receiver gnawed at his voice, Siyana, my love, I wished I were there for him, to hug him, to lift him into the air as if he were a little boy so he would be fooled and feel that his power was as great as mine. But right then I had no power.

But you know, don't you, that I'll be always thinking of you, of that beautiful, sad girl who would open the cupboard with the big maths books, pick one of them and read it so she could push the sadness away. At least I'm happy I bought you that oak cupboard. It was very expensive, but I bless every penny I paid for it. When I have no more energy, Siyana, I remember the girl who caught me secretly putting money aside and to whom I confessed that it was for her birthday. Today we panelled a room in a big new hotel with rosewood. I can't fall asleep for tiredness. But when I think of you, tiredness abates. I no longer write you letters in my head. You have no time to read them.

I've never wished for anything bad to befall you. Is it even possible to wish anything bad to befall happiness?

* * *

Only two of Staro Selo's houses stood proud behind the cornfields. Beyond them sprawled hawthorn and milk thistle, and all things with spikes. If you went through there you would waste a whole bottle of rakia pulling out thorns and disinfecting the wounds – so you'd better not go. But of course, if you're after hare, that's a whole other matter, since you might become a millionaire. In this neck of the woods, hares are more abundant than hawthorn and they are impudent too; in winter they sneak into your garden and eat the apple tree bark as if they were goat moths. Young pear and cherry trees fall to the sharp teeth of the long-eared savage. When you turn the soil in your orchard, he stands there, ten metres away from you, and watches you as if you were his employee and he was the manager around here. That's why people in Staro Selo had hunting guns, and if one of the long-eared savages got ideas of intelligence, they shot him in the head. Local folk hated wasting money on bullets and cartridges, but if they threw a stone the hare would only jump to the side and carry on watching them as if he were the boss.

The people who lived in the last houses next to the cornfields often saw a tall, skinny boy. They got a glimpse of him today as well, clutching something bright and yellow. 'What's that?' the men asked each other and stretched their necks just like the hare.

The boy marched through the thicket, and God knows how many thorns his mother would pull and how much rakia for disinfecting she would waste. It was Vasko, Valya's son. It seemed clear what he was after: butter mushrooms grow under the young pine trees. They're a bit of a nuisance, they spoil quickly, so we could do without them, thanks. But this fool wasn't after mushrooms. After a few minutes – though no one here takes 'minutes' seriously, maybe only old Dr Varbanov and the screwed-in-the-head healer Elena, because in their case a minute is crucial in deciding whether you'd go on breathing or you'd go six feet under, with the priest Palyo singing a eulogy at your funeral. Anyway, after a few minutes, a piercing screech tore through the pine trees. Was it a jackal shot in the back, or the cries of a child who had just spilt hot tea over their tiny leg? Was it a baby teething or a grandmother who had dropped the heaviest pot on the tiles? In fact, it was the nonsense blaring from the trumpet of the boy, Vasko, Valya's son, God bless his father. He had been a strong man; breakfasted and supped on bacon, that's why they buried him early.

This man's son was now wandering around holding his trumpet as if it were a sword. It was no sword, in fact it was hardly more than a pathetic penny whistle, as old as Dr Varbanov's teeth, scratched, pitted, looking like a poker that had pounded many heads.

Slowly, slowly from the jackal's howl, from the crash of the dropped pot and the teething screams, something began to take shape. The sounds resembled a pine sapling pushing through the soil to wave its green flag, a baby whose tooth has finally emerged and who is smiling, babbling, 'Mummy, Mummy'. After a few days, or maybe a few weeks – who gives a jot how long a day is around here – the battered old trumpet bore a melody, and in a month or so, people from the houses by the cornfield began straining their ears. To listen. You'd wonder how someone managed to tame that trumpet. It began pouring out songs, and even the youth recognised them. Old folk songs about Haiduks, which glided through the air somehow peculiarly, as if wanting to slice your heart into pieces and sew it up again. But it didn't hurt you at all.

In this wild place people say, 'The mare won't give birth to a lizard.' The tiny mosquito was Vasso's grandson, and have you heard how Vasso plays the trumpet? You'd think he plays for God, not for you and me. In fact, for ten seconds you feel as though you've turned into God yourself. Well, we won't count the seconds now… but it's beautiful, light.

Then, this boy, who was his grandad's grandson from the cap on his head to the sole of his shoe, began torturing the trumpet with something neither the people nor the corn had ever heard before. At the beginning it was gentle, then whatever got into the kid's head, the trumpet began kicking and jumping. You wondered where the melody wanted to go and wished for a quiet afternoon with a little drizzle. The boy would slip into the thicket – he'd already forged a path through the pines – and stand in his usual spot before beginning. Sometimes the trumpet brought the sun out and at other times it was as though someone had drowned in Munish and you were overcome by sadness. The skinny boy would play the battered trumpet for an hour or so and you'd wonder whether, just like when his Grandad Vasso played, God had perched to listen.

Who's paying this silly boy? No one. The people who lived in the two houses at the edge of town said that when they listened to the tiny grasshopper, even just for a minute, they sat by God's knee. They had no money, yet they would take out fifty lev and spend it on one of the beautiful bikes they sold in Second Chance, bashed around a bit, since even if they bought a brand-new one, the son would soon see to it. Right? That's what the battered trumpet brought: you may be relieved of fifty lev, but when you see your son smiling while riding his bicycle, you think to yourself, *Even if I had fifty million, I would still splash them on that bike.*

Dimo Zagoryaloto's birthday was in July. He was known from Pernik to Petrich. He'd had a stroke but his wife hadn't faltered. She stepped into the ring with the illness and saved him, begged God for a few more days for him and got them. He got his nickname, Zagoryaloto, because this one time, Dimo's wife roasted a lamb for the feast of Saint George and said: 'Come, Dimo. The children are hungry, let's eat.'

But Dimo clutched his trumpet and began playing. Maybe he'd helped himself to a few glasses of rakia, no one would tell the truth on that one. But when he started playing his wife and sons forgot all about the lamb in the oven. It burned. That's why they call him Dimo Zagoryaloto, *Dimo the burnt*, but no one got upset about the burnt meat. His sons and wife – even though you won't believe it about his wife, since she's a stingy raisin – kissed him and ate the lamb.

So now, on Dimo's birthday, Vasso grabbed the mosquito grandson by the hand and dragged him off.

'Where're you dragging that mozzie, Bai Vasso?' the neighbours by the cornfield asked.

'To the song master.'

'Who's that then?'

'Dimo Zagoryaloto. He's the only master around here.'

'Ahh, Bai Vasso, you're the master,' the neighbour said.

'You've seen a puddle, haven't you, Petko?' Vasso asked. 'But have you seen the ocean?'

'I haven't.'

'Well, you've seen the Black Sea though. I'm the puddle on the street and Dimo Zagoryaloto is the ocean – even though I haven't seen it, I know it's endless. I'm taking my grandson to Dimo, so the boy can hear the ocean.'

They say the mosquito and Vasso went to see Dimo Zagoryaloto. I've no idea what they fed the kid or what the two oldies drank, or what they had the urge to play, but the thing is that the whole Kalkas neighbourhood in Pernik came out to listen.

Do you know what it means to get someone from Kalkas to come out without bribing him with money? You have no idea how difficult it is! No one from Kalkas would even spit without money on the table. Even so, all the folk came out and carried Dimo Zagoryaloto in their arms. They picked Bai Vasso up too, shouting, 'More, more!' But it is quite unbelievable that the Kalkas folk carried even the tiny lizard, young Vasko in their arms. Who knows how much money the musicians earned, but they gave everything to a woman with four children whose husband had died just like that, even though he was as healthy as you and me.

'I didn't see all that with my own eyes,' one of the neighbours was saying, 'but a friend filmed it all on his phone. These men know how to make a miracle out of a battered trumpet! So good you'd think you were drinking rakia with God Himself.'

The boy marched along the stone wall – it was a really low wall, not a serious wall at all, so low that you could see what flowers crocheted and bloomed in Elena the Healer's garden. These flowers weren't tended by the healer's sinewy hand, but her husband's. The neighbourhood women thought this explained this man's beauty – he had soaked it up from the roses he tended. How was it otherwise possible for a man to be so beautiful?

The boy was walking along the stone wall, not from the side of the paved road but from the other side, where stinging nettles reaching up to your waist pushed against it. The Munish was trickling under them. You would be lying if you called it a river, but it wasn't a stream either. With November it would overflow and litter the fields with branches and silt, but now at the start of autumn it strolled along calmly, like a woman who had managed to put her baby to sleep and was finally able to rest her head. That's where the boy squeezed in, among the thickest nettles, along the banks of the Munish, ruffled by wind and sun. The boy clutched a trumpet – battered, yellow, without a spark.

The grasshopper began playing. The trumpet coughed a bit at the start, possibly it remembered its days as a baby trumpet; then it rushed to do all its growing elsewhere, much brighter. It was a song with lyrics, but how was the trumpet to say the words when it wasn't human? The melody tiptoed among the nettles, quiet as a child trying to walk holding on to his mum's pinkie.

Then suddenly the song raced off, full of joy, so very joyous that the girl in the almost-new pink dress on the other side of the stone wall began clapping her hands. Usually, she was a very quiet child. The trumpet liked the dress and swirled it into a lunar carousel. No, actually, it wasn't a carousel. The trumpet lifted the girl onto a Ferris wheel, and up there it was terrifying yet beautiful; you could see the fields and the proud peak of the Sklon, but when you started descending towards the nettles, it was scary. If it weren't for the trumpet and this crazy song, if it weren't for the brave rooftops of Staro Selo, the girl wouldn't have been able to stay even for a moment on the scary Ferris wheel that arrived all the way from Vienna on the melody's wings.

Finally, the trumpet went quiet as if it had bumped into the telegraph pole and could no longer see the girl standing astounded behind the frivolous low stone wall.

'Dame-Damyanka!' the boy called.

The girl remained motionless for another few moments. Then her voice returned to her, startled like a baby who had unexpectedly fallen, even though it thought it could walk.

'Vasko!'

The girl in the almost-new pink dress went close to the wall and stretched out her hand. Her fingers lay on the stones that left gaps between themselves so that the flowers could take deep breaths.

The boy, as thick as a paper clip, didn't mind the nettles. He dropped the trumpet and stepped forward; his hand, thin but strong, devoid of a flower or a chocolate from Café Solaris, lowered itself slowly and very carefully and touched the stone where the girl's fingers had been a moment ago.

The stone was hot.

The stone knew it all.

* * *

Rumour went around that Ginger Dimitar had a strong punch. Apparently, he could smash five or ten tiles stacked on top of one another with his bare hand.

'Damyan, do you remember how you pushed me on the street? I was flat out on the pavement,' Ginger Dimitar said. Rather it was his hair, reaching his shoulders, that said it. Perhaps it was an illusion, but his hair seemed unnaturally shiny. The curls on the right gleamed blood orange and those on the left were paler, like little kids who have just been to the dentist. His face was a small pile of straw. That's what money did to people in Staro Selo – made them into small piles of straw, no longer good enough even for the cowshed.

Was it possible that Ginger had dyed his hair? Who could tell? Around here the impossible was possible.

'Oi, dog, you remember how you hit me?'

'I do, but I'm not a dog,' Damyan said. He was in overalls. He didn't have time to get changed when he was called – one of the technician's cars had broken down. Damyan rushed over to help, but it wasn't one of the technicians. It was Ginger, Vova and Pavko. Between Vova and Pavko stood a child, a girl with bright eyes and a pink dress, almost new. A dozen girls in Staro Selo had those dresses, they sold for two lev-fifty each. Next to the girl protruded her grandmother, Elena the Healer.

'Vova, you ready?' Ginger's voice was a lake of hot chocolate.

Vova, taller than the pole of the national flag, stood swinging something in his hand – a dog collar with impressive spikes, brand new, unlike everything else in this neighbourhood.

'Put the collar around the old bag's neck.' All of Vova's hundred and twenty kilos swayed in a mass of sweat and muscles. The huge man stepped towards the healer, who, if she bent in two, could fit into his back pocket. His right hand grabbed her by the throat.

'Vova.' Her voice slipped out from under his steel grip. A flat monotonous voice. 'Vova, remember today's date. If you fasten this collar around my neck today, in seven days you'll be six feet under.'

'You too, but before that,' Ginger whispered.

Vova unclenched his fists, each as large as a melon.

'Vova!' Ginger said.

The melons continued to droop aimlessly. Didn't budge. The collar's spikes shone in the sun.

'Vova!' Ginger repeated, but there was no reaction. Muscles and tendons were silent.

Ginger smiled and stepped towards the man taller than the pylon of the national flag. The orange elbow only touched the giant's nose. Blood flowed, something quite natural around here, and even more naturally, Vova wiped it with his sleeve. His face was sure to recover after a week. Until then he would insist that he suffered from cold sores, because he often got them. Ginger grabbed the spiked collar, tied it around Vova's neck with lightning speed, then pulled the leash. It didn't hurt much.

'Pavko,' Ginger said. 'Will you put the collar around the old goat's neck?'

'Nope,' mumbled the man, just as tall as Vova and even stronger.

In this neck of the woods people were aware that Ginger breaks five, even ten tiles with one blow. Pavko began suffering from cold sores too, those special ones. Vova hung there with a collar around his neck. The blood on the spikes was already drying up. The young giant flexed his shoulders and stepped towards the child.

The pink dress wasn't moving. Wasn't sobbing. It was as if it was frozen.

'Mesechinke!' Damyan choked. His blue overalls flew forward. Vova or perhaps Ginger tripped him.

'Damyana, are you all right?' Elena the Healer asked.

The little one didn't say anything. Just stood there, hypnotised, petrified.

'It's gonna hurt,' Ginger whispered softly. 'Vova! Pavko, you too – tie up the madwoman.' They did the job in seven seconds, just as they had a year ago when they wrapped ropes around the barren cows and butchered them for meat in the village of Kralev Dol.

'Ginger Dimitar,' said the man in blue overalls with such a pretty face that people wondered how his beauty had managed to withstand the sludge in this backwater where the tarmac on the streets quivered with fear come dusk. 'Ginger Dimitar. Vova. Elena has been bringing you back from the brink of death since you were kids.' Beautiful's voice wasn't beautiful at all. 'She's saved your mothers too. Remember?'

Vova and Ginger Dimitar didn't remember. They watched his beautiful face without flinching, waited for him and didn't blink. People like this, even with smeared cold sores on their lips, had long ago become great. They had never needed saving. No one had yet invented a bigger saviour than money in your wallet. No one. Except God. But He wasn't around right now. He had gone on His travels to the other side of

Bulgaria. He had been called there to help; everywhere in this helpless land someone was asking Him for something: for love, for health, for money, to pass the exam, for the test results to be good, for the tumour to be benign, for the son to fall in love with a decent girl, for the daughter to not get divorced. God is good. He helps.

'Ginger Dimitar, your dad's heart stopped once. My wife saved him,' the man in the blue overalls said. 'You're tying this woman up as if she were an animal.' Then Pavko, a mountain of a man who was going to suffer two weeks of cold sores, grabbed Beautiful just where it hurts most.

'Did I permit you to crush him?' the paler part of Ginger's face asked.

Damyan didn't turn towards the three men. Beautiful Damyan was staring ahead, but there was nothing there except a grey wall, three metres tall. This wall rose almost to the sky – perhaps it was a shooting range or part of an abattoir where they cut up cows that would never calf again. Strange, why Damyan looked so old and so beautiful right now.

'Dog!'

'I'm not a dog,' repeated Damyan.

'Damyan, the gentleman with the space shuttle Maserati kicked Siyana out. Your daughter-in-law is his ex, already. You've got no backing, man. No one's looking out for you. I'll skin you, man. I'll slice you all the way down to your kidneys. To the innards. To the socks. Let the plebs learn who's been pushing Ginger Dimitar. If they like it, they might try it for themselves.'

'Dimitar,' Elena said flatly, without haste. 'I'm looking at you. Seven days after you've skinned my husband to the innards, you'll regret not having eaten your own innards. Not only in Radomir, but everywhere you set foot, you'll be a laughing stock.'

'Well, well, see how knowledgeable the old crow is, huh!' Dimitar laughed. 'I won't skin you, Elena. You spat in Siyana's brain. I won't beat you. You'll just watch.' Ginger spoke gently as if talking to a toddler. 'Go on, Pavko.'

Pavko was one metre and ninety-three centimetres tall, with a dark brown beard. There was an old belief in Staro Selo: if a boy lives in a house over which the Sklon casts its shadow in the morning, he will easily reach two metres. The girls he'll sleep with will have beautiful eyes, like the doe Pavko shot when he was thirteen. Ever since then, it had been clear that as well as being a strong man, he was a good shot. So now that strong man with a good shot, Pavko – who on Saint George's Day ate, for a bet, a whole twelve-kilo lamb in one sitting – squeezed the fingers of the girl in the almost-new pink dress and pressed her hand over a wooden block. That wooden block was in fact a useless old railway sleeper, but in Staro Selo nothing was ever useless, everything could be put to work.

'Elena, look,' Ginger said. 'Siyana left me. This is what happens to her daughter.' The ginger face gleamed with a smile. Then the ginger fist, as powerful as thunder, landed on the tiny arm, just above the wrist, or maybe over the wrist itself.

Many people in Staro Selo had seen how Ginger Dimitar smashes five tiles, stacked one atop the other, with one blow.

The child screamed.

The grey wall shuddered.

The blue overalls dived forward, so fearlessly that their sleeves burst at the seams. Vova tripped them. Good job Pavko was holding Elena with a nylon rope, the same kind they used to tie the breeding bulls.

Exactly at that moment... what a moment, damn it!

No one knew exactly when it happened. A ball tumbled from the three-metre-high wall. How did this happen... who knows? A boy, as slim as scissors, light as a black tomcat, rolled over the useless sleeper, an ordinary wooden block. This boy didn't look at the block; he threw aside an ugly, battered trumpet. The boy had probably lost his mind. He bent down. He bit one of the legs in the orange jeans. He bit so hard, so viciously, disgustingly, that the strong cotton cloth tore apart.

A few drops of orange blood trickled from beneath the thick orange cloth. The jeans were neither soaked nor reddened.

* * *

Golo Bardo is *golo*, naked, in name only. There are puny pines, thorny bushes, hawthorns and some tiny ash trees covering it. The thing with the wolf pack happened in the winter. Mind you, winter's gone crazy too – in January you're walking around with a thin jacket with no idea when a blizzard will hit you. Snow or not, you live as if your wallet is large enough. Otherwise, you tighten your belt. It's been a long time since such a phenomenon occurred in Staro Selo. A sound like that had never before resounded in the surrounding miser hills. The predators were tightening their ranks and row upon row of bloodthirsty throats and cubs with their fur still soft dragged their hunger to the bigger mountains. There was no sound of beasts' footsteps, no wheezing. There were no mind-chilling shadows. Nothing.

This year wolves descended into the village from the puny thicket of pines (waiting to wither from some green flea plague but still hanging on to life on Golo Bardo). People were not frightened of beasts; they are something natural – wolves are winter's caterpillars. But their howling was terrifying. Did they feel they'd starve to death? There were no flocks of sheep or herds of goats or cows. The wolves howled. The whole slope – they called it Gnida Planina because dark things happened there – shuddered. Most of the pines had been cut down one by one, even some of the puny ones were chopped to the ground. What do you care when you sell them and pocket the money? OK, fine, it stopped raining in summer.

So what? Here the pensioner is bullheaded and doesn't give up on planting gardens. Vegetable prices are sky-high – a third of your pension goes on two tomatoes. You only throw that kind of money around if you're mad! The geriatrics pricked pepper and tomato seedlings into the sandy soil. If you get a kilo of peppers, you have food for a week. Whether it rained or not was as important as a cigarette butt trampled on the pavement. The grannies dragged buckets of water from the river. The grandads dug trenches and argued about who was going to water their vegetable patch first.

But that howl was annoying. The wolves had completely lost their minds. In the evenings, sometimes all night long, the air boiled from their footsteps, their rough mouths – cracked and bloodthirsty – gaped. When the howling exploded the air shrivelled, houses, windowpanes and people shivered. What was going to befall those long-suffering people? Some took out guns and rifles, others paid hunters from Radomir to chase away the grey plague. All in vain. After the hunts, the howling intensified. It tore the valley. Snowdrifts buried and quenched the desire to fight the starving wolfen jaws. The snow snapped the branches of the plums, and the plums were the future rakia. Life on this side of the Struma is possible without air, but not without rakia.

These wolf wails.

Ugly.

* * *

'You'll be fine, mesechinke moya. Your hand will become even stronger. Your grandma and I will make an ointment for bones. Your wrist will heal.' Someone else might've found it hard to carry his daughter in his arms and walk around with her as if she were a baby, but that was precisely the reason Christo had returned from Spain. It wasn't that difficult. 'Let's dance the Radomir horo together, hey,' he said and very carefully, so as not to wobble the hand in its stiff cast, picked the horo's steps – two forward, jump, two backward, jump, jump, jump.

'Tell me the story from when I was little again,' the girl with the bright eyes said. 'Tell me about the shoelaces and Mum's students.'

'OK then, mesechinke moya.' The tall man sat on the bed still cradling the girl. 'Well, two of your mum's students had come over so she could help them with some equations. Your mum is brilliant at maths, your mum is the cleverest woman ever, Damyana. So these two girls had come for a lesson, otherwise they would fail their examination.'

'What's an examination, Dad?'

'It's when you're given lots of maths equations to solve and you have to do it on your own during the lesson.'

'Will I get things like that?'

'Yes.'

'Were you good at maths?'

'No, I wasn't.'

'Is that why you married Mum, so she could solve your equations?'

'Yep.'

'What happened with the shoelaces?'

'Well, your mum helped the girls, they worked out the equations and it was time for them to leave. They got up to go, went to put their shoes on and ohlala! The shoelaces were missing. What were they to do! Here shoelaces, there shoelaces, gone! As if they had hidden underground.'

'Ohlala!' the child exclaimed.

'Ohlala!' her father repeated. 'At one point your Grandma Elena looked at you and what did she see?'

'What was it?' the girl asked, trying to get up, her face twisting.

'Go easy, mesechinke. You're not supposed to move your hand. So, your Grandma Elena looked at you and saw your cheeks were about to burst. You always made that face when you didn't want to eat. You would put one tiny mouthful in one cheek, another in the other, then pretend to be Red Riding Hood or the Golden Apple or Cinderella… You wouldn't chew and that was that. But your grandma carefully examined your puffed-up cheeks and spotted the end of a shoelace sticking out.'

'Ohlala!' the girl said and laughed, then winced again.

'So there we go, you had taken the shoelaces and stuffed them into your mouth. See what a cheeky little devil you were?'

'I was,' the girl said contentedly.

'Then I asked you, "Damyana, why did you stuff the shoelaces in your mouth?"' her father said quietly.

'Ahh, Dad, you've never told me this part before.' The girl livened up again. 'What did I say?'

'You said, "Daddy, I put the laces in my mouth because I wanted the girls to solve more equations with Mum. Seven and a hundred more." "Why, mesechinke?" I asked you.' Christo paused and gently stroked the cast on the girl's wrist.

'Tell me, tell me what I said. You've never told me this story before.' The girl wriggled again.

'"When Mum solves equations, she smiles." That's what you said, mesechinke.'

It was dusk outside. When you mix twilight with a child's smile, the night tiptoes and leaves beautiful dreams in people's eyes.

★ ★ ★

Is it possible to sit next to a random girl in a café and for that girl to know in advance how to proceed? She unbuckles the belt first. With her teeth. Under the table.

Then comes bliss.

Where do they raise these soft-lipped girls?

Autumn and winter are vicious seasons. The town's folk are even more vicious. But they are cunning too. Ingenuity makes smart people bow. Down, lower, to the bottom. Bow before the powerful. Chapeau. Bravo.

Bravery is for the stupid.

Yet...

Masons didn't build this town for it to bow. If this town

ever breaks, let the earth beneath it open its cavernous mouth. Let its people pour their poison elsewhere, let them cut their own throats.

A person should not be unbuckling an orange belt with their teeth. The town should not be bowing.

Well, you would think Staro Selo (apparently a neighbourhood despite its agricultural name) was the most subdued place. The backwater of backwaters. Someone's taken people's nerves out, put them into the soup instead of noodles and boiled them. And the morons in Staro Selo drag their sorry asses along the street, seeing nothing, hearing nothing, only glancing sideways to make sure no ginger specimen sits beside them, lest trousers have to be pulled down. Anyway, everyone knows what Ginger prefers…

Truly trampled-upon people you'd say – no brains, no nerves, a people skinned to the bone, here in Staro Selo. They must've had enough. From here onwards it only gets deeper and eviller. Someone was heard reciting the other day:

Rose
from the troubled dark
of their own lives
and wrote in their own blood:
FREEDOM!

Well, prattle. That's what that is – everyone around here is a master of prattling.

* * *

Ginger Dimitar came out of his spaceship. He looked great, sublime, invincible. He marched towards the town hall in Staro Selo, where, perched on two equally high pylons, the Bulgarian national flag and the European Union flag were embracing. Plebs crawled around in grey jackets, black gilets, brown coats. Everyone was getting on with daily life – finding out what's the fee for a divorce; hiring a private maths tutor since the son might fail his final exams this year; checking their sugar levels at the doctor because stress is hitting their weakest spot; arranging a lawyer for the division of the apartment because Grandfather, its owner, had long since kicked the bucket and the trial has been dragging on for seven years.

Ginger Dimitar didn't look at anyone. This scum – mean-spirited, stingy – was transparent to him. He was approaching the post office. He was planning to buy the building in a few months. His nose was high in the air; he had no interest in the morons crawling about. Ginger couldn't find anything to be excited about in this sour backwater.

Suddenly, behind his back, a wolf howled. Blood-curdling. Some fool had put his stupid phone on loudspeaker. Ginger regarded this as supreme insolence. Was the fool unaware of his presence? Leave it out. Ginger rushed over to put him in his place, but somewhere very close to the town hall, behind his back, another howl rang out. The wolves were thrashing about – a tooth for a tooth. Someone's throat was being ripped violently, quickly. Another muppet had increased the volume on their phone to the max. Idiot! Ginger was going to stuff his stupid brain where the sun didn't shine. Immediately.

'Enough!' Ginger Dimitar shouted.

The iPhone stumbled. The device's dumb memory growled, panicked, dug into the ground, whimpered and shut up. Phew. Ginger sighed. Very well. Next to the little path, deep in the mud under the footsteps of people who had no time to walk around it, another crap phone howled.

No way.

'I said enough!' Ginger Dimitar ordered.

But the filthy phones weren't shutting up. Baring their teeth. Left. Right. Behind his back. In front of him. Insolent. Heedless.

The wolves in them bit, tossed, whimpered, barked. Bared their teeth.

They surrounded him.

Threatening.

Howling.

Howling.

Howling.

Bastard wolves.

'Now listen, Damyan.' Vasso stood up, a mountain of a man. 'Stavri, who played the drum next to me, cleared off to Holland. My favourite drummer cracked his whip and left! People here rarely want music for weddings nowadays. Stavri went to Amsterdam to dig canals, ditches and sewers. Got up and left. I want to pull my hair out – what a drum that man was! When he started drumming, you'd think Golo Bardo had ruptured and the Struma had changed direction; before you knew it, it'd started flowing towards Burgas because of his drums. But the man left and that's that.'

Damyan was still beautiful. They beat him up, battered his face yellow and purple; the yellow drains like dirty water, but the purple takes its time.

'So here we go, Damyan, I've got an accordion, he's my cousin, but drums… I thought and thought and apart from you, I couldn't think of anyone else, man. I know you've got two left hands; the difference between you and Stavri is the same as between a rocket and a screw on the doormat outside the rocket. But you see, I don't have a drum, and I don't trust anyone else. The drum has to listen, and my people are drunkards, always jumping into fights. You're a sane man, Damyan. Never mind you're incompetent in the ear department. You're a good person. That's what matters.'

Damyan was listening to him. Even though his face was battered after the beating – black around the eyes, yellow around the chin, like the shirts of Pernik's football team, the Miners – it was still beautiful.

'Go on, man, go on, say yes! These are christenings. Babies! Our music is meant to dig channels in people's minds. Go on, say yes.'

Damyan was quiet.

'We'd each get a hundred lev for that christening. You'd be able to put it aside to buy your granddaughter gold earrings. What a sweet child. That bastard… But it's a wrist, not a drum to burst forever. An arm bone heals like a dog's leg… Come on, say you'll do it.'

Damyan still didn't say a word, but something like a smile flitted in the purple around his eyes then in the yellow around his chin. But who knows whether under this black and yellow football shirt there was a smile or a knife? Vasso, mountain of a man, wasn't hanging around. He slapped Damyan on the shoulder and mumbled, 'Sorry, brother, I forgot they beat you up.'

Apparently, the people of Staro Selo – who had truly seen all there is to see – lifted their hands in amazement; but then again, how could anyone have seen anything in Vasso's narrow plot, where the two oldies sat next to the ragged hens under the wonky shed roof? Anyway, one of them, a skyscraper of a man, blew the trumpet and the other one, yellow and purple in the face, started beating and hitting the drum so that the skyscraper man threw the trumpet to the floor and shouted:

'You're bloody deaf in your brains and in your bones, Damyan!' Five minutes later, he screamed, 'Oi, get in rhythm, otherwise I'll beat you up, deafy.' The purple-yellow man left the drum and got up. The skyscraper grabbed him by the shoulders and said, 'Forgive me, brother. Go on, pick it up again so I don't add some blue to your jaw too.'

Damyan, in his blue overalls, reconsidered. He picked up the enormous instrument and timidly tapped it with the batons.

The mountain man threw the trumpet onto the grass and groaned:

'Oi, oi Stavri, why did you drop me in the shit? You out there with the ditches, and I, here tortured by this deafy. A beautiful, gentle man, but the moment he touches the drum, it all turns ugly!' The man who was purple-yellow in the face got up to leave again, but the skyscraper told him, 'Oi, don't you goose up now. That's why I asked you. I thought to myself, *If Damyan can live with that Crazy Elena then he can cope with me teaching him the drums.*'

The lessons carried on, Vasso swore, asked Damyan to bring him some water, then asked him to go fetch him a glass of rakia from Valya, his daughter-in-law. Damyan did as he was bid. He was on sick leave and didn't have to go to the locomotive depot for everyone to see his blues and greens and yellows and feel sorry for him.

'Damyan, you're a good man, but when it comes to music, you're a bit simple. Never mind. Don't take it to heart. When you hear me picking high notes, don't even bother with the drum because you'll piss me off and I might kick you one even though you're a decent man,' Vasso told him. 'Music heals, brother!' he suddenly shouted. 'Look, since you've started hitting that drum your bruises have faded.'

Just then a tiny shadow, as thin as a stalk of grass, joined the music lesson.

'Grandad, is it true music heals?'

'Well, if music doesn't heal, what does? Music and this trumpet belong to God,' Vasso the mountain said. And if you want to know Vasko, you goose, God has kept Dimo Zagoryaloto's trumpet next to his heart.'

'Is that true!'

'Have I ever lied to you?' Vasso said.

'Well... you've been buying me a bike since I was three.'

'I'll buy it, boy, I'll buy it. Just let us get paid for that christening.'

Damyan nodded his head, sweat trickling over his bruises; he drank half a bottle of water and then a third of a bottle of rakia.

'Does music heal bones?' the boy asked. He too was a little green around the neck and the chin after those bastards smacked him about, but he got better quickly. Crazy Elena gave him a jar with a foul-smelling potion to rub in.

'Damyan, stop scratching behind your ears,' Vasso snapped. He was taller than the Sklon. Darker too. 'Go on. The Radomir horo. Watch out what you hit and how you hit it! You understand, deafy?'

There are other ways to save money. You tend your garden. Dig. Weed and water. Feed it. You hope someone doesn't come and pick all the tomatoes you've raised from seed, that someone doesn't come and lift the garden bench, the metal door handles and the electricity cables, that they don't rob you on your way back from the village shop. If they only robbed you, you could swallow it, but often you might also get kissed by a brick on the back of your head. That's bad. For peace of mind, always carry a few lev on you. The thieves pocket them, then they're happy, their work hasn't been in vain. If you're lucky, they might reconsider and there won't be a brick kissing your neck.

These were the thoughts swimming in the head of Granny Angelina, a woman of seventy-four. She, in honesty to her own self, wasn't very brave. Every now and then she would drop her guard, imagine something nice, pull the devil's tail, and before she knew it even murkier, darker thoughts nested in her head. She didn't call the thing she imagined every so often a 'dream', because in Staro Selo there are no such things as dreams. Cheese costs money. Friendship lives inside your wallet. You know better than to dream. Still. You could ask God for something. That's why they've put God up there, so He can understand us. But what if you ask Him to kill someone, would He really erase them? Could you pray for someone's death? From time to time Granny Angelina asked herself things like that, then she went to church and asked God for forgiveness.

Ginger Dimitar is a scumbag. God would understand why she buried those scumbag dreams deep in her heart.

The thing that was constantly on her mind – was it a dream? What could she call it? Before falling asleep, her thoughts kept tripping over the same image, and it was there again as soon as she woke up. She thought she heard what people were saying, and out loud at that:

She found them in front of Solaris, that old Angelina, the café's cleaner, did. Yes, that quiet granny, seventy-something, her hair as white as vanilla ice cream. She's a gentle woman, she steps aside to let a worm pass, she's only ever killed one slug in her garden. She's never lifted a hand to do harm, never stolen a coffee or anything else, even though she's been washing dirty cups for ten years now. She collects the coffee grounds. That's her bonus – she pours the murky, brown residue over the roots of her tomatoes. Her veggies are divine, that's why they get stolen so often.

The old Angelina is not that daft and senile, people would say. *That old crone won't be able to protect her veggies on her own, she's worked it out and gives half of her salary to Pavko. Pavko, that local boy, one metre ninety, brown beard, strong. He lifts his left pinkie and people lie on the ground.*

It's only because of Pavko that the woman can take her tomatoes home. No one dares touch a leaf in her garden any more. True, she chooses the best, biggest, ripest fruit and presents them packaged at his door; she even makes him salad. But there's always something left for her.

Well, not just something – she made two hundred bottles of tomato puree, but she didn't dare boast about it. In twos, in threes she carried the bottles to the cellar and covered them with old rags. Around here, if they spot you taking something to your cellar, you might as well forget about it the following morning; you'd be skinned to the bone and your cellar destroyed too... but let us not get distracted. If Pavko is protecting you, you have tomato puree, a cellar and peace. Thank the Lord!

So, this woman with the best tomatoes in Staro Selo fantasises from time to time. All sorts of impossible nonsense creeps beneath her white locks: she finds them, all three of them, drunk – plastered – and prostrate behind Café Solaris. It's happened before; she's found drunk girls alongside the men, girls who'd been delivered by Jeep from Sofia for belote tournaments. It is possible to tip a glass too many and smoke the other kind of cigarettes. What can you do! Kids nowadays have money. The girls sober up. But sometimes, in fact every day, Angelina with the cream-white hair wished for other things. For example: to grab her head in disbelief.

God! she wanted to call Him, because He was her only hope; her sons were in Sweden.

Sometimes Angelina closed her eyes and turned to Him.

God, I know You're overworked. You make it so that the earth gives us bread, and You give us our children, rain and tomatoes. I know the things I see beneath my closed eyelids are bad, God. They are twisted, crooked and profane, and if you see sinful things beneath your eyelids, your soul digs up black silt and then it withers in black drought. I've been seeing this horrible image for months now. Please, if You can, wipe it from my brain, God. This is what I think, I don't wish it, but it's what I see when I close my eyes:

Ginger Dimitar, Vova and Pavko... strong boys, each pushing two metres in height. They're lying prostrate. Really ugly, next to them glitter puddles – small, not very deep – and not red but brown in colour. I've been washing the floor in Solaris for ten years now and I know when the blood has congealed, whether it has come from a nose or a lady's parts. I'm not scared of blood any more, God.

I see the right hands of Ginger Dimitar, Pavko and Vova...

God, You the most merciful, the poor woman called to him again, *please chase away these images, cleanse my thoughts.*

... the wrists.

You know God, you've seen it, a little girl's broken wrist, Damyana. Elena the Healer's granddaughter.

Those three are driving cars as wide as the town hall and girls bend down to their shoes. I don't want to see the things I see every day, please God. I'm grateful to You I don't have a daughter. If they made her do the things all these other girls did for them, I would've poisoned her with my own hands. I admit this sin, God...

There's no one to stop them. You're not stopping them, You, most merciful. Why not? We must've sinned before You, the whole neighbourhood. That's why I'm seeing this horrible image. Forgive me. I'm seeing their wrists broken. I don't want to see these things, God.

The woman with hair as white as a hospital bed sheet made the sign of the cross.

* * *

... a town can stay trampled for a few months. If people's nerves are taut, sucked out and boiled into a soup, it could stay trampled even for a year. But then – humiliated, despondent, with nerves wrecked beyond reprieve, lower than a beggar – someday some year some century someone will rise from the troubled dark of their own life and write in their own blood: FREEDOM.

* * *

The winter came to an end. A crazy winter – no snow in January, warm, not January at all. January ought to kiss June's dust, since June was cooler, colder. No spring around here – it got frightened and ran away, no one saw it. Winter arrived in March, then April picked it up, but afterwards a ferocious sun conquered the sky and people moved from fur coats to T-shirts. Something happened. People couldn't believe their ears at first. But the human mouth blabs – that's why God created it – buttered words to Ginger. You kiss Pavko's arse too, then you go back to Ginger and drop your colleague in it. The colleague gets fired from the brewery; you keep your job. That's why God gave you a mouth – to lick shoe soles with lips and words.

When your nerves are wrecked beyond reprieve, when you've had enough of licking shoe soles and dropping your colleagues in the shit, the mouth begins saying other things.

Mouths like that tend to get in trouble on this side of the Struma, but they can't stay shut forever.

Ginger Dimitar wasn't driving a car, but a fighter jet. A Mercedes with six cylinders, maybe twenty-nine – in fact, a hundred. As he was driving his starship, Ginger Dimitar decided to stop for a whisky and to have a piss. Well, he's a human being at the end of the day, a man is born to drink, right?

Here, on this side of the Struma, when people see a ginger head they lean forward and stare at their shoes. The local folk have learnt, women and men; everyone knows about the belts and the trousers. Nothing wrong with that, right?

Of course, the ginger prince has his own parking space. If some misguided specimen turns up and parks their car in too close a proximity to that particular section of asphalt – because of their innate stupidity, ignorance, et cetera – quite by chance the sinful, insignificant vehicle bursts into flames. Second-hand cars are ever so unreliable. Best not to touch them. You barely have to look at them and BOOM! A fire breaks out. It's an interesting physical-chemical phenomenon, isn't it?

Ginger Dimitar parked his Mercedes-beast in its designated slot and smiled with satisfaction. But the moment his foot touched the ground, suddenly, out of nowhere, a howl reverberated — suddenly wolves were howling, petrifying, as if it were winter and blizzards had returned to Staro Selo. The whole street stiffened, the pavement shrieked, the asphalt squealed. The air trembled and turned into cast iron. Around here we can do without air, but lying prostrate before Ginger Dimitar we cannot. Ginger Dimitar kicked the tyre of his spaceship. Ginger Dimitar shivered. Not a soul could be seen on the street. There was only the vile howl.

'Fuck it,' concluded Ginger Dimitar. It was unlikely that he meant to use such a culturally sophisticated phrase. Around here, if someone mentions your mouth, they inform you what they are about to shove in it. After a while, Ginger concluded that he'd wipe out every member of this repulsive tribe in this repulsive town.

But the howl — ahh, this savage, nasty, yet beautiful howl — wasn't stopping. The street howled. Staro Selo groaned, Gnida Planina whimpered, and for the first time since they chopped down its pines, it didn't look hideous.

Ginger was cursing. Oops, swearing rather. He kicked the kerb and the wheels of his fighter jet, trampled on the asphalt, yet the sound boomed even more grotesquely.

At one point Ginger noticed where the dog was buried, so to speak. He detected the source of the filthy trick. The whole car park drowned in the howl. The attention of his Ginger Highness was drawn to a dirty black nylon tape, rumpled in places, stretched between two pylons. The wind blew it and Ginger realised something was howling from its direction, as viciously as if the tape was spewing wolf mince and tallow. Fuck it. Ginger spat on the pavement. He pushed the tape, kicked it carefully and saw a camera, two sensors. Leave it out! No tricks like that on him. Stupid, prehistoric models, primitive boxes, ancient, mould growing on them, mounted side by side. Their colourful wires quivering. Pouring their poison over earth and sky, beast and nature.

'Which moron did this?' Ginger screamed amid a sea of curses, pardon – swear words. Furious, his mind asked only one basic question: WHO? Who's the idiot who cooked up this filth? Probably an adolescent, an art-nouveau technician. There'll be broken necks. Tonight.

Then – ahh, God, I do love You for granting us mouths – a child whispered:

'Did you know what Elena the Healer told Ginger Dimitar? That he would turn into a laughing stock in front of Radomir, in front of the whole cosmos and of Pernik. A laughing stock.'

Everyone in Radomir knew the cosmos was in fact the true name of God and every courageous person in the town.

* * *

'Dad!' The cast was as heavy as an anchor and the skin beneath it itchy as hell. Her father hugged her but not too often because pain is pain, and you need to dissolve yourself in it. When you dissolve yourself in the pain, it can't find you and then it stops hurting. 'Dad, please tell me about how when I was little, I splashed into the Munish.'

'I told you that story yesterday.'

'OK, tell me just half of it and then you read me a bit of *Pippi*. When you read, the book is wonderful. When I read, the letters are like a plough. I can't lift them off the page, the story turns into a snail and crawls... But first tell me how

I nearly drowned in the Munish and how Mum got me out of the mud.'

It was around five in the afternoon, light and warm.

'Let's go for a walk,' he offered. 'Let's go to the Sklon.'

'It's too steep,' the girl moaned.

'I'll carry you,' her father promised.

'That's not fair. A child should climb on their own, otherwise how's that a peak! Tell me how I fell into the Munish.'

'Well, there was no bridge over the Munish back then. It had rained. You know what the Munish is like, you give it a little rain and it turns into the Monsterish. And back then, there was only a thin pipe across the water.'

'How thin? As thin as a loaf of bread?'

'No, a little thicker. As thick as your grandma's watering can.'

'OK. Then?'

'Your mother had dressed you in your newest pink trousers.'

'From Second Chance?'

'Yes, but they were almost new. Basically new,' her father said, just like everyone in Staro Selo was saying when they came out of Second Chance with full bags. 'You were walking on the pipe, because you were too lazy to walk around the town square to the main bridge. Then you dropped into the mud – plonk – you and the new trousers sank into the mud all the way to your waist.'

'And?'

'Your mum pulled you out. She was dirty up to the waist too and you were crying about the new pink trousers. You didn't stop for two days.'

Exactly at this point of the story – what a time to interrupt – behind the window which had forgotten it was five o'clock and it was light and warm, and from the direction of that Munish (usually calm as a newly hatched chick, but which had now turned into the Monsterish), it was exactly then that a trumpet solo resounded. A trumpet!

At the beginning it was quiet like a girl with almost new trousers who wants to cross the wild Munish. She is really frightened but wants to do it and climbs onto the pipe, but in the trumpet's melody the girl doesn't drop into the mud and her mother doesn't get dirty up to her ears rescuing her.

No. The trumpet had a different point of view. The melody pulled the girl out of the silt of fear – she tiptoed along the pipe, then, full of courage, ran up and further up and further up the steep, sawlike slope all the way to the Sklon. The girl climbed to the top. It is a well-known fact that from there you can see the Struma, Staro Selo's brave rooftops, even your mother, down there along the banks of the Munish which has swollen and grown into a real river. The melody was peaceful, soulful, yet it was steeper than the Sklon. It had the sky within it, and silt, and ten clouds where the girl was flying as if in an aeroplane. But she didn't manage to stay long in the white-bearded clouds because the music stopped.

A boy – we all know who it was – carrying Dimo Zagoryaloto's giant trumpet walked into the room with the story about the girl with the most beautiful pink trousers.

'Dame-Damyanka,' the boy said quickly, as if he was chasing a wolf, even though the wolves had long left the Sklon. 'You know what? You're better now, I'm sure.'

'Hello, Vasko!' The girl's smile was so broad that it contained both the town's gorgeous weather and the Munish itself.

'Music heals bones. Grandad Vasso said so. He doesn't lie. He'll even buy me a bike.'

'And we'll cycle together to Stefanovo,' the girl said happily. 'The road there is as smooth as butter.'

'Hi, Uncle Christo,' the boy said belatedly. 'Mum said you've returned from somewhere... I don't know where. It's good to have you back.'

The man nodded and said: 'That's an amazing trumpet. Is it your grandad's?'

'No. It's another man's, an even greater virtuoso's. If Grandad is the brick, that man is the house built with two million bricks. His name is Dimo Zagoryaloto. He's from Kalkas in Pernik.'

It was already five-thirty in the afternoon, and that's the hour of silence. In this silent hour, in this interesting place, the boy – bruises on his neck and chin still visible – suddenly asked:

'Uncle Christo, have you heard this thing... for example... is it possible another kid can become dearer to you than Grandma Maria's only gold coin, or milk, or even Dimo Zagoryaloto's trumpet? If you can hear music about this girl, is she your special friend, will she be your friend forever?'

The boy spoke quietly and the room became very warm, as warm as if the stove was lit and someone was baking potatoes on it. Perhaps that's why the boy and his trumpet were soaked in perspiration.

The man got up, stretched an arm and tousled the boy's hair. Not that there was much hair to tousle after Valya, the boy's mum, had cut it almost to the skull.

'That's right, Vasko. When you hear music about someone, you love them all your life.'

Outside – who knows what time it was – it was beautiful, the breeze rustled the air and the Munish came out of its bed to peek through the window and see what was going on.

Nothing was going on. In the room there was only a girl with her hand in a cast, a boy with a trumpet and a man who didn't even have a trumpet.

* * *

She walked into Solaris and suddenly everything went quiet as if someone had been shot. She was dressed as usual – blue trousers, a blue blouse. Silver-grey hair tied in a ponytail; dark, high forehead; a tall woman, as thin as the gaze of a starving man.

The woman stepped towards the bar and said: 'A rose hip tea.'

The barman, a boy with a sparse beard, didn't budge. His eyes flew to the man with ginger hair and sank into the blood-red locks, scarlet and cocky on the right side, crushed and matted on the left. The ginger hair continued sipping whatever was in its glass and didn't move.

'Boss, shall I serve her?'

The boss didn't answer. Turned his right thumb downwards. The gaze of the barman with a sparse beard jumped to the door, then he turned his head to the newcomer. Two men with broad shoulders drank in the café. They sat by the window, a small bowl of hazelnuts in front of them. The barman swayed. His clever fingers rushed to brew the rose hip tea. The sparse chin had noticed a thumb unexpectedly, fractionally, raised – a thumb belonging to the biggest man around here.

One of the gentlemen, the one with broader shoulders, got up first. Maybe a second later, maybe less than a second, the other stirred and left his comfy seat. They looked alike even though they weren't related. The men's iron elbows blocked the door behind the woman's back.

She didn't wet herself from fear. She walked over to the ginger man, reached out, took his hand and shook it for a long time. Then she turned and with slow steps, as flat as hewn stone, began walking towards the two giants.

'What was that?' Ginger grated the syllables as though he carried a smoothing plane in his throat. 'Wait a minute, Elena. Oi, wait!'

Three other men joined the two big elbows, and the barman with unconvincing facial hair came out from behind the bar and pushed her. Elena smoothed her blouse carefully, as though, if she didn't remove the fold that had just appeared, something would explode.

And it exploded.

'What d'you want, hag?' Ginger's voice was a muddy avalanche.

His muscles doubled, his arms, shoulders and neck tripled in size. Two skulls were tattooed on his left arm. In black ink on his right arm, the tattoo master had carved an English inscription into the skin: SIYANA LOVE.

The arm with the skulls grabbed Elena's elbow.

'What're you doing, draggin' yourself over here?'

'I fancy a rose hip tea,' the woman said flatly, without looking at him.

'If I whack you one, you'll piss yourself,' Ginger said.

'Try,' the woman invited him.

'They'll find you dead in a ditch tomorrow, you dumb cow.'

'They'll find me. In your dreams.'

'I'll trash you, bitch.'

The barman with the sparse beard pushed her again, the man with the broadest shoulders tripped her. The blows weren't strong, she didn't even waver. The woman lifted her head, slowly reached for her tea, then slowly sipped from the tea, then again, very, very slowly, maybe she wanted to enjoy its aroma. She straightened. Looked even taller. That's how people recognised her from a distance on the street.

'Ginger Dimitar, if I were you – mark my words – if I were you, I would pay this "dumb cow", as you just called me, a visit.'

The barman retreated as if stung by a wasp. The man with the impressive shoulders hid his fists in his pockets.

'Why the fuck do I need to visit you?' Ginger Dimitar's voice was glass shards.

'Because your brain is shifting into an ugly vortex. Madness is a big place. It will swallow you. Your skin is yellowing. Your fingers tremble. You can't sleep, can you? Upset stomach. Vomiting.'

'Nasty, nasty filth.'

'I may be nasty, but you got cold feet and didn't dare put a collar around my neck,' the woman said.

Ginger clenched his fists. Fourteen fists followed. The air vanished from the café. Muscles were about to burst. Waiting.

'If I were you, Ginger Dimitar, I wouldn't thrash Elena the Healer. In the hospital they'll examine you for a long time. Once upon a time they called it "melancholy", nowadays they call it "depression". Boredom lulled to sleep with a glass of something strong destroys the brain and insides, and that's especially true for you.'

'Blah-blah,' Ginger snapped and the flame on his head licked at the forest of fists.

'Blah-blah,' the woman responded calmly. 'But if I were you, I wouldn't be thrashing Elena the Healer right now. If you pop over to hers today, before three in the afternoon, you could drink something nasty, sickening. You'll choke. You'll spit. You'll cuss. Every eight hours for twenty days. You might even lose consciousness. But when you finish the last drop in the jar, you'll sleep. Every night. The skin on your chest and bottom will itch, but really itch, even bleed, I promise you, but sleep will return to you. Your breathing will steady. I could mix you this potion. Your head will spin when you hear the price, I promise you that too. If you come after three, even a minute later, you won't find me.'

'Filth!' Ginger grated.

'Filth who can mix potions.'

'Fine. Make it. Start stirring. Right now.'

'Ginger Dimitar, make a note – no one orders Elena the Healer. You can break her hand, true. You can kill her too. Any idiot can do that. So what? I've got a condition and I'm announcing it in front of your henchmen. Come to Elena the Healer, but I want you to make cuts along your right arm before you do. You'll start from here,' she said slowly and touched Ginger's wrist. On his forearm, right on top of the huge muscle, lay a name written in English, SIYANA. 'You'll cut SIYANA from the elbow to the fingers of your hand. The same way you would score a steak.'

'Hollow watering can. Cow!' The voice had lost its glass shards. Only the rattling remained. 'I'll tear you to shreds. I'll feed you to your dog.'

'Goodbye,' Elena said calmly. The young men, led by the barman and his sparse chin, looked at her, all of them big, strong and powerful.

'Oh, and one more thing: I left something for you by the door,' Elena said over her shoulder. 'The wooden block. You broke my granddaughter's wrist on it. Use it to support your wrist. Cut.'

Ginger glanced at his right arm – SIYANA stared at him in Latin script.

Grey-hair, not a person but the barrel of an old rifle, walked past. In measured steps she walked towards Solaris' exit.

The men's powerful muscles didn't block her way.

She stopped by the door. Pulled out a mobile phone – greenish, as fancy as a luxury hotel. She pressed the display a couple of times.

The screen began howling. The hunger of not one but a hundred wolves tore the green silence. The phone sizzled, the wolves in its electronic stomach pounced – desperate, beastly souls thrusting their bloody teeth into the vodka bottle on the counter.

The howling twisted. Crawled. Croaked. Pressed on.

Crushed.

Unbearable and black. Terrifying.

A beautiful howl.

★ ★ ★

They could be making it all up, the people of Staro Selo; they're not to be trusted. They look at the moon and try to convince you it's noon. Their lies run deep and evil. Caverns:

you can't jump over them, it's impossible to bypass them. You fall into them. You sink. Wounds open, bitter and angry. But tomorrow, when your anger passes, you think to yourself: *Hey, crooks, what a lie! I take my hat off! Top people!*

Who knows when the first rumour – as fat as a steak – exploded: one of the local bandits was done for. People were terrified to say his name out loud. He went mental. He frothed at the mouth, ears, nose and elsewhere too. Imagine! The man concerned happened to be ginger.

He, the liars of Staro Selo say, had apparently made cuts across his arm all on his own. He'd cut it as if he were scoring a steak. He'd been told to do that by that one, you've heard of her, the crazy healer, Elena.

All sorts of people flocked here – from Sofia, Pernik, Kyustendil, all the neighbouring villages – and they'd all seen it with their own eyes: a specimen the size of a walk-in fridge, muscle over muscle, not a man but a mountain ridge, his hand wrapped in bandages, boozing in Café Solaris.

'Is it true what they say?' Elena's neighbours asked.

'I have sworn before God and my mother's grave that I will not give a deadly poison to anyone. I don't mix death in my cauldrons,' Elena snapped.

For about a month now bunches of flowers have appeared by her gate: lilacs, primroses, wild roses and small bunches of dandelions. Common flowers, cheap.

The people from the neighbourhood with the village name picked the flowers from the fields or their front gardens. That's what the locals in Staro Selo say. But can you believe them? You want to, but can you? You listen, you watch and before you know it, you see a vehicle, longer than Dida and Dona's shop. Behind the steering wheel sits a ginger gentleman.

Take a good look, but watch out that he doesn't spot you staring at him. I warn you, the neurologist in Radomir retired. Who's going to send you for a scan? Mind you, that might not be necessary. Most likely, the morning after the beating you'll wake up dead.

But you're young and green and simple. You believe in miracles. You run to the field. You pick wildflowers. You don't know their names. You fashion something like a bouquet, and when you walk past Elena's house, you leave it outside her gate.

That woman has pulled so many people out of pain into the light. She deserves it.

★ ★ ★

'Find her!' ordered the man who had just crawled out of the shining Maserati. He didn't cast a shadow; he was thin, elongated. Not even whitish. Colourless. Odourless. Bloodless. No hair on the legs, no bones in the pelvis, just an ordinary fly with the Latin name *Musca domestica* stuck to the bumper of the majestic vehicle. In fact, it was more of a castle than a motor vehicle.

According to the *Encyclopaedia Britannica*, the fly in question is ten million times more sensitive to sugar (and according to the elite, to women) than the human tongue.

'Bring her over.'

The insect's word vanished into the manicured lawn.

'Yes, Si...'

'And a priest.'

The redhead bent down. Swallowed his own spleen and arse. His gaze licked the knees of *Musca domestica*.

'But...' The bowed red head suffocated in its own voice. For a moment its breath ceased to polish the cufflinks of the elongated gentleman standing before him. Was it right? But then again, what's right in this chaos? 'But Siyana... You chucked her out... Sir... I don't know where to...'

The newcomer spat. 'Non compos mentis,' he articulated flawlessly. Then touched his belt with transparent fingers. 'I want her here in six minutes.'

His words developed fever, ready to scourge everything around them. But flames weren't necessary here. No enemies stood before the fly.

'I'm getting married.'

The redhead jumped. 'Yes! Sir. Mister. Tennku. For... for your trust ... Tennku. I'll try find her.'

The colourless fibril wanted to spit again. Didn't. He was proud of his privileged upbringing. 'Stop gawking. Move.'

Musca domestica stuffed a piece of chewing gum into its mouth. The vigorous movement of the jaw was going to calm its heartbeat. Seventy-eight yews were planted and fashioned into perfect topiaries beside the fence outlining the redhead's mansion. The redhead's face was also a yew. Greenish. Pruned to perfection.

* * *

A silver Jeep with wheels from the ground to the sky, a powerful specimen, pulled up – not in front of Solaris, but in front of the one-storey house of Crazy Elena, the healer. Someone big from Sofia? Big but not from Sofia. The students from the Secondary School of Food Technology and Management – in other words, from Mangiata – who had managed to get average grades in English, deciphered *UK* on the number plate. One of the boys knew very well what *UK* was because he had been there – a whole summer long, helping his dad with mincemeat deliveries around Manchester's supermarkets. They'd had to get up at three o'clock in the morning.

UK means the United Kingdom, England, Brexit. Had they really heard of Crazy Elena all the way over in the UK? Well, it was about time Staro Selo became famous for something other than robberies and shady dealings.

However, no one from the UK alighted from this monolithic Jeep, a vehicle the locals hadn't seen around these parts before. A woman in jeans and a blouse appeared. A blouse not unlike those Granny Sara sold in Second Chance, only it was the real deal. A white blouse; the students from the fashion design classes often sketched such ethereal phantasmagoria. The neighbours knew the haughty creature shoved into the jeans – Siyana, the spiteful maths teacher.

All the students from the School of Food Technology and Management, the School of Mathematics and the School of Fashion Design and Innovative Technologies in Radomir had been left wailing in unison, since to pass her mathematics class you needed a score of 300 per cent instead of the 3 per cent you'd need if you had a normal teacher.

Only one girl mourned her when the mathematics miracle disappeared to the UK – Petya, glasses, boots without heels, nails without polish, a girl clogged as a vacuum cleaner bag. The nerd even wept when the maths genius left Radomir. People say Siyana had paid for the vacuum cleaner to try her luck at the Olympiad in Munich, with her own money too. The glasses won second place.

This clogged Petya had borrowed thirty lev from her granny to buy a bouquet for the geometric reptile, but the other students had grabbed the roses and smacked Petya's head with them, breaking her glasses. End of story.

It may not have happened exactly like this – if you make the people of Staro Selo work, everyone gets sick immediately, but if they have to tell a lie, everyone perks up. They wax such lyrical lies that in ten years' time you still remember them. The same Pythagoras python in jeans and a white blouse (purchased in London and not from Second Chance if the destroyer parked on the street was anything to go by) quickly-quickly slunk into Elena the Healer's garden.

This was reported by two respectable women in the house to the left. One of them, Dona, happened to be on her balcony, looking through her binoculars very discreetly. Her twin sister, Dida, also happened to be on her balcony with a telescope; she did it inadvertently, quite unintentionally, without imposing her action on anyone's attention. The ladies offered the local population an authentic version of the event. Their words were more plausible than a postal order amounting to a thousand lev, more unshakable than the former mayor's headstone in the town's cemetery.

Whatever Dida and Dona said was as if it had been announced by National Television. After all, these girls thoroughly investigated every minute detail, as well as the information in its entirety.

'Christo,' Siyana had said, 'how are you?'

'Fine,' Christo, the healer's son, had responded. What else was he going to say? They knew what a muppet he was, you could torture him and he'd still say, 'Thank you'.

'I'm fine too,' Siyana had said, but she looked more than fine. The skin on her face was stretched, gleaming like a laminated floor. Her hands – white bread. Not wholemeal, which is all brown due to the added calcium, colouring and all sorts of chemicals. 'Aren't you going to invite me in?'

'No.'

She had pulled out money. Dida and Dona were certain of it – lots of money. A wad. A fat one. Frighteningly so.

'I have money,' Christo had replied. 'I've earned it.'

Earned! Wind and fog, if you ask Dida and Dona. These two knew every fairy tale about every man in Staro Selo. Especially Christo, Siyana's husband. Shame he's so handsome. He has no backbone to speak of. Weren't they divorced though? No, I don't think so. At least there has been no mention of it in the neighbourhood.

'How's Damyana?' Siyana had asked and stuffed the wad of money into his pocket.

'Fine.'

The weather was lovely. The hollyhocks were casting shadows, although not very dense, in the afternoons.

'Christo, you told me a story once. About the tears of the girl who becomes your special friend for life,' Siyana said. That's exactly what she had said, the twins heard her very well and exchanged glances. They sell the thickest milk, the softest bread and the most honest sausages in the whole Pernik region, and scanners, X-rays and magnetic resonance imaging machines bow to their hearing abilities. You can trust them. 'Do you remember when you told me this story?'

It became very quiet. You could hear the hollyhocks' shadows creeping across the paving slabs.

'You're not that girl,' Christo said, took the wad of money and tried to give it back to the mathematician. She didn't take it. The money took off into the air – a flock of bewildered birds. At least it wasn't windy, it was a quiet day.

Then the banknotes fell as if they were chicken feathers – you pluck a chicken before gutting the bird and portioning the carcass. Bloodied feathers lay on the pavement.

'Not like feathers,' Dona corrected her sister. 'They looked like baby's socks.'

Dona, as it is known in the whole of Staro Selo, is the kinder of the twins.

At that moment, outside Elena the Healer's house stopped another Jeep, the size of an ocean liner. Everyone recognised Ginger Dimitar's dinosaur. He revved the engine, the asphalt perspired, the pavement swayed.

When Ginger put his foot on the street, an unpleasant sound tore the heat. Howling wolves, tearing at something tough and sinewy. According to Dona, not just tough but certainly disgusting too.

Look at my eye! Dida thought.

In fact, it was a cement pylon howling. The same one Damyan the Beautiful had fastened the old grapevine to not long ago. A feeble schoolboy from Mangiata had whispered something to Crazy Elena and, according to Dida and Dona's testimony, the conversation lasted ten minutes. Dida, the more alert of the twins, caught the words 'sensor' and 'cameras' flying out of the pimpled teenager's mouth. If you think you're going to hear something leave Elena's mouth, you'd be better off shooting yourself.

The twins hadn't even sat for their lunch that day when two skinny, beardless teenagers turned up clutching a ladder.

Clearly Crazy Elena has reached deep into her pocket, thought Dida. *I wouldn't have given a penny to the charlatans.*

Rumour has it, and Dona confirmed, that the installation cost an arm and a leg. The only thing I'm not sure about is whether or not the kids installed the wire so that the camera automatically recognises the ginger tick's Jeep, or if it's one of the cheap IT brooches for poor cousins like us. Anyway, respect to your graduates, Mangiata. That's the kind of children Mother Bulgaria has birthed and continues to birth here in Staro Selo.

The howl bit Ginger.

This was the point Dida and Dona noticed the beauty flowing from the wolves' throats. It seemed to them the wolf pack was singing.

Wolves, you are real men.

Ginger Dimitar fumed on the street. The priest Palyo poked his nose from the car, he wasn't drunk, just tipsy, but polite.

Dida, a sober shopkeeper, could have sworn that in his state of anger, Ginger Dimitar announced: 'Siyana! The threadworm is here. With a priest. The priest will marry you to the threadworm.' After that Ginger politely (as if!) turned his attention to Elena. 'Oi, you, filth! I'll demolish your house. I'll stuff your beams up—' ('Pardon us but we couldn't possibly repeat that. We're well-brought-up European ladies from Staro Selo.')

The twin Dona, a kind creature with a penchant for peppering her narratives with poetry, pointed out that Ginger Dimitar took out a rose hidden under his shirt and cried: 'Siyana! Take the flower! For f—'s sake.'

The reply of the once-upon-a-time mathematical tempest, the vicious Pythagorean priestess, remained unknown.

Before sitting down to their afternoon coffee that day, Dida and Dona bowed to the scientific progress achieved by humankind. The two European ladies were convinced of the importance of computer technologies in the life of Staro Selo and after a powerful explosion of commercial energy put their minds to new business projects...

Onwards!

Howl, wolves, howl. We will howl with you.

* * *

Two kids strolled along the street, bathed in sunlight – not a street but a treasure trove, all the house windows were diamonds.

It was hot. The boy looked at the girl with messy hair. He looked at her for about a minute. Who cares if it was a minute or not?

'I couldn't find the comb, Vasko,' the girl admitted guiltily. 'I've got a haystack on my head. Don't look at my hair, look at my shoes.'

'Your tiara's pretty, Dame-Damyanka,' the boy said finally.

'Tra-la-la-la,' the girl protested. 'Don't be silly.'

The kids didn't know God often stops by in Staro Selo and even more often transforms into a tiara and shines in a girl's beautiful hair. Like this, her face is clearly visible even after dusk.

* * *

Christo Damyanov was printed on the envelope.

No postal address. No sender name. The envelope wasn't even sealed. The man, bearded, tall and thin, in an old but lovely shirt, turned it in his hand.

'What is it, Christo?' a tall, very thin woman with grey hair asked.

He didn't respond.

He pulled a piece of paper out of the envelope. On it, with a blue pen, was written an ordinary equation:

$-3y + 4x = 11$

$y + 2x = 13$

The man flinched. Stared at the numbers. Ran his fingers over them. Once. Twice.

Under the equation, with the same blue pen, was inscribed:

You. The rest is loneliness.

JANUARY 2022
STARO SELO, PERNIK, RADOMIR

 MUNKEN

Learn more about the paper we use:

www.arcticpaper.com

Arctic Paper UK Ltd
8 St Thomas Street
London
SE1 9RS